THE DUCHESS OF DRURY LANE

THE DUCHESS OF DRURY LANE

Freda Lightfoot

This first world edition published 2012
in Great Britain and 2013 in the USA by
SEVERN HOUSE PUBLISHERS LTD of
19 Cedar Road, Sutton, Surrey, England, SM2 5DA.
Trade paperback edition first published
in Great Britain and the USA 2013 by
SEVERN HOUSE PUBLISHERS LTD

British Library Cataloguing in Publication Data

Lightfoot, Freda, 1942–
    The Duchess of Drury Lane.
    1. Jordan, Dorothy, 1761-1816–Fiction. 2. William IV,
    King of Great Britain, 1765-1837–Relations with women–
    Fiction. 3. Great Britain–History–George III,
    1760-1820–Fiction. 4. Great Britain–History–George
    IV, 1820-1830–Fiction. 5. Great Britain–History–
    William IV, 1830-1837–Fiction. 6. Historical fiction.
    I. Title
    823.9'14–dc23

ISBN-13: 978-0-7278-8246-2 (cased)
ISBN-13: 978-1-84751-464-6 (trade paper)

All Severn House titles are printed on acid-free paper.

Severn House Publishers support the Forest Stewardship Council [FSC], the
leading international forest certification organisation. All our titles that are printed
on Greenpeace-approved FSC-certified paper carry the FSC logo.

MIX
Paper from
responsible sources
FSC® C018575

Typeset by Palimpsest Book Production Ltd.,
Falkirk, Stirlingshire, Scotland.
Printed and bound in Great Britain by
MPG Books Ltd., Bodmin, Cornwall.

Prologue

1816

The winter sunshine is too weak to take the chill from my bones or ease my cough as I sit gazing out upon two dreary cypress trees. Nor does it lighten the gloom of these shabby rooms. Saint Cloud is proving to be as much a disappointment to me as was Marquetra or Versailles. The rooms at our lodging house are cold and bare, with but a few pieces of old furniture, nowhere comfortable to sit apart from the small couch upon which I recline. Not that my surroundings trouble me greatly, since what house could possibly compare with my lovely Bushy? My thoughts, as always these days, are with my darling children. I ache for a letter from Lucy telling me how her latest pregnancy is progressing, from dear deluded Dodee or even foolish Fanny. And from my boys of course. If I can depend on nothing more, I can be certain of the love of my children. They will ever sustain me.

But yet there is no post again today, and I worry over why that is.

'Has Frederick visited you recently?' my visitor asks, as if reading my thoughts.

I sit up a little and talk of the last time I dined with my son only a week ago, which always cheers me. 'His regiment is not to remain in Paris long, but may move on to Cambrai soon. Should that happen, then I shall follow, if my health permits. Paris is an odious place and I shall not be sorry to leave it. George and Henry write to me of the wonders of India. Lolly is at sea and Tuss at school. And my darling girls . . .' I pause, not wishing to admit why it is so difficult for them to visit their mother, that their father in fact forbids it.

'They are too young for travel, I should think,' she agrees.

'Quite.'

'But as a widow, Madame, you surely need your family about you at this sad time.'

I inwardly smile at her artless questions, well aware it is the natural curiosity of a newspaper reporter, as much as friendship, that inspires them. My dear Sketchley has painted me as a grieving widow. This masquerade she has created is as a Madame James who was supposedly married to a businessman, now deceased. It suits me to play this role, and am I not adept at acting a part? But I welcome all visitors, usually fans who have guessed the truth of my identity. They often call at Number One rue d'Angoulême and I am happy to see them, including Miss Helen Maria Williams, for all I have reservations about her motives.

'You speak true. It is not, believe me,' I say, 'feelings of pride, avarice, or the absence of those comforts I have all my life been accustomed to, that is killing me by inches. It is the loss of my only remaining comfort, the hope from time to time to see my children.'

'I'm sure your daughter will visit, once the baby is born, and your other sons when they return from active duty.'

'Another frustration,' I tell my sympathetic listener, 'is based upon my inactivity. I have never been one to lie about doing nothing,' and I return my gaze to the dank, overgrown garden, far too tired and sickly to venture out.

'Have you done any writing lately?' she gently asks, silently acknowledging my solitude. 'It is ever a comfort to set down one's thoughts, I find. Perhaps it may cheer you if I read you my own latest effort. I would welcome your critical opinion.'

'That would be delightful.'

Poetry is an interest we share, since we are of an age, and each with a past filled with emotion and nostalgia. Our chat about poetry is often interspersed with tales of Napoleon, a favourite topic of conversation as Miss Williams' politics are somewhat militant. Even now she is relating some anecdote of the revolution. I respond as best I can, understanding little of what she says, but glad enough of her company, the presence of another human being in my empty life.

I listen to her poem, making one or two comments, mainly of praise since I do not care to risk damaging any artist's sensibilities. Have I not personally suffered at the hands of my peers whose opinions were warped by jealousy, or have whipped up animosity in an audience for the same reason? 'Thank you, I enjoyed that. You have a natural way with words, and I have a gift for you too.' I reach for a small volume set ready on my side table and hand it to her. 'Miss Sketchley kindly arranged for my collection of poems to be printed. I thought you might care to have a copy.'

Miss Williams takes the book from me, eyes shining. 'Oh, how very kind of you, Dora.'

I wince slightly at the use of my first name, not something I have encouraged while in France, but after several visits perhaps we may be called friends now. I am, of course, aware that my charade has not fooled this woman. She knows full well who I am, and no doubt how I came to be in these dire straits. What she does not know is that I have known poverty before, and view it rather as the return of an old friend, not exactly welcome but most certainly familiar. And Miss Sketchley's recent visit to London did not bring the news I had hoped for. Barton promised to help but seems to be having little success thus far.

'Do you intend to stay in France long, Madame?'

'Only until my health improves,' I assure her. 'My dear Sketchley fusses over me like a mother hen but I hope to return to the stage soon. Acting is my life, you understand.' I go on to speak warmly of the leading men I've worked with: John Bannister and John Kemble, to name but two. The former being very much my favourite as the latter has caused me no end of trouble, as did his sister, Mrs Siddons, in her day.

'You must indeed miss it, having enjoyed such a long and successful career.'

'I was most fortunate.'

'Did you always wish to be an actress?'

I give a soft laugh. 'Not at all. I was something of a tomboy, more interested in climbing and boasting to my brothers that I could jump higher down the stairs than they dared even try. Acting never occurred to me. I left that ambition to my sister

Hester. I was perfectly happy working in a hat shop, but then tragedy struck our little family and our lives changed for ever.'

She edges forward in her chair. 'So how did it all come about? Do you remember the first time you ever stepped on to a stage?'

'Oh, indeed, I remember it only too well. I was absolutely terrified.'

One

Spring 1778

How could I ever forget that night? My debut leading role was to be in Henry Fielding's farce *The Virgin Unmasked* at Crow Street Theatre in Dublin, for which, if successful, I was to be engaged at the princely sum of twenty shillings a week. I stood frozen with fear in the wings, listening to the chatter, laughter and ribald jokes of the audience just a few feet away, growing increasingly impatient with the delay. The pit was crowded with young bucks, no females allowed, and beyond that was the two-shilling gallery. While up in the boxes, or lattices as they were called, sat the toffs in full evening dress. They had paid twice that sum and meant to savour their superiority by looking with disdain through their opera glasses down upon everyone else. And above all of them came the one-shilling gallery and the slips. Hundreds of people all gawping at the stage where I was about to make a complete fool of myself. I was scared stiff, utterly petrified.

'Get on with it!' I heard a voice cry. 'Where's the farce?'

'Aye, come on, we're eager to get an eyeful of the new gel,' yelled another, followed by yet more jeering laughter.

I turned on my heels and fled.

'Dolly, Dolly, don't go!' I could hear Mama calling to me, but ignoring her I hitched up my skirts and ran pell-mell to the women's dressing room. My one desire was to escape what I saw as a baying pack of wolves out for my blood. I huddled shivering in a corner, feeling sick to my stomach, knowing in my heart that it was hopeless, that I couldn't do it. I simply could not walk out on to that stage.

I doubt I would ever have been an actress had not my mother chosen to tread the boards before me. As a profession the stage is both insecure and unsettled, as actors are constantly on the move. Actresses are also the subject of public disapproval since they're generally considered to be disreputable and immoral. Yet my own mother suggested just such a career for me, a girl of only sixteen.

I had vehemently protested. 'Hester is the one who wants to act, not me. Why can I not continue to work as a milliner's assistant? I hope to be allowed to learn the art of hat making myself soon.'

'Hester has tried, and found herself too beset with stage fright, so Mr Ryder has generously offered you a trial. You will earn far more on stage than you ever would in a hat shop.'

Under her maiden name of Grace Phillips, Mama had set out as a young girl with her sister Maria for Dublin, both intent on becoming actresses. That was back in the 1750s when strolling players visited every town, and the two girls had often enjoyed being taken to the theatre in Bristol. So for some reason they'd fallen in love with the notion.

Their father, a rector in Haverfordwest in Pembrokeshire, South Wales, had died when they were quite young and the family was largely brought up by a married cousin. But despite an education of the highest quality, far more so than my own, and coming from a respectable family of means, the stage was all Mama had ever dreamed of.

Why the Phillips sisters chose Dublin, I do not know, but the Smock Alley Theatre was under the management of Thomas Sheridan, a famous impresario at the time. Mama loved to tell stories of her years at Smock Alley, how she played Juliet to Sheridan's Romeo, but then one day he returned to London and the theatre closed down. Having little choice in the matter, Grace and Aunt Maria likewise moved to England, but sadly never starred on the London stage or realized their ambition of fame and fortune. They spent almost their entire working lives touring the provinces, until Mama finally gave up acting for motherhood. Despite seeing myself as Irish, I was in fact born in London near Covent Garden in 1761, no doubt where my stage-struck parents were seeking work at the time, and where I was baptized Dorothy Bland. Our dear King George III had only recently come to the throne so a whole new era had begun.

'Why do *you* not return to the stage, Mama?' I suggested. 'Since you love it so much.'

'Don't be foolish, Dolly. I am far too old to play pretty parts now. And who would care for your siblings if I were not around? James is working hard but will have his own family to keep soon. Francis wishes to join the army, and George will do his bit, for all he is young. Hester may try again with small parts, but you can sing and are an excellent mimic. You are now our best hope to provide for the family.'

'But I wouldn't dare go up on stage, I swear I couldn't do it,' I cried.

'Yes you could,' my sister Hester protested. 'You have me crying with laughter by your antics, you do really, Doll.'

Mama's expression had remained implacable, her face tight with suppressed emotion. She'd been this way ever since Papa had left her. My father, Francis Bland, an affectionate and well-meaning man but clearly weak, had abandoned us, his beloved family, some years before when I was but thirteen. My darling Mama had never recovered from the shock. Theirs had been a love match and she had believed in him utterly.

Papa was a captain in the army, until he took up his wife's profession, but his family, being gentry, considered that he had married beneath him. Mama never spoke of that time, but I believe that as the lovers had been underage, his father had the marriage annulled. Despite this setback my parents stayed together for sixteen years, living largely in Ireland, long enough to produce several children To all outward appearances they were a devoted couple, although they never troubled to legitimize the marriage by going through a second ceremony.

Following his departure Papa moved to London to marry an Irish heiress, no less, perhaps at the behest of his family. Our situation as a consequence grew ever more precarious. We stayed with Cousin Blanche in Wales for a while before returning to Dublin and taking lodgings in South Great George Street. But then came the worst news of all. Papa's health had broken down and having set out for France to recuperate, he sadly died at Dover.

If we had been poor before, we were now penurious as the small allowance he'd paid us, his first family, had stopped.

'Perhaps Papa has left you a small inheritance,' I'd suggested, striving to keep hope alive in my mother's sorely bruised heart. 'Have you asked his widow or the Bland family if that is the case?' Mama had turned her face away from me to busy herself studying a handbill which listed coming productions.

'I have put in the necessary claim with the Bland family for the sake of my children, but you know full well, Dolly, that I would never demean myself by asking such a question of that woman. I have my pride, if nothing else. We can depend only upon ourselves. Remember that always. But we must eat, and I also need to send money for Lucy's keep and a physician to attend her.'

My younger sister, Lucy, was causing concern as she too was sickly and was even now being cared for by Blanche. As my mother's first cousin and one-time surrogate mother, Blanche was ever ready to offer a haven of comfort to us at her home, Trelethyn, near St David's in South Wales where she lived a quiet, rural life with no children of her own.

But even dear Cousin Blanche could offer us little in the way of financial assistance.

'Fortunately,' Mama continued, resolute in her plan, 'my standing in the theatre means that I carry some weight still in the acting community. It is all arranged as I accepted Mr Ryder's kind offer on your behalf. You start at Crow Street next week. Now, what shall be your stage name?'

In the face of such family trauma, how could I refuse?

I chose to be named Miss Francis after my father, as Mama insisted Papa's family would object to my using the Bland family name. Nor had she any desire to cause confusion among the public by the use of Phillips, her own former stage name. But my agony in choosing now seemed irrelevant as I had failed my greatest challenge by refusing even to go on stage.

A hand caught at my arm and gave me a little shake. It was Mr Ryder, the manager, a kind and generous-hearted man who had found me hiding in the dressing room. 'Dolly, you *are* going on that stage, if I have to carry you on myself. You know your words. You can act. You *will* do this. Do you hear me?'

And so I was dragged back and shoved on to the stage, the audience almost ready to riot as they'd long since lost patience with waiting for the farce that normally followed the main play.

For a terrifying moment I stood transfixed, illuminated in that pool of candlelight. Then I took a breath and as I spoke my first tremulous lines the noise died away, the audience sat hushed and expectant before me. In that instant all fear left me. It felt as if it was the most natural place in the world for me to be.

It was like coming home.

I was playing the lead in a farce about arranged marriage, a popular theme. The girl, Lucy, obstinately refused a succession of suitors suggested to her by her rich father, only to finally admit that she'd secretly married a handsome footman. To my surprise I found that I delighted in the role, playing her as pert and cheeky, albeit with an air of pleasing innocence.

When the audience laughed at my antics I felt my heart swell with pride and excitement at this amazing discovery that I could indeed entertain. It was the most wonderful sensation in the world for a plain tomboy such as myself, one slightly short-sighted who was often obliged to carry spectacles on a chain about my neck.

Never considered to be a classic beauty, my nose and chin being somewhat too prominent, yet I was young and fresh-faced, with a cupid's bow mouth and rosy cheeks. And with dark eyes some men might consider meltingly warm, even alluring. I must have possessed some charms as I had received and rejected one proposal of marriage already, aged fifteen. The press were later to describe me as more agreeable than handsome, not particularly tall but with a neat, elegant figure with interesting *embonpoint*, which was a polite way of saying I was full-bosomed and shapely. They were not always so generous, as like all actresses I suffered from bad press as well as good.

Fortunately, I had the kind of expressive features that were perfect for this comic role. As was my mop of brown curls, generally a nuisance to control but creating the right comedic look beneath a mob cap.

And the applause I received at the end of my performance felt like a kind of ecstasy, a warmth that flowed through my veins like wine. Utterly intoxicating!

My first appearance on stage at the tender age of sixteen brought about a complete sea change in my attitude. I worked hard in the coming weeks, learning lines, watching how other actors performed, picking up tips and wrinkles. I felt so inadequate that I knew I must learn my craft quickly. Mama, of course, was in her element, I hadn't seen her in such good spirits in an age. She would sit with a pile of newspapers on her lap and avidly scour them for reviews, pointing out the good ones to me.

'Listen to this, Dolly, you are described as "a most valuable acquisition to the public stock of innocent entertainment". And when Sheridan's daughter Betsy came to watch you the other day, she said you surpassed what could have been expected. She even claimed that one day you would be a favourite and the first in your line of acting.'

I laughed. 'I think you exaggerate, Mama, or she does. Stop reading such nonsense.'

'Don't be unduly modest, child. All the reviews are good. Read them for yourself, dear.'

I refused absolutely to do so, blushing at the very thought. Throughout my career, reviews, whether good or bad, were anathema to me. I hated them. But I was relieved to see my dear mother content.

I next played the simple-minded shepherdess, Phoebe, in *As You Like It*, which was great fun. I was also allowed to speak the prologue and epilogue. One was written for me specially in the character of an Irish Volunteer, for which I was required to wear a soldier's uniform and strut about the stage with sword in hand. The performance always brought shrieks of laughter and loud applause from the young folk of Dublin.

Hester was given a few small parts, and George too was dreaming of an acting career, meanwhile helping out backstage where he could.

My heart was now set upon the theatre. I was finding more fulfilment and happiness in my work than I had ever anticipated, gaining in confidence every week. My mother was right, I did have a natural talent for acting, particularly with comedy, and if I could use it for the betterment of my family, then I would do so, and bring myself pleasure at the same time.

Two

'A treasure to be nurtured'

Thomas Ryder, our manager, owned both Crow Street and Smock Alley. He constantly complained that times were hard, and was struggling to make both pay. 'Dublin doesn't have the capacity for two successful theatres,' he would moan whenever the moment came to pay our salaries. There was the odd week when we received no pay at all or 'the ghost refused to walk', as it was termed in the trade. 'We need to attract greater audiences, if I could but think how to pull them in,' he would say, holding his head in his hands in despair.

Mama would fall into a faint if I came home with nothing. 'And what are we supposed to live on? How am I to buy bread, or send money to Blanche for Lucy? There are doctors to pay, medicine to buy.' Lucy was failing, and this was a cause of great distress to poor Mama. We had to do all we could to save my little sister, no matter what the cost.

I kissed her soft cheek. 'Do not fret, dearest Mama, I will find the money for Lucy.'

One of my fellow actors was a Richard Daly. He was tall and rather dashing, an elegant dandy who was always impeccably turned out, ruffled, beribboned and curled, pea-green being his favourite colour. He might even have been classed as handsome were it not for a cast in one eye, which was really rather off-putting when he looked at you. He was a member of the Fire-eaters' Club and an avid duellist. It was said that his opponents could never be certain whether or not he was focused on them, which was apparently why Daly didn't have a scratch on him. He generally wore a somewhat battered looking brooch pinned to his chest which was said once to have saved his life by taking the bullet.

I didn't much care for the fellow myself, as there was an

arrogance about him, and a flirtatious insincerity which I did
not entirely trust. He was forever under my feet when I came
off stage, would lurk in the wings so that I'd be obliged to
squeeze past him as he made no effort to move.

'When will you allow me to take you out to dine, or to walk
by the river?' he would whisper in my ear as I slithered by.

I might have said when I was old and grey and had lost all
common sense, but instead I confined myself to a polite smile
or a little giggle. He was, after all, an actor of some renown
in the company who frequently played the lead, while I was
a mere newcomer. He was forever bragging about his time
studying at Trinity College, so was undoubtedly a gentleman.
Rumour had it that he'd been obliged to turn to the stage
having gambled away much of a personal fortune, although his
skills in acting were not particularly well thought of.
Nevertheless, he would readily dip into his ample pockets to
help tide over his fellow cast members, particularly the young
ladies of whom he was rather fond, so perhaps there was some
good in him, I thought.

Today he offered to help me with my lines.

'I thank you kindly, sir, but Mama does very well at that
task. She was once an actress herself, if you recall.'

'Ah, but we need to rehearse our love scene. It is vitally
important that we get it right.'

I gave him a doubtful look, wary of this offer since I knew
his reputation as a skirt-chaser. Yet I was badly in need of a
small loan, not only to see us through the week but also for
Mama to send money for Lucy's treatment. 'Perhaps we could
quickly run through it this afternoon, before the evening
performance,' I agreed.

'Gladly. What a delight you are, Dolly.'

'Dora. Dolly is the name my family use. My stage name is
Dora, or Miss Francis.'

'Ah!' His eyes glinted as his gaze roamed over me, allowing
it to linger on my breasts as men so often did. 'Excellent
choice, *Miss* Francis,' and he flourished a bow as if I were a
courtly lady. 'We will foregather at one o'clock precisely in
the props room where we might hope to find some peace and
quiet.'

I took my sister Hester with me. 'Do not,' I instructed her, 'on any account leave me alone with this man. I do not trust him an inch.'

'You're a fool even to agree to this,' she said, in her usual scolding way.

Hester had no time for men, a prejudice presumably caused by a neglectful father. And in this instance she may well have been right, as I could see at once that Daly was displeased by her presence. Giving him no time to object I handed Hester the script, announcing that she would act as prompt. 'Now we can concentrate on the action without worrying about forgetting our lines.'

He frowned at me, but then of a sudden put back his head and laughed out loud. 'Keep your chaperone if you must, dearest Dora, for now. But I am not fooled by your maidenly blushes. I am fully aware that you find me irresistible.'

'Shall we begin?' I said, deliberately cool.

Hester sat in the corner, barely glancing at the script she held in her hand as she watched open-mouthed the 'love scene' performed before her eyes. I do not care to recall the number of times he insisted we go through it, far more than was strictly necessary. And on every occasion came 'the kiss'.

'No, it still isn't quite right, you must sink into my arms, lean back when I hold you. Like this.'

'Like some fainting virgin?' I caustically remarked.

'Exactly. Is that not what you are?' His good eye fixed me with a challenging glint, but I managed to slide from his arms with some of my dignity still intact.

'I think that's enough for now, don't you? I feel confident we know this scene well enough, and I'm in need of a rest before the first performance. Thank you for sparing the time to help me.' I was invariably polite, although fearful of seeming to encourage him, and pointedly avoided joining in his banter. 'Before we go, there is just one matter I wish to discuss with you.' I cast a quick glance across at Hester, who instantly jumped up to start tidying away the props that we'd used, deliberately keeping herself busy as we had agreed. 'I wondered if I might ask a small favour.'

'Your wish is my command,' he simpered, taking my hand,

the moistness of his lips leaving an imprint of his lingering kiss long after I had gently withdrawn it.

I quickly explained about Lucy and the need for money to pay for a physician and medical care. 'I wouldn't ask otherwise, but we have no way of raising the necessary funds, so a small loan would be most appreciated. Well, not too small. Physicians are expensive and times have been hard for Mama recently. Twenty or thirty pounds perhaps?' I timorously suggested, thinking of the creditors whose accounts we also needed to settle. 'I will, of course, pay back every penny, perhaps in regular instalments if that would be agreeable?'

He smiled. 'I am so sorry to hear of your sister's illness, and only too happy to help. We can discuss the exact terms later.'

Perhaps, I thought, Richard Daly was not so bad after all. But I had no wish to repeat that 'love scene' save on stage.

To my great relief, by the following year of 1779 I learned that Daly was engaged to Jane Barsanti, a leading actress of note whom he was to marry, which meant he'd be unlikely to trouble me again, or so I thought. She was a widow, her former husband, Lyster, having died. I guessed he'd left her sufficient funds to add to her attractions, certainly so far as Richard Daly was concerned.

Once she was his wife, he offered to take the Smock Alley lease off Ryder's hands. Our poor beleaguered manager clearly had mixed feelings on the matter. While still struggling to maintain both theatres Ryder was nevertheless aware that with money behind him, Daly would prove a powerful rival. He therefore put up little resistance.

'I am sorry to see it go, but have done all I can think of to make it pay,' Ryder mourned. 'I've engaged at considerable expense the finest that the London stage has to offer in such actors as Mrs Abington, Sheridan and the Barrys, all to no avail. You are welcome to it, Daly.'

'He does not mean it,' my mother whispered. 'Poor Ryder fears Daly will bankrupt him, for it is true what he says, Dublin cannot sustain two theatres.'

Perhaps Mama was right in her surmise as Ryder made a

sudden decision to put on a comic opera, as if in a last valiant effort to survive.

'I intend to stage *The Duenna*, but we'll switch all the characters, making men play the ladies' parts, and vice versa. It will be a completely transvestite performance and we'll call it *The Governess*. It will be a travesty and a delight.'

I was given a leading role, dressing as a man in the character of Lopez, and although I say it myself, I, like the show, was a great success. The audience loved it, and my part in it. Perhaps I radiated more charm than usual; my laughter certainly bubbled up straight from the heart, so much did I enjoy myself. I love playing these comic roles and dressing up as a boy. Certainly the men enjoyed a rare view of my legs in breeches. Whatever the reason, I attracted attention other than that of a satisfied audience. Richard Daly himself returned to see me perform, and apparently liked what he saw.

He cornered me, as was his wont, when I came off stage, but on this occasion followed me to the dressing room. I stood holding the door, deliberately not permitting him entrance. He smiled in that squinting, devil-may-care way he had. 'You're wasted here, Dora dear.'

'I disagree. Thomas Ryder was the first to offer me a trial as a green girl, and is generous in giving me excellent parts. I have no complaints.'

'And does he pay you well? Do you have the three guineas a week he promised?'

I looked away, not wishing to admit that despite his best efforts Ryder had been unable to keep his promise on wages. 'We are hoping for good houses all week for this comic opera,' I stoutly remarked, in the manager's defence.

Daly sadly shook his head, making a little tutting sound. 'It will not be enough, Dora. Crow Street is on its way out. You are a good actress, and I would welcome you at Smock Alley at any time. I intend to engage Sarah Siddons, John Kemble and other star names for future productions, and you could be part of that success.'

He pestered me time and again in the weeks and months following, which put me in a terrible quandary. My darling sister Lucy had sadly died, despite all our care of her, so there had also been the funeral to pay for. Ever since her death, Mama had slipped into a decline, and rarely ventured out of bed. I was deeply concerned over her state of health. Losing a husband and a child in one year had all been too much for her. I certainly needed to earn more money, painfully aware that I was falling behind with my repayments on the loan Daly had made me.

Yet I felt a loyalty to Ryder as he'd been the one to take me on and give me my first chance.

'I can't just walk away,' I would say, still hesitant to commit, and wary of throwing in my lot with Daly.

Finally, he issued an ultimatum. 'This is your last chance. You must decide now or find some other way to repay the loan.'

And so I went to tell Ryder about the offer, wishing to be open and honest with him. He gave me a measured, rather sad look. Then after a long moment of silence, came his reply.

'Take the offer, Dora. Daly is right, the doors of Crow Street will be closed for ever by the end of the year. Sadly, I don't have a rich wife to back my enthusiasms. I wish you every success in your career, and am glad to have been a part of its inception, but there is no future for you here. You must go to the Smock Alley.'

Only when I heard these words did I realize how very much I had longed for a different reply. There was something about Richard Daly that sent shivers down my spine, but I had no choice. I must accept his offer, or my family would starve.

Three

1780

It was soon apparent that Daly revelled in his new position of power, and the company trod delicately around him, obeying his every word for fear of losing their place. He had not the care or respect for women usually found in an Irish gentleman, and it was not uncommon to see some weeping female leaving with her carpet bag via the stage door. Or, for that matter, an actor storming off in a fury. Daly certainly meant to keep us all on our mettle. And he continued to wait in the wings, watching me closely.

I began with the role of Priscilla Tomboy in Bickerstaffe's *The Romp*. It was a naughty part, some might call it very slightly vulgar, but I did my best to give her a warm heart and good humour.

'I would as lief marry the old-clothes man . . .' I said to Young Cockney, bringing a roar of laughter from the audience. '. . . I won't kiss him, I would spit in his face first.'

Words I could easily have said about Daly, remembering that earlier rehearsal.

The audience loved it, and by association, me. I am sure it was no more than that, but I was delighted by my reception. Daly too was well pleased, pecked me a kiss on each cheek and gave me a warm hug of approbation. His reaction was such that an idea suddenly came to me in the glow of the moment.

'I wonder, may I have a benefit? If the audience likes me and we manage to fill the house, it would help with the repayment of my debt.'

He gave me his squint-eyed look. 'There is absolutely no hurry to pay that off, Dora. Have I harassed you about it in any way?'

'No,' I admitted, unwilling to say how it unnerved me when he sometimes refused to accept the meagre sum I was able to offer him each week by way of repayment, as if money were of no account to him. 'It is most kind of you to be so generous, and so patient, but I would welcome the opportunity of a benefit.' Since all the profits from such an event went directly to the actor concerned, I saw it as an excellent way to resolve our financial difficulties. Mama might rally then if the debt were paid off and we had more cash for the family each week.

He winked at me, and playfully chucked my chin. 'You are worrying unduly, dear girl, but if that is what you wish then I will arrange one for you.'

For the first time, even though I hated this habit he had of seeking any excuse to touch me, I responded to the gesture with a beaming smile. 'Oh, thank you, sir. I shall be forever grateful.'

'I'm sure you will. An expression of gratitude is always pleasant, if directed in the correct manner. And there is really no need for you to call me sir. Richard will do fine.'

'Thank you, er, Richard . . . sir.'

He rumpled my curls and went off laughing, but the glow of satisfaction I felt inside did not diminish and I ran to our lodgings with wings on my heels to share my good news. 'We will soon settle this debt,' I promised Mama, and the thought of a benefit inspired her sufficiently to rouse her from her bed to help me learn the lines.

Daly chose the play, one I'd never heard of, and a tragedy rather than the comedy I would have favoured, which was disappointing. But I was so excited, so keen to do well that I rehearsed and studied for long hours, with Mama's help. She also guided my choice through a selection of songs, including 'Melton Oysters', one of my favourites, which I would do at the end.

The night of the benefit arrived and despite some nervous flutters in my stomach, I was filled with excitement, eager to begin, constantly peeping through the curtains to check on the audience.

Sadly, there was barely a soul in the place save for the young bucks in the pit. I was not as popular as I had imagined, which seemed a salutary warning not to believe what one reads about oneself in the press, however good the reviews.

I performed the tragedy as best I could, considering the paucity of the audience and no sound of the laughter I was so used to, but it was heartbreakingly difficult. I rallied sufficiently at the end to sing 'Melton Oysters', as agreed. My voice was not trained but had a sweetness to it, and the song allowed me to lift the mood a little.

> *There was a clever, likely lass,*
> *Just come to town from Glo'ster,*
> *And she did get her livelihood*
> *By crying Melton Oysters.*

This was much better received, but not enough to save me.

'I'm sorry, Dora, but there will be no money for you,' Daly coolly informed me. 'The expenses of the production far outweigh what we have taken at the door.'

I was deeply disappointed and hugely embarrassed.

'Do not blame yourself, child, this is no fault of yours,' Mama soothed as I sobbed in her arms backstage. 'It was a poor choice of play. Tragedy is not your forte, and there was precious little in the way of publicity for it.'

Well used to her ranting and railing against Daly, I paid little attention. Who else could I blame but myself? Having pinned my hopes on a large enough sum of money to pay off our debt, to me the failure of my benefit was a huge blow. The £50 he'd so generously insisted I borrow had seemed like a fortune at the time, but was now all gone in doctor's fees, funeral expenses, grocery bills and the cost of footwear and clothing for my siblings, not to mention costumes for myself for each production. Were I being paid £5 a week, as was John Kemble, there would have been no problem, but there was little change from my twenty shillings by the time our landlady had been paid, and the family fed.

'You sang your little songs most charmingly, dear, and there will be other opportunities, I'm sure.' As Mama dried my eyes and tenderly consoled me we became aware of a growing noise in the pit. As custom dictated, the manager had gone out on stage to inform the audience of the result of their munificence in attending the benefit. The young Irish bucks were far from happy to hear that no profit at all had been garnered, and there came a huge roar of disapproval.

'Then give Miss Francis another benefit,' called one.

'Aye, we like her singing. Give her a second chance,' came a chorus of approval.

'I fear that cannot be done,' Daly said. 'Every actress has only one opportunity in any given season for a benefit, and this, our first season, has not been a profitable one. Miss Francis was unfortunate and there is nothing to be done about that.'

'There's something *we* can do,' shouted an aggressive voice from the gallery. And Mama and I looked on in horror as a group of bank clerks joined the young men in the pit, and the whole tribe of them began to break up the benches in their fury.

'Stop this at once!' Daly roared, but his cries went unheeded. My supporters, which is what they chose to call themselves, even turned on the orchestra, who were making a pitiful attempt to drown out the hubbub by sawing on their violins and blowing loudly into their trumpets. The result was bedlam, until one young man put up his hands to his comrades for silence and began to address Daly in a calm, clear voice.

'These are our demands. You will agree to give Miss Francis one more chance, a proper benefit this time with posters put up around the town to publicize it. And she must be allowed to choose her own play instead of that tragic drivel you put on tonight.'

'And if I do not agree?' roared Daly.

'Then we will rip this theatre to shreds, and you will have more to worry about than the loss of one night's profit.'

Fearful that they might carry out their threats, Daly was forced to concede to the pressure. He had little choice. 'See what trouble you have brought upon my head,' he snarled, as he brushed past me and strode away in a rage.

Mama, who was looking happier by the minute, hugged me tight. 'Another benefit, and this time you will do well, I know it.'

She was right. My second benefit, this time a comedy, was

riotous in that it proved to be a huge triumph. My supporters were there in droves. The theatre was full to bursting and I pocketed the princely sum of £40. I took it straight to Daly's office and laid the entire wad of notes and coins on the desk before him, the glow of success still warming my heart. 'There, does that settle what is left of the debt I owe you?'

He picked up the notes and counted them one by one, even though he knew the amount as he had himself put them into my hand. He then counted the shillings and sovereigns, every single sixpenny piece, before setting it all in a tin box and locking it back in his safe. Then he came around the desk to stand before me, a wry smile on his handsome face, his squinting eye wandering elsewhere while his good one remained fixed upon my face. 'It settles about half of it,' he said in calm, soft tones.

'*Half?* But I only borrowed fifty in the first place and I have paid a fair amount back already, scraping by each week on a pittance in order to do so.'

His laughter was a low rumble deep in his throat. 'You are forgetting interest, my dear, which is considerable for any unsecured loan.'

I looked at him blankly, not understanding. 'Interest?'

'A bank would charge you considerably more than I, even were one willing to lend to a young, unknown actress such as yourself with neither means nor reputation.'

I felt sick to my stomach. In my naivety I had given no thought to interest, nor made any provision for it in my reckoning. Our budget was tight enough, so slim that I could see no way of increasing my weekly repayments. And there would certainly be no hope of a third benefit. 'How will I ever repay it then?' I cried, unable to keep the fear and misery from my voice.

I was so young, so naïve, so utterly innocent.

'I am quite sure,' he said, with a soft chuckle, 'that you will think of a way.' Then, lifting my chin with one finger, his mouth came down upon mine. To call it a kiss would be a misnomer. He devoured me. I was shocked to the core, revolted even, and quickly attempted to step back, out of his grasp. But his arm came about my waist, pinioning me against him, and while his other hand stroked my throat, the assault continued. I was not so innocent that I wasn't aware of the fact that many young actresses were willing to exchange their favours for a particular choice role. I was not one of their number. Summoning all my strength, I thrust him away.

'I think you mistake me, *sir*,' I snapped. 'My virtue is intact, and I mean to keep it that way.'

His laughter was still ringing in my ears as I stormed from his office and up the stairs, in high dudgeon.

Daly never left me alone after that. Wherever I went he seemed to be hovering right behind me, or would appear unexpectedly out of nowhere. 'You are sweet as a cherry,' he would say, capturing me in his arms, or lightly graze the bloom of my breasts above the neckline of my gown with the backs of his knuckles. 'Ripe for the picking, so deliciously vulnerable. Utterly irresistible!'

I loathed his hands on me, constantly touching and caressing, trapping me in some shadowed spot just when I thought I had escaped his attentions. 'I beg you to leave me alone.'

'Why do you pretend indifference when you are equally captivated by me, as I am by you?'

'That is a mere figment of your imagination,' I told him as sharply as I dared.

'Besides which, do you not owe me considerable gratitude?'

'I shall pay you in cash, as agreed. What would your new wife say were she to discover how you pursue me?'

'Fortunately, my dear beloved does not control every corner of my life, try as she might. In any case, I believe it is you who pursues me,' he airily remarked. 'I cannot seem to go anywhere without running across you. I wonder why that is?'

I longed to say because *you* never leave *me* alone, but could not quite find the courage. The tittle-tattle in the green room about Daly's reputation for seducing young actresses was becoming common gossip. Many a girl had been unable to resist his advances simply because he was her employer, acting often her only means of earning a living. And he was nothing if not persistent. I, however, was determined that much as I feared losing my job, I would not succumb to these seduction tactics.

'I believe you are anxious to repeat that little love scene, in very truth this time, rather than a mere rehearsal.'

I tossed back my brown curls. 'I am no such thing. I do assure you I have no wish ever to repeat the experience.'

'Oh, come, shall we say one kiss to reduce the debt by one pound?' he teased.

I stared at him in astonishment. 'One pound!'

He chuckled. 'Very well then, what value would you put upon a kiss? Two pounds? Three? I'm open to suggestions. But it must be a proper kiss, with feeling. Let me show you.'

He pulled me close in his arms, his mouth again devouring mine, his tongue almost choking me this time as it probed and licked. Desperate to free myself, I gave him an almighty heave and pushed him away. 'Leave me be. I vow I shall be obliged to tell your wife if you do not desist.'

His laughter was harsh and cruel, for he knew as well as I that I would never risk such a thing.

The new Mrs Daly was a good actress and well regarded. She loyally supported her husband in running the theatre, and her brilliance was the main reason Smock Alley had survived as well as it had this last year. But she was known to keep a tenaciously close eye on who her husband chose to play the best parts, and to be utterly ruthless with those who transgressed her trust.

'You would not dare to tell her, my sweet. You know full well how fierce my Jenny can be with young actresses who stray on to what she considers to be her private territory.' He smiled at me with that devilish, squint-eyed grin. 'But perhaps you could offer a little more than a kiss? I would make it worth your while.'

'Not while I have breath in my body to resist,' I hissed, shocked by his audacity, yet needing to remind myself constantly that this man was my employer, and that my future career, nay, my family's survival, lay entirely in his hands. His reputation as a tyrant in charge of his own minor universe was becoming increasingly evident, and as a gentleman he naturally considered himself above the law. My fears grew that I was indeed his next victim.

'In point of fact, I pity your poor wife,' I snapped, and sticking my chin in the air walked away, head high, fully expecting him to shout after me that I was sacked. But he only carried on laughing, as if biding his time for the next spat between us.

In the months following I was kept busy with a variety of minor roles. I tried not to mind but was deeply disappointed not to be cast in quite so many good ones, with few leads offered. Other people should be allowed a turn, after all. Mrs Daly naturally took most of the leads, but then it was her money which ran the establishment and she was a gifted actress, so how could I object?

Daly continued to tease and flirt in that mischievous way of his. 'Why are you so cruel as to deny me a little of your time and attention? Can you not see how heart-sore I am for love of you?'

'I see you are a rogue of the first quarter,' I announced, growing braver in my efforts to put him off.

Fortunately he made no serious advances upon my virtue as he became increasingly distracted by a newly pregnant wife who was constantly sickly. I rather hoped he had finally accepted my refusal, although I would sometimes find him watching me with that odd, squint-eyed stare. And occasionally, he would still hover in the wings and whisper to me as I passed by.

'Have you reconsidered my generous offer?' he would ask. 'You cannot deny it is a good one. You know how I long for you. Why not pay me in kind instead? Think of the relief you would feel at being free of the debt.'

Daly's constant harassment flustered and enraged me, making me come close to hating him at times. But I studiously ignored his persistent badgering and without fail relinquished five shillings each week, a quarter of my earnings, which barely covered the extortionate interest he was charging. At least Hester was bringing in a little money too now, if not as much as she would like. Following the death of Lucy, Cousin Blanche had asked for my brother Nathaniel to come and keep her company. She treated him as an adopted son, which was good for Nat, and meant one less mouth for us to feed. But Mama was still not well, which was of great concern to me. Better parts might lead to an increase in wages, so it was frustrating always to be the simple shepherdess.

'You realize why Daly is reducing your parts,' my sister warned me one day after a further disappointment. 'It's because you continue to resist him.'

I looked at her askance. 'He would surely not be so vindictive.'

'Don't be naïve, Doll. Richard Daly will allow nothing to stand in the way of his desire. And he wants you.'

I ruefully admitted that she was most likely correct, and recklessly challenged him on the subject. 'Why am I never given decent parts any more?'

'All in good time,' he said. 'Such favours need to be earned.'

'But you said I would be a part of Smock Alley's success. What of the three guineas you promised me? Am I not working as hard as I can? Was not the theatre full on the nights I played the lead?' I was learning to stand up for myself a little more, fighting for the facility to clear my debts and see my family secure.

'Have you thought again of my offer? What price a kiss?'

I scoffed at this nonsense. 'If I am not allowed to play leading roles, how am I ever to gain the necessary experience?'

He squinted darkly at me from beneath his tricorn hat, then leaned close to whisper in my ear, the gold tassels on his pea-green jacket brushing against my breasts. 'I am not a man accustomed to spending my nights alone, so were you to be a touch more generous you would not find me ungrateful. I am quite certain you and I would do well together. When are you going to give in?'

I turned on my heel and walked rapidly away, privately vowing never to mention the matter again, no matter how annoying it was to see others given preferment. I concentrated on improving my acting skills still further, resolute on learning my craft, on giving my utmost attention to every part, however insignificant it might seem.

As Mrs Daly's pregnancy advanced, like all actresses afraid of losing her favourite parts to rivals, she continued to appear on stage. But by November 1781 even the stalwart Jane Daly was forced to retire. Surely now, I thought, I would be granted better roles.

* * *

One night Hester was waiting for me as I entered the dressing room. We'd been rehearsing all day, followed by two performances, and keeping up a level of concentration so that I didn't miss the few lines I had was strangely tiring. I was eager to clean off my make-up and go home; the prospect of the warm soup Mama would have waiting for us was most appealing.

'Mr Daly has sent for you,' Hester told me, looking anxious, as she knew how fervently I avoided his presence.

I groaned. 'But it is almost midnight and I am bone weary. Whatever it is must wait for the morrow. Help me out of this gown, Hester, I ache for my bed.'

Our lodgings were an easy walk from Smock Alley, and, as always, we hurried home arm in arm, giggling over whatever incidents had gone wrong on stage that night, as we so liked to do. There was always something, a door that had not opened when necessary, a knock not delivered on cue, or a blank moment when one of the older actors had forgotten a line and I had been obliged to cover it up by paraphrasing it for him. We were laughing over Benedick's wig having fallen askew in the main production of *Much Ado About Nothing*, which had not at all been intended, when a smart phaeton drew up beside us.

'Miss Francis, I believe I ordered you to my office.'

I stared in dismay at my employer. 'Mr Daly, it is late. I thought the morning would be soon enough.'

'When I demand attendance from an employee I mean it to be at *my* convenience, not *theirs*. Pray, step aboard. Since you chose to disobey me, we must have our conversation here and now.'

'But it is past midnight . . .'

'Therefore my patience is thin. If you please . . .'

My heart skipped a beat. Climbing into a phaeton with Richard Daly at past midnight was not a prospect I relished, but I could see no escape. 'My sister . . .' I began.

'. . . can surely see herself home for once. She is not a child, and you will not be long after her. I dare say you value your position at Smock Alley, do you not, Miss Francis?'

I cast Hester a pained look. 'Hurry straight home. I won't be long.'

'I'll wait for you . . .' she began, but I shook my head, knowing there was no way I could refuse. I had evaded his attentions before and believed myself capable of doing so again. 'Go home, or Mama will be worried. I shall follow shortly.'

She nodded, then put down her head and ran, hating to be alone in the dark. I offered my employer a bleak nod of assent and climbed into the carriage beside him.

Four

'. . . our little arrangement'

If I had hoped that he would indeed conduct the conversation there and then, before releasing me to my supper and bed, then I was fooling myself. Daly snapped the reins and set off at a brisk trot, heading away from the town centre.

'Where are you taking me?' I asked, struggling to hide the tremor in my voice.

'Somewhere I can have your undivided attention.'

'I would rather you take me home at once,' I insisted, furious at my own stupidity at climbing into the carriage with him, but had I not done so, he could as easily have dismissed me on the spot. And with nowhere to go now that Crow Street had closed, where else could I find employment to feed my family, and pay for the physician needed by Mama? Besides which, I had signed articles with Daly. There would be huge penalties to pay if I left, or if he dismissed me for insubordination, and I was already in hock to him. 'Surely, whatever the problem is, it can wait till morning?'

His rumble of laughter was chilling. I clasped my hands tightly in my lap and sent up a silent prayer.

It was not answered. The horse clipped along at a pace that precluded any hope of my jumping out. The night was black and silent, save for the rustle of leaves, the creak of branches in the wind. We were soon far from the busy thoroughfare, and I could tell by the sound of the horse's hooves we were now on unmade country roads rather than cobbles. *Where was he taking me?* Panic was clawing at my insides, rapidly turning to cold terror. The journey felt as if it had taken hours, although it was probably no more than twenty minutes or so.

When he finally stopped the vehicle I made a valiant attempt to escape but he leapt upon me, pinning me down with the weight of his body.

'You're the very worst sort of tease, do you know that?' he snarled, ripping my gown at the neck in his eagerness to paw at my breasts. I screamed, although instinctively aware there was no one to hear me, let alone come to my rescue.

'I swear I am not,' I cried. 'I have begged you time and again to stop pestering me. Please let me go. I don't want this. Let me be.'

He wasn't listening. He thrust a hand into the warmth of my bosom and squeezed it hard. Then he was pushing up my skirts, his fingers exploring my private parts, and in my shock and horror I knew all was lost. When he finally shoved his member into me, the pain was hideous. I was quite certain he was ripping me apart. And he kept on thrusting, over and over again, panting and gasping, and all the while grinning his squint-eyed leer at me. I was sobbing, screaming, fighting him with every ounce of my strength, but it wasn't enough. My efforts were feeble by comparison with his lust.

When he was done with me, he thrust me aside, a sobbing heap in the corner of the carriage. Then he calmly adjusted his clothing, clicked on the reins and drove home at a much more steady pace.

By the time we had reached the door of my lodgings I had my gown in some sort of order. I was so desperately afraid of upsetting Mama were she to see me in this state that I'd even managed to stop crying, determined to regain control of my emotions. He flung open the door and I was only too eager to depart. Even then, at the moment of my release, he gave me yet further orders.

'You will make yourself available whenever I call for you, at whatever hour. I may find us somewhere more comfortable than this small vehicle, but you will do as I ask, without question. Understood?'

I stared at him in horrified disbelief. Perhaps I had thought this violation was some act of revenge on his part for my resistance over the long months he had pursued me. Now I saw that it was but a prelude to a more devastating plan.

'What is it you want from me?' I asked, my voice cracking beneath the strain of what I had just endured.

'Whatever takes my fancy, and I rather fancy you, *Miss* Francis.'

His emphasis on the 'Miss' was most derogatory. It implied that I was no more than a woman of the streets. 'If you value your job, you will come when I say, without question. Oh, and I will reduce the debt by – um, shall we say five pounds for this night's service, less interest?' And with a final leer he drove off into the night, leaving me shivering with shock on the cobbles.

I made sure that neither Mama nor Hester were ever told of what had occurred that night. Where was the point in upsetting them, I thought. We were stuck here at Smock Alley, at least for the length of my contract. Years of servitude to Daly's every whim stretched ahead and I shuddered at the prospect, my mind desperately seeking some way of release. Yet what escape could there be? If I walked away Daly could sue me, and my family would starve.

Later that day I spoke to him, quite cold and matter-of-fact, as if we were discussing a business meeting. 'I will do as you ask, since I have no choice in the matter, but I would be obliged if you refrained from using Hester as a go-between. I have no wish for my family to be privy to this affair, or whatever you choose to call it.'

'I was thinking much the same myself,' he casually remarked. 'I have no wish for my wife to hear of our little arrangement either, so I'll find us a room in an hotel next time. I will let you know the day and time.'

And so began our 'affair', our 'little arrangement' as he termed it. Twice a week throughout that endless winter, he would take me to some seedy little hotel down by the quay. It stank of sewage and fish, and stale sweat, and I could hear odd little rustling sounds behind the wainscot. He would instantly strip to his under-drawers then order me to do the same while he watched. I always kept my eyes averted, not wishing to look at him, shivering as I peeled off my chemise, sick to my stomach with loathing. So much so that afterwards I would often physically vomit into the chamber pot. This always amused him, calling me his fragile little flower.

'Are you sickening for something?' Mama asked me one day in spring. 'You seem oddly quiet and paler than usual. Where have your rosy cheeks gone, my dear?' And she patted them in that gentle motherly way.

I managed a smile to reassure her. Mama herself had been unwell for some time, and I had no wish to add to her worries, and thereby risk making her worse. 'I am simply tired with doing two, sometimes three plays a week. My head spins at times trying to remember all the lines.' How could I tell her the true cause of my distraction?

'Nonsense, you have a wonderful facility for learning. You are far more likely to forget to eat properly than not study your part.'

'I confess I actually dried in the farce at the matinee today; my mind had gone a complete blank. It was alarming.'

She frowned. 'That is most unlike you, Dolly. I shall coddle some eggs and stand over you while you eat them. And tonight I shall have Scotch broth waiting for your supper.'

But no amount of coddled eggs or Mama's delicious Scotch broth was going to heal this sickness. I had not seen my monthly courses for some weeks now, and much as I might deny the fact, I knew, with a horrified certainty, that I was pregnant. Was I not familiar enough with the symptoms, having seen Mama through several of her own pregnancies?

I so longed to tell her, to seek her guidance and support, but dare not. Apart from the fragile state of her own health at this time, shame ate at my soul, even though I knew I should bear no guilt over what had happened to me. I'd had no choice in the matter but to do as Daly ordered or risk starvation for my family. Lucy was dead, and James was married, of course. Francis had joined the military and Nathaniel, a bright, intelligent boy, was at school receiving the kind of education that Mama had always dreamed of for him, his fees largely paid for by the small inheritance from Papa that had finally come our way via the Bland family. As both boys spent their leave or school holidays with Cousin Blanche, they cost me little. Even so, I sent what money I could, for all she insisted it was quite unnecessary and to look to our own needs first. Which indeed was true, as there was still Hester, George and Mama to be cared for out of my purse.

And soon there would be a fourth member of the family dependent upon me. A frightening prospect for a girl only just turned twenty.

My reward, if you can call it that, came in the improvement of the roles I was offered. Throughout that spring of 1782 I was given the choicest parts. I played Adelaide to John Kemble's Count of Narbonne, Lady Anne to his Richard III, and Katherine to his Petruchio. My reputation began to rise as a result, soaring ever higher, albeit at only twenty shillings a week, which left little spare to pay off my debt, the interest increasing the outstanding sum faster than I could ever hope to reduce it.

I made every effort to keep out of Daly's way, to avoid him and protect myself. But without fail the summons would come, and of necessity I would obey. I did my utmost to detach myself mentally from however Daly chose to use my body, or rather abuse it. Fortunately it never took him very long before he was done, and he'd then be anxious to return to the theatre in case his wife noticed his absence.

But after several weeks of this treatment I was finding it harder to tolerate his attentions. He was growing bolder by the day, and becoming ever more demanding. I think he enjoyed humiliating me, certainly didn't see me as worthy of any kindness or consideration. On one visit to that miserable little room, he ratcheted up the degradation still further by insisting that I take his member in my mouth. I was so appalled, so ashamed, that I stoutly refused to perform what seemed to me a vile act.

'I will not do it. I am not some street whore. You expect too much of me, and why is my debt still not settled? I have done all you asked, surely it should be paid off by now.'

'*I* will say when the debt is settled, not you, some twopenny actress.' He was so enraged by my refusal that he shoved me down on the bed and took me with such a fierce violence, I cried out in agony.

'It was your own fault, Dolly,' he warned, as afterwards I struggled not to weep. 'Had you done as you were told I would never have lost my temper and accidentally hurt you.'

Hastily I pulled on my clothes, my anxious need to escape even more urgent than usual. 'That was no accident, it was entirely deliberate on your part. You love to hurt and humiliate me. You are a sick, sad man and I hate you. The very fact that your victim is unwilling is what gives you the most pleasure! How much longer must this go on?' I demanded somewhat recklessly.

'Until I grow tired of you,' came his calm reply, smilingly unruffled by my little tantrum.

I could not go on like this, behaving like a strumpet for a man I loathed.

But a week later he again issued his usual order to meet him that afternoon at two o'clock. I did not go. I bravely, or perhaps recklessly is a more accurate word, ignored his instructions. He was furious.

'Where were you? I waited an hour and you did not come. How dare you disobey me?'

I stiffened my spine to stand as tall as I could before him. 'I dare because I have nothing more to lose. For the sake of my family I have tolerated your ruining my career and my life, completely at your mercy as you stole my innocence and degraded me, but I will not willingly subject myself to violence. You are a cruel tyrant, a despicable, immoral man who cares for nothing but his own selfish desires. I don't care what you do to me, I'll have no more of it.'

I expected a tirade of fury but he showed no reaction at all, save for a slight tightening of the mouth, and his right hand falling to where his sword would hang, as if he were about to fight a duel. The silence went on for so long that I began to tremble with fear, my new-found courage quickly evaporating. At length, when I was praying for the ground to open and swallow me, he spoke. 'Have you ever heard of a Mrs Eston?'

My heart began to pound, for of course the scandal had been common gossip in the green room at the time. The poor lady had been deserted by her husband, but she was young and pretty and Daly had been rather taken by her. It was said that at first he was most kind, lending her money to help her recover from her abandonment, but then had caused her to be arrested for non-payment of her debt. Had she too refused him favours? I wondered. Why had I not paid more attention to this gossip?

'It was a most sad case,' he said, his handsome face with its cock-eyed gaze as inscrutable as ever.

'For which you were vilified in the *Dublin Evening Post*,' I daringly challenged him.

'The chit had some supporters, it is true,' he agreed, somewhat dismissively. 'But it didn't greatly help her in the long run. The debt remained, you see, and although some may think me vengeful, I am surely entitled to be reimbursed for my generosity. As she could not repay the loan, then debtor's prison is sadly where she ended up, as must you, my dear. One way or another the price has to be paid. You owe me a considerable sum, Dora dear, and if it is not settled . . . if you are unwilling to give me any sort of recompense for my kind generosity, then . . .' He let out a heavy sigh. '. . . then the debtor's prison it is.'

My knees went all weak and I very nearly collapsed. 'You cannot seriously mean to have me arrested and put into prison? My family would starve.'

'I do and I will. You have twenty-four hours, Dora, to consider your options. Be careful you make the right decision.'

That evening I wept as I confessed the whole truth to my mother. She had never seen me cry, save for when Papa had left, and later when we'd learned of his death. But this was grief of a different sort. I wept for my lost innocence, for the seed Daly had planted in my body which would mature in the fullness of time, and for the terror of prison. The words spilled out, the whole sordid tale, for I could keep the secret no longer.

To her credit Mama did not castigate me. She was a woman of the world and knew well enough the fragility of our situation, as well as the lot of young actresses. She put her arms about me and held me close to the warmth of her motherly breast. 'Do not fret, child. We shall never allow him to use you thus again.'

'How can I stop him? He is no gentleman, for all his fine dandified ways and fancy education. He is a tyrant, a bully.

And now, because I have refused to obey his orders any more, following his further recourse to violence upon me, he has threatened me with arrest. There is nothing to be done.'

But I had greatly underestimated my mother. Grace Phillips, the woman who had run from home to join a theatre, and then married against the wishes of her bridegroom's family, was no feeble-minded weakling. She was a woman of pride, ambition and great courage. Now, with commendable composure, she considered our options.

'Your father's Irish family will be of no use to us. My erstwhile mother-in-law made it very clear when she handed me that not particularly generous legacy from your father's estate for the boys, there would be no further help from that quarter. And we can ask nothing more of dear Cousin Blanche. She would offer you a home, without doubt, where you could safely have the baby. But there is no hope of employment in South Wales. No theatre within miles. Nevertheless, we must leave.'

I stared at her, slightly bemused by all this reasoning. 'Leave? How can we leave? You have already said there is nowhere for us to go.' I, not unnaturally, was in such distress that I could no longer think clearly.

She patted my hand. 'I still have contacts, friends in the theatre world. We will go to my sister in Leeds. Maria is with the Tate Wilkinson company there. I worked with him many years ago, played Desdemona to his Othello in 1758 at the Smock Alley, under the management of Thomas Sheridan. Tate is a most generous-hearted man, I'm sure he will agree to give you a trial.'

Hope fired in my breast, a fragile spark of belief that perhaps I had a future, after all. 'Do you think he might take me on?'

'We can but hope, and are you not a far more experienced actress than you were two years ago? Make no mistake,' Mama reiterated, 'your dear Aunt Maria will also help us. Now hurry, we must gather our few possessions together and leave at once. First thing tomorrow we will take passage to Liverpool and make our way across country, walking if necessary, to Yorkshire.'

'Across the Pennine hills? But Mama, you could never manage to walk so far.'

'I would walk across the fires of hell if that were necessary to save you, Dolly,' and she kissed me, the most loving mother in the world.

I was overwhelmed by the suddenness of this decision, and by her determination. Yet bemused as I was, and ever practical, I continued to seek out problems and difficulties. 'I should collect my wages. We cannot leave without money.'

She frowned a little at that, but then shrugged it away. 'That is unfortunate, but we cannot risk asking for wages. In any case, what difference will a few more shillings make? We must make do with what I have saved in my purse.'

'And all my costumes are in the dressing room at the theatre. I cannot possibly go without them! I have spent a small fortune, and Hester many hours on stitching them.'

'Then you will both have to start afresh. We cannot risk your going back merely for costumes, dearest. Were Daly to guess what we are about, he would have you arrested this very night. Now call George and Hester! There is no time to be lost. We take only what we can carry and leave.'

So it was that early the following morning we boarded a ship bound for Liverpool, albeit with mixed feelings. Delighted as I was to escape Daly's control, the question of the debt remained worryingly unresolved.

Five

'. . . the exquisite and plaintive melody of her voice'

We arrived in Leeds on a wet day in early July 1782 after a gruelling journey across country. We'd begged whatever lifts we could, but walked far too many of the hundred or so miles from Liverpool, taking the better part of a month to do it. I had spent a deal of time throwing up in ditches, where we'd generally spent the night. I was sick to my stomach with fear of being followed, as well as from the effects of my pregnancy. Footsore and weary, Mama alone was in high spirits. She had astonished me by her unflagging zeal, and entertained us through the long miles with yet more anecdotes of theatre life, most of which we had heard many times before. But she did also fill us in on Tate Wilkinson.

'He's the son of a Doctor of Divinity who was once chaplain to Frederick, the previous Prince of Wales. Sadly, as Tate's father went on to solemnize marriages in defiance of the Royal Marriages Act, the poor man was sentenced to transportation to America.'

'What on earth is the Royal Marriages Act?' I asked.

'It was brought in by George III in 1772 to ensure that royal princes and princesses marry appropriately, with the King's consent. His Majesty disapproved strongly of some of his brothers' marriages and concluded greater control was needed so that the dignity of the monarchy could be preserved. Which means they are only permitted to marry ugly foreign princesses instead of lovely young actresses.' And we both laughed, not for a moment thinking that this very act might one day impinge upon my own life.

'I believe Tate's father died at Plymouth before the ship had barely left port. Tate himself, however, you will find a most charming man, and well educated, having been a pupil at Harrow School.'

'Then what on earth made him choose the theatre as a career?' I felt compelled to ask the inevitable question, my earlier hope in my own new career now rapidly fading as I grew increasingly weary.

'Because in spite of all the social prejudices against actors, he chose this most reviled profession so that he might indulge his love of mimicry. He is not the greatest actor in the world, and those he impersonates do not always take kindly to his shrewd observations of them, but he is a most polished and kindly gentleman.'

When we at last reached Leeds we found cheap lodgings and Mama quickly dispatched a note to Tate Wilkinson, requesting a meeting.

'It will not be long now,' she assured me. 'I have every confidence he will take you on.'

I couldn't stop blaming myself for the time I had wasted keeping my secret. Why had I not trusted my mother, instead of hiding behind my shame? Now I was worried that my condition, at four months gone, would damage my chances of being given even an audition.

'Make no mention of this matter for now,' Mama insisted, when I expressed this concern to her.

'But that would be cheating,' I protested.

She scoffed at this. 'Actresses fall pregnant all the time. We will leave off mentioning you are increasing until he has seen the value of your work.'

The following day we received a note saying that Wilkinson would be happy to meet us at a local inn.

The moment he walked through the door I knew at once that I would like him. He was not handsome in any way, nor young, being in his middle years. He was short and rather stocky with an awkward gait. Mama had explained that he'd once fallen off stage and broken his leg, which had been set badly. But his round, homely face was wreathed in a broad smile, and his eyes twinkled most merrily.

'What a happy chance to see you again, Grace,' he cried, smacking a kiss on each cheek. 'Not quite the waif-like Desdemona of yesteryear, but not unhandsome, no indeed, not unhandsome at all. In fact, bearing up better than most, I should say.'

My mother blushed delightfully at this flattery and quietly introduced George, Hester and me. I realized of a sudden we must look a sorry sight indeed: travel-stained, bone weary, and really rather shabby. I deeply regretted the loss of my basket of stage costumes, essential for any actress, and one I'd invested in heavily over the last two years. But afraid of alerting Daly's attention, as he might then prevent our departure, I'd been forced to agree with Mama that we walk away with only the clothes on our backs. Nor did we have much money, and I saw at once that Wilkinson recognized our penurious state.

Dejected, miserable, close to tears, I was suddenly overwhelmed by shame and shyness. How foolishly naïve of me to imagine we could just up sticks, cross the Irish Sea and find a place in another company.

Genuinely delighted to see her old friend again, my mother was bubbling over with high spirits. Over-compensating for my gloom she at once began to sing my praises, painstakingly listing the productions in which I'd played the lead, emphasizing the good audiences, the well-received songs, even the benefit, leaving out any mention of the first failure. I listened in cringing silence, hating the fact that my brother and sister were witness to my embarrassment. I could sense Hester fidgeting beside me, jealous of the fact she was being overlooked.

'Harrumph!' Wilkinson muttered at last, also embarrassed by this outpouring of maternal pride and anxious to stop the flow. He appeared reluctant to take on the responsibility of an actress who looked so unprepossessing, and who could blame him? He turned to me at last and asked, 'And what is your speciality: tragedy, comedy or opera?'

'All,' I said, too deeply depressed to be bothered to answer properly.

He looked astonished, eyebrows raised in some surprise. 'Well, I should need to reflect on the matter most carefully.' Upon this remark he quietly withdrew, presumably to think of some excuse to be rid of us, and I turned upon my parent in a fluster. 'This was all a terrible mistake. How could you embarrass me so, Mama?'

'Be calm, my dear. He is a fair man and has not yet given us his verdict.'

Nor did he immediately do so when finally he returned, bearing a bottle of Madeira and several glasses. He placed these on the table, then cleared his throat.

'Normally, my response would be in the negative. I am most particular who I take on these days as business is not as brisk as it might be. But because of my fondness for you, Grace, my old friend, and the undoubted bond between us, I may well be prepared to offer your daughter a small part, just to try her out. That is, if I like what I hear, you understand?'

'Oh, I do indeed, Tate, how very kind of you. That would be perfectly acceptable, would it not, Dora?'

I said nothing.

Mr Wilkinson smiled. 'May I hear a sample of your work, my dear, so that I might taste the quality, as it were.'

My throat was so choked with emotion, shame and fear, that I could barely speak. 'I would rather have a proper audition on the boards at some other time, if you please, sir.'

'Ah, would you indeed? Well, I dare say that could be arranged.' Picking up the bottle of Madeira he began to pour a little into each glass. 'But since I am here, let us drink a toast to friendship and to old times.'

We each sipped our wine and soon he and Mama were laughing together as they shared memories of their youth. Mama regaled him with her own marital tale and he spoke fondly of his wife and five children. As the conversation moved back to their shared passion, the theatre, the wine was beginning to warm me, staving off the constant gnawing hunger we'd all endured these last weeks, and I began to relax a little and smile at some of their tales. George was asking questions about stage sets, and Hester urging him to say more about the famous actresses he'd met over the years. It was all most pleasant. Then he turned to me and again asked me to recite a few lines.

'Choose something you know well. I'm not a harsh judge and will make all due allowances for the lack of a stage from which to project your voice.'

I caught Mama's encouraging smile and as the Madeira had

boosted my courage a little, I agreed. 'Very well. I shall do a speech from *The Fair Penitent*.'

Nodding, he sat back, glass in hand, and listened most carefully as I recited the lines. When I stopped, there was a small silence. Not one of us dared speak, and I could hardly breathe. Even the volatile Hester had the sense to see that our family's future rested on his answer, and held her silence.

At length Wilkinson spoke, addressing his remarks directly to my mother. 'Have you tutored her, Grace?'

'Not excessively so,' she protested.

'If you have, then you are to be congratulated. I am astonished by the exquisite and plaintive melody of her voice, her distinction of articulation, as well as her truth and sincerity of feeling.'

I actually gasped. Never had I been granted such high praise. It quite boosted my dull spirits. 'If I can please you, the manager, then I should have no fear of pleasing an audience,' I said. 'And were I to achieve public favour then you would not find me ungrateful for the help you have afforded me. I would work hard for you, sir, always.'

Thinking I'd perhaps sounded a mite too full of myself before, I flushed a little as I tried to explain. 'When I said earlier that I could do all, what I meant to say is that I have performed in all, although I prefer comedy, and the opera was of the comic variety.'

He nodded, dismissing my rudeness with a wave of his hand. 'My only concern is that in all honesty I can only pay you fifteen shillings a week, hardly enough to keep the entire family.'

Mama hastened to say how that was of no account, as if we had no need of money; that George too could sing and would willingly help backstage. 'And Hester could play small parts and help with costume, would you not, my dear?'

'Of course,' she agreed, eyes bright with hope.

Wilkinson seemed reasonably satisfied with this, and offered me the part of Calista in the very play from which I had quoted, the very next Thursday. 'To be followed by the role of Lucy in *The Virgin Unmasked*.'

I was overwhelmed, and thanked him profusely, while privately recognizing the irony of such a role.

Mama was casting me telling glances, urging me to keep my secret a while longer, until I had proved myself. 'And may she sing too?' my mother pressed. 'She does a wonderful rendition of "The Greenwood Laddie".'

Wilkinson looked somewhat surprised by this request. 'How can Calista die pathetically and then come on all alive and singing a pretty ballad?'

I hastened to assure him there would be a slight pause, and that I'd make a complete distinction between the two performances.

He still looked unconvinced. 'I shall consider the suggestion, but are you quite certain you can handle comedy as well as tragedy?'

I fully understood his reservations, as he'd seen little sign of the merry side of my nature in my miserable, bedraggled appearance at the inn. In addition, he was well respected, not only in the local community but nationwide, and had a reputation to maintain. As Calista was a role usually given to a serious actress of note, not a young newcomer, I again expressed my gratitude. 'I will not let you down.'

'Then the matter is settled. I shall expect you at the theatre first thing.'

The rehearsals were long and much tougher than I had ever experienced before, though this was no bad thing. I wanted to work, to learn and improve. I spared no effort to attain a high standard, and fortunately I still cut a reasonably slender figure, not showing much at all, as yet. The slight swell of my stomach could easily be disguised with a full-skirted gown. And I loved every moment of it. *The Fair Penitent*, a Restoration drama in blank verse, was very popular with audiences and I gave of my very best, wishing to do the power of the words justice.

To be fair, Wilkinson stood by his agreement to allow me to sing at the end of the performance, and changed the programme accordingly.

When the first night arrived I was, as usual, terribly beset with nerves, which thankfully vanished the moment I went on. The play was reasonably well received, although it was a small house since folk don't turn out for a newcomer, and the Yorkshire cotton workers in the audience were not an easy public to please. At the end I jumped back on stage, dressed in my frock, with my mob cap atop my mop of brown curls, and sang 'The Greenwood Laddie' without accompaniment.

To my complete delight, the Leeds audience loved it. Not only that, they leapt to their feet and applauded. The reviewers the next day said that I possessed the necessary vivacity, confidence and natural stage presence required, and that my voice was strong and clear and true.

Mama was jubilant at my success and I was duly granted a benefit by way of a launch, playing to a packed house early in August. Following this success, Tate Wilkinson offered me a contract.

'Before I sign I should tell you, sir, that I am with child.' I flushed with humiliation at having to reveal my loss of innocence, but the moment for honesty had come.

I saw the disappointment in his eyes, the way his mouth tightened as if he had heard this too many times in the past, and had not wished to hear it from me.

'It did not happen of her own free choice. She was ill-used,' Mama hastily put in, unable to restrain herself.

He gave Grace a quizzical look, but asked for no further explanation. Then just as I expected at any moment to be given my marching orders, he asked, 'Are you fit to work?'

'I am, and will continue right to my time.'

'Then sign. I want you in my company.'

I gladly did so, too overcome with gratitude to find any words to express it.

Six

'. . . the horse and foot'

The season being over the company set out for York. According to Mama, Tate Wilkinson was lessee of theatres at York, Leeds and Hull, as well as touring the company around Yorkshire and earning himself the title of The Wandering Patentee.

The company walked around Yorkshire on foot like strolling players. Actors, of course, were accustomed to living on the road and not having a settled home, carrying everything they owned with them. But having only ever worked in town, at one or other theatre in Dublin, this way of life was new to me, and came as something of a challenge.

Wagons carried the scenery and props, as well as some of the children, who found it all rather exciting. Occasionally the women too would ask for a lift if they were tired, or beg rides from passing farm carts. I managed to do this on several occasions, if only for the sake of Mama. Hester, of course, was always quick to complain if she grew weary. My sister is kind and helpful at heart, but not the most patient soul, and with a quick temper. The men rode on horseback, assuming they were rich enough to own or hire such an animal, and sometimes allowed my young brother a ride now and then, if they felt like a walk.

So off we went, bag and baggage, trudging across country, over hill and dale. Beautiful as they undoubtedly are, the Yorkshire moors are bleak and windswept, rough, rock-strewn and boggy. A remote part of the country indeed, with nothing more to guide our way than sheep trods, and the well-worn paths of previous years. A stout pair of boots was essential, not to mention good health and strength.

It was a far from ideal situation for a pregnant woman, but fortunately I was fit and healthy, my spell of morning sickness long past. I did, however, worry about Mama, who was less robust, and barely recovered from our earlier trek from Liverpool.

'Are you feeling all right?' she asked, coming alongside as we plodded along, equally concerned about me.

'I am very well, Mama, really quite enjoying the warm summer sunshine.'

'You aren't worrying about Daly, are you?'

'I try not to, but it isn't easy,' I confessed. 'I wonder sometimes what his reaction was when he discovered I'd escaped his clutches. More than likely he would be angry. Nor will he easily let me go. Were he ever to discover where we are he would most certainly demand recompense for his loss, penalties on breaking my contract, and the repayment of my debt.'

She thought about this for a moment. 'One advantage of this peripatetic life is that it makes it harder for Daly to find us.'

'But not impossible.'

'No,' she admitted. 'The theatre world is a small one, so not impossible.'

Wilkinson joined us at this point to ask how we were faring, and I smilingly thanked him for his concern. He was ever a kind, generous-hearted man. 'I am well, thank you, kind sir.'

'You look sprightly enough, praise be, but it is not easy for you, I know from my own wife's labours. The horse and foot travels over one hundred and fifty miles a year,' he blithely informed us.

I rather liked this description of us, as if we were a military troop rather than a troupe of strolling players, proud to be living and working together.

'Are you hungry, dear ladies? We'll be stopping in Tadcaster shortly where I know of a good inn.'

Fortunately, our rather rotund manager was fond of his food, and arranged regular stops at inns where he made sure 'the horse and foot' was well fed.

Those who could afford it would stay at the inn, while the rest would find cheap lodgings as close to the theatre as possible, hoping food would be provided and that the beds would be bug free, which I have to say was not always the case. Whenever we stopped to rest, or to prepare for the next production, I spent every free moment copying out or learning lines, making or mending costumes. Although I greatly depended upon Hester in this respect as she was far better with a needle than I. She would scour market stalls in every town we passed through.

'See, I could trim a gown and bonnet with this,' she would say, pouncing on a length of tatty looking gauze curtain. 'And if I cut the sleeves off this old jacket it would make an excellent waistcoat for your part in *The Romp*.'

Whether I needed a hat and breeches for a page boy, mob cap or fancy gown, my talented sister could turn the most inauspicious looking garment into one that could easily have graced the great Sarah Siddons of Drury Lane.

'What would I do without you?' I told her. 'I am so proud of you.'

'And I of you,' she answered, in a rare moment of sibling affection. As sisters we were fond but not overly sentimental.

My main task was to learn, as quickly and efficiently as I could, all the standard parts in our repertoire, from Shakespeare to Fletcher, Steele, Dryden and Cibber, as well as the regular farces we used. One day I might be playing Phoebe, the next Calista, or perhaps Maria in an extract from *The School for Scandal*. I might even perform in both main play and farce on the same night, sing a ballad or do a recitation during the interval. Just writing out the lines took an age, although Mama helped with this chore, as she had schooled me in my letters as a small child.

'I've finished writing out the part of Rosalind for you,' she told me, as we went to our beds after an excellent supper at the Sun Inn. 'Which I'm sure you will play before too long. It is entirely suited to you.' That was another thing about Mama. Her complete and utter faith in my talent and ultimate success.

I was so grateful to have my mother and sister with me for support. Surely we were now far enough away from Dublin to feel ourselves safe from Daly's reach.

The company moved on to York for the races. The Yorkshire circuit was carefully planned to coincide with race meetings, assize weeks, fairs and markets. This was because the town in question would be buzzing with people who'd come in from the countryside around to enjoy the great event. The military, sailors, even fishermen also proved to be a loyal audience, and they too were taken into account when we chose our stopping places.

But it was hard work, our performances carried out in less than perfect conditions, often in rooms behind inns, or in stables and barns. The rare occasion when we acted in a real theatre was a treat indeed.

Once we were settled, there would be rehearsals every morning, and often in the afternoons too. Doors opened at four, allowing ample time for the audience to gather, and performances often lasted from six until midnight. It was an exhausting schedule but not for a moment did I complain. Wilkinson was paying me one pound, eleven shillings and sixpence a week, which I greatly valued.

My first stage appearance in York was with a part at which I excelled, and I soon had the audience shrieking with laughter at my favourite role of Priscilla Tomboy in *The Romp*. They loved her cheeky audacity, and the vitality I put into the part. It was exhausting but I always came off stage in high spirits.

I next played Arionelli in *The Son-in-Law*, a part normally played by a man, which greatly offended a Mr Tyler, the actor who had played him before. He had acted opposite me in *The Fair Penitent* and when he objected to my being cast in this role, Wilkinson told him that if he had any complaints then he should try some profession other than acting. The poor man left, but a sense of ill will against me lingered long afterwards, as if I were in some way responsible for his dismissal.

While in York we took the opportunity to pay a call upon dear Aunt Maria. Sadly we found her sick in bed, a jaundiced look upon her face, and clearly close to death. Mama whispered to me that she thought the cause to be either drink or laudanum, or possibly both.

As if to echo these private comments, my aunt regarded me with a feverish gaze. 'I did not deal well with the strains and stresses of theatre life, nor the disappointment of my lack of stardom in the capital. Other than that I believe I did rather well for myself. But I hope that you, dear niece, will do better, and learn from my mistakes.'

She was delighted that I was to follow her in the profession, and bequeathed her entire wardrobe to me.

'That is most generous of you, Aunt,' I cried, excited by the prospect of new costumes to replace the ones I'd been forced to abandon in Ireland.

'Sadly, I've been obliged to pawn most of them, but I still possess some of my favourites, which may be of use to you.'

'I'm sure they will.'

'And I can alter them to fit,' put in Hester.

She was distressed to hear our tale of Daly and learn of my condition. 'I urge you most strongly to use the title Mrs, not only for the sake of your reputation but as a means of protecting yourself against unwelcome advances from would-be suitors.'

'I will indeed.'

'Nor do I care for the stage name of Francis, as I never had much time for your father. He let my dear sister down badly.' Aunt Maria was equally adamant that I should not use her own name of Phillips. There was much more advice she gave me, to which I avidly listened, eager to soak up everything I could in order to build a good career for myself. And sadly, a week later she died, but true to her wishes we discussed with Wilkinson a change of name.

'It cannot be Bland because of family problems,' Mama pointed out. 'Nor Phillips. My sister made her objections very clear on the use of our maiden name, as it may cause confusion, or detract from her own place in posterity.'

'Then what shall it be?' Wilkinson wondered, tapping his chin thoughtfully with the tip of one finger. 'Dora we have, much better than Dolly or Dorothy, but we must come up with a new surname.' He thought about this for some moments, as did we all. But then his face broke into a smile. 'I have it, the perfect name for a new beginning. As the son of a clergyman it occurs to me that dear Dora here has in effect crossed the water. She has been rescued from her days as a slave and reached the promised land. So we will call her Jordan. Dora Jordan. How would that suit?'

'Perfect,' I agreed, smiling happily. My new career had begun.

Seven

'the fly in the ointment'

The entire company was humming with excitement. Mr William Smith, an actor with the Drury Lane Theatre, was coming on a visit. Wilkinson had opened the new Theatre Royal in York in 1770, and its reputation had grown since those early days. It was very often a place London impresarios such as Richard Brinsley Sheridan, or their agents, would come to seek out new talent. Gentleman Smith, as he was known, was in York because it was race week, but naturally everyone hoped to be noticed, perhaps even offered a contract. An opportunity to star at such a famous London theatre was every actor's dream.

I was playing in *The Romp*, and afterwards the gentleman himself came backstage to congratulate me on my performance. 'You would do well at Drury Lane,' he said, making me blush.

'I think you flatter me, sir.'

'Not at all. You are wasted here, touring the provinces. The capital is where you should be displaying such a rare talent.'

Before I could answer, Wilkinson suddenly appeared at my elbow. 'How kind of you, sir, to compliment my actors. Such appreciation of our efforts is always welcome. But I would tactfully remind you that Mrs Jordan is articled to my company, and has no plans to leave it.'

No one was more aware than I that I could not break my contract without incurring penalties, but Gentleman Smith had planted a seed in my head that would continue to grow.

'No indeed,' I hastily agreed. 'I am most happy here.' Which was certainly true. I took care to note that my admirer did not miss a single performance that week, and then left without making offers to anyone, which was a great disappointment to all.

Wilkinson was so alarmed at the prospect of losing me that he at once doubled my salary and gave me another benefit.

I was delighted, as it is always good to feel valued. He also promised to draw up longer articles, once the tour was over. Sadly, being granted a second benefit so soon did not go down well with fellow cast members, and only added to their jealous mutterings.

Perhaps as a result of this conversation with Gentleman Smith, and while we were still in York, Wilkinson introduced me to a Mr Cornelius Swan. He was quite elderly, a Shakespearean scholar and drama critic of renown. He too most charmingly praised my performance, and soon became a great friend.

'May I, dear lady, offer my services as tutor, or perhaps coach would be a better word. Mr Wilkinson believes you show great potential but would benefit from a few lessons. Perhaps I could be of assistance.'

He was indeed of the greatest assistance, taking me through my lines, pointing out where the emphasis should lie, explaining the exact meaning in Shakespeare's poetic words, which I found most enlightening.

He called me The Jordan and if I was feeling unwell, which I sometimes was due to my pregnancy, he would sit by my bed with Mama's red cloak about his shoulders and instruct me in the character of Zara, in the tragedy of that name by Voltaire, although he introduced me to the part using the English version translated by Aaron Hill.

He later told the manager, 'You must revive that tragedy, Wilkinson, for I have given the Jordan but three lessons and she is so adroit at receiving my instructions that I declare she repeats the character as well as Mrs Cibber ever did. Nay, let me do the Jordan justice, for I declare she speaks it as well as I could myself.'

I could not help but smile at this evidence of pride in his own acting skills, appreciating the great critic's help even as I insisted that comedy was much more my forte. Life was indeed most pleasant and it felt good to stay in one place for a while and have more time to study.

Our contentment ended when one morning Mama came rushing in bearing a letter. 'It is from Daly, I know his hand well.'

My heart seemed to stop beating. But she was correct. Daly had discovered our whereabouts, no doubt thanks to the excellent press reviews I'd received while playing in York. He was ordering me to return upon the instant of receiving this letter, or he would have me arrested for debt. He was also claiming a full penalty of £250 for breach of contract, plus repayment of the original debt, with interest. Fear overwhelmed me and I burst into tears.

'Oh, Mama, what are we to do? I can no more pay such a debt now than I could before we left, and the sum has grown worse. I shall be incarcerated in a debtor's prison after all!' It was too much for a young girl to cope with.

'Dear me, what is this?' Our new friend had arrived for my next lesson, and seeing me in such distress he insisted on hearing the whole sorry tale. I spared him few details, and his jaw tightened in angry disapproval as the true reason for my condition was finally revealed. When I was done, he leapt to his feet in a rage.

'The man is a scoundrel and shall be dealt with most forcefully. He must not be allowed to destroy either your career or your life. I will settle the debt myself.'

I gasped. 'Oh, but I could never ask such a thing.'

'You have not asked it of me, I offer the service most willingly. I am a man of means and can easily afford such a trifling sum. You have become like an adopted daughter to me and if by this small service you can be free of that charlatan, it would be a small price to pay.'

And so my debts were generously settled by my new friend, with no return favours attached, and I was at last free of Richard Daly.

As we progressed across Yorkshire, putting on our productions in venues large and small, I continued to study hard, to observe my fellow actors closely. I was eager to learn from their greater skills. It was, of course, the same old story. They did not welcome the presence of a new rival in their midst, competing for the best parts. I soon recognized that the other women were wary and resentful of me, in case I should prove to be more successful than themselves.

'Who is this Mrs Jordan?' they would whisper to each other behind their hands. 'Where did she come from, and why has she risen so quickly to be granted such excellent parts?'

They would scrutinize my every performance, and be quick to point out any perceived mistakes.

My greatest rival and sternest critic was a Mrs Smith (no relation to Gentleman Smith). Until my arrival she had played all the comedy leads. For this reason, and because she was well connected, the lady thought rather well of herself. And she too was pregnant. The difference between us being that her circumstances were somewhat more comfortable than my own, since she was in the happy position of having a husband.

There was precious little in the way of privacy in the claustrophobic little village halls, old barns and inns in which we often performed, and changing behind a blanket strung up on a washing line was often the best we could manage. Mrs Smith would frequently take the opportunity to express her opinions to her friends in strident tones, knowing I could hear every word, as, with Hester's help, I prepared to go on.

'Are we ever to be graced with the presence of *Mr* Jordan, I wonder?' she would loudly proclaim to fellow cast members, who quietly tittered at her daring. 'Does he in fact even exist, or is the *Mrs* merely a courtesy title?' Her caustic laugh rang out. 'I doubt that is a courtesy baby she carries in her belly. More likely a bastard.'

'Enough gossip, ladies. Five minutes to opening,' I heard Wilkinson say as I froze, mortified with embarrassment. He was ever coming to my rescue.

Once on stage, of course, I easily put the jealous mutterings of my fellow cast members out of my head and concentrated on the character I was playing. It was of vital importance that I become that person, that she, or he, appear real to the audience. That only worked if I believed I was that character too.

This was my big opportunity, and I meant to make the most of it.

I certainly had no intention of being upset by the Mrs Smiths of this world. Hadn't I endured far worse than malicious gossip in my short life? And no matter what I had suffered in the past I was determined to love this baby I carried below my heart, whether it be a bastard or no.

'Pay her no heed,' he assured me later. 'I've made it clear that your marital status is none of her business.'

As always I was grateful for his protection, but rather feared his intervention may have made matters worse, not better.

We next toured Wakefield and Doncaster, planning to go on to Sheffield, but the undercurrent of jealousy continued to fester. The dreadful Mrs Smith was so anxious for me not to steal her roles of Lady Teazle and others, that as summer turned into autumn and she came close to her time, she clung on looking anything but a virginal heroine. Eventually, for the sake of propriety, she was ordered by Wilkinson to retire. Even so, some ten or eleven days following the birth of her child in September, and stubbornly determined to play the part of Fanny in *The Clandestine Marriage*, she attempted to walk the eighteen-mile journey from Doncaster to Sheffield. Sadly, she injured her hip as a result of this foolishness, and was again forced to retire.

As I am able to learn a part in twenty-four hours, it was I who played the role. It's a convoluted comedy about arranged marriage, and I gave a spirited performance which went down well with audiences. But my success only added to the lady's bitter dislike of me.

In October matters took a turn for the worse when a huge wooden roller, that held up the scenery, fell within inches of myself and Mr Knight while we were seated at a table as chambermaid and footman in *The Fair American*. We could easily have been killed outright. Somehow I kept my nerve, believing the show must go on no matter what. But I did wonder if there was some mischief afoot.

We left Sheffield at the beginning of November, moving on to Hull for Christmas where we stayed at Mr Dunn's in Myton Gate, in rooms above a shop. And it was here that I gave birth to my daughter Frances just before I turned twenty-one. Mama was there to help, but it was a straightforward birth and all went well. Despite my little Fanny being Daly's child I loved her on sight, perhaps even more so, since she had no father.

'Now do not make Mrs Smith's mistake of rushing back to work too soon,' Wilkinson urged me. 'You stay safely in the straw until you are fully recovered. I always insist upon it with my own dear wife.'

He was ever kind in his treatment of me, as with all his cast. But unbeknown to me, Mrs Smith took advantage of my absence to spread her malicious gossip.

The play chosen for my return, *The Fair Penitent*, was, as it turned out, somewhat unfortunate. Calista is in love with the disreputable Lothario despite having been seduced by him, and not in the least penitent. He refuses to marry her, and in the end she is desperate to salvage her lost reputation, only it is too late.

As the play was performed on Boxing Day the house was a good one, but the audience received it with cold disapproval. It seemed that the good wives of Hull had been regaled with the story of the birth of little Fanny, and with no husband in sight I was seen to be re-enacting my own shocking tale. This naturally affected my performance, which I confess was indifferent and uninspired. I do not do well when I feel no warmth radiating from an audience. Not only that, but I could hear loud whispers being exchanged, see fingers pointing at me. It was utterly humiliating. When I went on to sing 'The Greenwood Laddie', I was actually hissed. As always Wilkinson came to my aid. 'Bear up, dear girl. Do not allow them to unnerve you. This is all down to the Scandal Club.'

I did not need to ask who the instigator of that cabal was.

He put out a more benevolent explanation for my situation, painting me as a victim rather than a strumpet by pointing out I was not parading a lover but rather living with my mother and caring for my siblings. Following his intervention I gradually won over the ladies of Hull and was forgiven, but it was an unsettling experience.

'We seem to be caught up in an endless spiral. Why did Wilkinson not put an end to this peevish jealousy when it first began?' I asked of Mama.

'Because Tate is not against a little competition between players. He believes it makes them strive all the harder to give of their best.'

'That seems to me an odd way of viewing the matter.'

Mama laughed. 'That is because you are conscientious, my dear, and Mrs Smith and her cronies are not.'

The company then returned to York where, properly recovered from childbirth, I donned male attire once more to sing the part of William in a rustic operetta, *Rosina*. The theatre was sold out.

The Scandal Club, as Wilkinson called it, was once again in action at Sheffield a year later in 1783. By this time Mrs Smith had a new ally in a Mrs Ward, who had recently joined the company, her husband being in the orchestra. There was also a Mrs Robinson who loved to show off her neat and graceful figure, resenting the fact that I captured all the breeches parts, that rare opportunity for an actress to reveal her legs. The venom of those three women soon spread, and they would huddle together at the open stage door, or in the wings like the witches in Macbeth, chattering in loud voices in an attempt to disconcert me and put me off my lines.

Sometimes I would play them at their own game, and creep on stage with an air of great distress, as if bravely battling against tears. At this sad sight the audience would exclaim in horror, wondering what on earth might be the matter. Was I hurt, had something dreadful happened to my child? But my friends would send round a whisper explaining the mischief being done to me by my fellow actresses, and they would sigh crossly, and warm to me in sympathy.

I am not called a good actress for nothing.

In the end, Wilkinson grew so irritated by their behaviour that he had all the doors locked to confine the coven in their proper place, which put an end to the ploy, or so I hoped.

That winter Mrs Smith and her husband held a benefit, and I made what I thought to be a kind offer. 'Is it not time that we ended this foolish vendetta? I am more than willing to offer my services in your benefit, if it would help.'

'I'm sure we can manage well enough without digging in the gutter,' Mrs Smith snapped.

'Ladies, ladies,' said Wilkinson, quietly attempting to placate everyone. 'I'm sure Mrs Jordan means well, and you must have some other actor on stage with you, so let it be she. It can do no harm.'

The house was a good one, and I believed my own part in the production helped to contribute to the large sum pocketed by the Smiths.

The lady herself was less grateful. 'I'm sure we did well enough, although I'm certain we'd have done better had Mrs Jordan not been the fly in the ointment.'

Fortunately, not everyone behaved in this manner towards me. There was in the company a fine young man by the name of George, who was the stepson of Elizabeth Inchbald, an actress of note. And to him, I tremble to admit, I gave my heart.

Eight

'Mrs Jordan had better remain where she is and not attempt the London boards'

Hester had made her first appearance at Leeds not too long after my own, and it was she who now used the name of Miss Francis. She'd begun with a simple song, progressing through various small parts until almost two years later she was playing roles such as Polly in *A Beggar on Horseback*, and Juliet in *Measure for Measure*. My versatile young brother would happily perform walk-on parts as a messenger or halberdier. Very occasionally he would join me in a duet, as he had a fine voice. George added little to the family coffers from his efforts, but dreamed of playing comic opera one day, so was content to serve his apprenticeship in any way he could. Mama, of course, was kept busy looking after Fanny.

On stage I enjoyed the attention of many admirers, including a Member of Parliament who was apparently a close acquaintance of the Prince of Wales. He would sit in his box ogling me night after night, and then come backstage hoping to entice me to dine with him. I always refused, paying him no heed, as George Inchbald was the one I liked to think of as my new beau. George generally played the male lead, and he and I had performed many a 'love scene' together on stage. Rumour was rife in the green room that these were also taking place offstage. Sadly for me this was not at all the case, although there was an undoubted attraction between us which even my sister remarked upon.

'I see you have yet another admirer now in Inchbald. What happened to the MP, the man with royal connections who was madly in love with you?'

I laughed at her teasing. 'Charles Howard was a man more in love with the arts than with me. He was interested only in watching how my career progresses.'

'He liked to watch far more than your career, Doll. The fellow was besotted. I do, however, have my reservations about George Inchbald. He, I think, is more in love with himself.'

I busied myself with tying ribbons in my hair as I could feel a betraying warmth on my cheeks. 'He is most attentive, but it is of no interest to me whom he loves,' I airily remarked, which was a bold-faced lie. But then I had no wish to admit how much I liked him, how often I watched his broad-shouldered figure stride across the stage, my heart beating fast and with open admiration in my eyes. I could most easily fall in love with him.

Every day he would come to my dressing room to console me against my rivals' mischief-making. 'Take no notice of the Scandal Club,' he would say. 'They are only jealous of your skill and beauty. You are by far a better actress than they will ever be.'

His consideration and support was most flattering.

'But then you do realize I adore you, Dora. Your happiness means the whole world to me.'

I would blush with pleasure at these kind words, then let him kiss my hand while aching for him to pull me into his arms as he often did on stage, and kiss me for real this time. But, ever the perfect gentleman, too much so perhaps, he would simply smile and talk of other things. He loved to sit and watch me take off my make-up or pin up my hair for the next act. He would walk me home to my lodgings after a show, often coming in for supper to chat happily with me and my family for hours. Actors are notorious night birds as it always takes a little while to come down from the heights of a performance.

And he so loved to tease. 'Do you know what the press call you?' he asked me one evening following a performance of Nell in *The Devil to Pay*.

Anticipating some flattering remark, I blushed bright pink and shook my head.

'The humble Nell of the York stage.' He laughed, and I laughed with him, but then the more I thought of it, the less of a compliment it sounded.

'Meaning what, exactly?'

'Well, there is all the malicious gossip about your apparent lack of morals that the Scandal Club has spread about you. And of course, you do have a child.'

I held my cool with difficulty, mortified that we should even be having this conversation. 'Not all ways of getting with child are pleasant ones,' I quietly remarked, and for a moment Inchbald was silent as he digested this comment.

'Are you saying—'

'I am saying that I am not some common little floozy. I have never willingly taken a lover, royal or otherwise. Nor do I ever intend to, so how am I to be compared with Nell Gwyn, if they are indeed comparing me with her? Why would I earn such a sobriquet?'

He appeared very slightly embarrassed. 'You cannot deny being pursued by that friend of the Prince of Wales, son and heir to the Duke of Norfolk no less.'

'For goodness sake, you make too much of what was no more than a passing acquaintance, and I gave the fellow no encouragement. I shall probably never see him again, thank goodness, and I certainly never expect to set eyes on the Prince of Wales. Can you imagine a royal prince ever visiting the Theatre Royal in York? I very much doubt it. Although, who knows, one day I may move to London and become famous.'

He beamed at me. 'If that happens, I shall be honoured to claim you as a friend.'

'I hope you are honoured now,' I teased, batting my eyelashes a little, and instantly forgiving his comments, which must surely have been born of jealousy. 'Not for a moment do I imagine such good fortune could ever come my way, but a girl can dream.'

Right now my dreams were centred upon George Inchbald, on romance, marriage and more children. If in some quarters I was not considered quite respectable, because of little Fanny, marrying a man such as George Inchbald would surely set the matter right. I rather thought he would make a good father for my little girl, and a devoted husband for me.

'It is the idea of marriage you are in love with,' my sister scoffed, shrewdly guessing the direction of my thoughts. 'Not George Inchbald.'

I was quite sure she was wrong and missed no opportunity to spend time with him, to flirt and tease, and tempt him to linger a little longer over those stage kisses, hoping to encourage him to risk one backstage.

George, however, while happy to go along with the game, showed no sign of wishing to take our friendship further. Why did he never make a move? I wondered. Mama thought him a fine young man. And I knew that his own stepmother, Elizabeth Inchbald, approved of the match. I began to wonder if perhaps Hester might be right, that he cared more for himself than for me.

Was I simply desperate for respectability in order to put an end to these nasty rumours about my alleged immorality? Surely not. It was love that kept me tossing and turning in my bed at night, and my days gazing doe-eyed at the man I adored.

Gentleman Smith came again, and as always on one of his regular visits, anticipation and excitement mounted. There were the usual jealous mutterings, reignited whenever he was seen watching one of my performances, or came backstage to speak to me.

'I am continuing to maintain an interest in your career,' he assured me. 'It appears to be progressing well.'

George was also excited. 'He may watch the performances of the other actors, but it is you, Dora, who most impresses him. He will offer you a place at Drury Lane this time, I'm sure of it.'

At the end of the week, Gentleman Smith returned to London as he always did, and I waited anxiously, watching the post each day, hoping for that much longed-for offer. It took a week or so, but gradually, it dawned on me that no such offer would be forthcoming. Perhaps he was simply flattering me and being kind, while seeing me only as a provincial actress as my mother was before me.

It was about the time that I was recovering from this disappointment that a new realization dawned upon me. It occurred to me that George had not visited my dressing room, nor walked me home to our lodgings to take supper with me, ever since Gentleman Smith had left.

'Why is he staying away?' I asked Hester, genuinely puzzled. 'We were getting along so well. Have I done something to offend?'

My dear sister looked at me with a cynical sort of pity in her eyes. 'How naïve you are, Doll. George Inchbald is a cautious man, prudent and careful, and rather conservative in his views. I'm afraid he is reluctant to take on a woman with a child, unless, of course, that woman were a rich and famous actress.'

I stared at her in dismay. 'Are you saying that were I to be offered a well-paid position at the famous Drury Lane, then he would ask for my hand? Otherwise . . .'

She nodded. 'Otherwise he would never risk such a commitment.'

To my utter shame, my eyes filled with tears. 'But he was so attentive, so kind, so loving. I believed he was smitten, as was I, I do confess.'

'Oh, Dolly, what a dear affectionate soul you are, but far too trusting.'

To be let down again by Gentleman Smith was bad enough, but to be disappointed in love at the same time was a double blow. I fell into a depression. I had so taken George's attentions for granted, believing that he truly did adore me, as he claimed, that I fondly believed I'd found the love I so longed for. Now I felt dispirited and listless, as if I carried the whole world on my shoulders, and the sameness of the parts began to pall. As a consequence my performance began to suffer; either I felt unwell, or was quite unable to give them the concentration and care necessary. Naturally I upset fellow actors with my inattention, and I confess public adoration cooled somewhat on occasions. I also suffered badly from migraines, and on one evening actually collapsed on stage. But that was the fault of Wilkinson.

It was March 1785 and I was to play in a benefit performance of *Cymbeline*. I was also billed to sing 'The Poor Soldier' at the end of the third act, as well as play in the farce. My head was pounding and I felt quite certain I was about to be sick. It was suddenly all too much and I told Wilkinson that I was not well enough to sing, begging him to lighten my load by cutting out the song after *Cymbeline*. He refused.

'You know that I cannot change the programme at this late stage. The audience expects a song from you, Dora.'

'You must announce that I am sick.'

He strode away but returned moments later, looking most flustered. 'They refuse to do without it. They are demanding your presence. Can you hear them, they are baying for you. You cannot let them down.'

I was lying on the couch in the dressing room with a cold cloth on my forehead. Having struggled through the play I now felt utterly drained, yet he was ordering me to go on again. 'I will not risk my health merely to warble a ballad, and if they are disappointed, so be it. Nothing in the world shall alter my mind.'

'They feel that if you were fit enough to play in *Cymbeline*, you are also fit enough to sing. And I have to say I agree with them.'

'Why will you not believe me when I say I am ill?'

'You are a fine actress, Dora dear, but you cannot fool me. You may be heartsick, but your body is perfectly capable of working. Had you truly been ill you would have stayed at home and called a doctor.'

'But my throat hurts. My head aches and I . . .'

He turned to Hester. 'Fetch the costume for Patrick. She has two minutes to change, then she goes on and does the song.'

So I staggered on stage, began to sing 'In the prattling hours of youth . . .' and fainted.

In the spring of 1785 Wilkinson decided to stage *The Country Girl*, being Garrick's revised version of Wycherley's *The Country Wife*. It was as full of wit as ever, but he had toned down the somewhat outrageous immorality to a level more acceptable to today's audience. The play had proved to be controversial for its sexual explicitness even in Restoration days, as it concerned the libertine's trick of feigning impotence in order to ingratiate himself upon married women. But then a young and inexperienced country wife comes to London, who catches the eye of a rake. The leading part was played by a Mrs Brown, and I confess I fell in love with the play and the role on first viewing. It was an utter delight.

'I intend to make this role my own,' I told Mama, as I sat dandling darling Fanny on my knee one evening at the end of the week, having watched and studied Mrs Brown's performance on every single night.

'Ah, yes,' Mama said, 'I remember playing in the original when I was quite young. It was the greatest fun. Your dear father rather liked the play and gave it a revival, but I agree it fell out of favour again as Shakespeare came back into vogue. Bring me a copy of the new version and I will copy out the lines for you,' she offered, ever ready to help.

I learned the lines, making notes of my observations from studying Mrs Brown's performance, and how I might improve upon it by giving the part my own personal interpretation. Mama discussed the role with me at length, the play on words and nuance of character, and encouraged me to read the original version so that I could see how Garrick had made changes. Solid preparation, I believe, is essential before taking on any new role, and one day I hoped to shine in this one.

It was late in the summer of that year when Gentleman Smith visited during race week, as usual, and this time there was no prevarication on his part. He came straight to the point.

'I'm here to make you an offer, Dora Jordan. We are seeking a new understudy for Sarah Siddons, and Sheridan has accepted my recommendation and is prepared to offer you four pounds a week if you will take the position.'

I could hardly believe what he was saying. My chance had come at last. Not perhaps quite what I had hoped for, for I'd no real wish to play second to anyone, not even the great Siddons, but it was the opportunity I had longed for to go to London and make a name for myself. It was certainly not one I had any intention of turning down.

'I shall be delighted to accept,' I told him, without a moment's hesitation.

'Excellent, then I will speak to Wilkinson and arrange your release.'

A few weeks later Hester rushed into the dressing room in

a state of high excitement. 'Guess who has deigned to pay a visit to our humble theatre?'

We all sat silent, unable to guess at a single name which would produce such enthusiasm in my sister.

'The great Sarah Siddons herself.'

Mrs Ward gave a bark of cynical laughter. 'She has come to observe your performance, Jordan, and may well put an end to your dream if she does not care for what she sees.'

This was so very true I heartily wished that my dear sister had not told me. The very prospect of acting before this famous actress had me shaking in my shoes before ever I reached the stage. I felt sick, longed to turn and run as I had once before.

Sensing my panic Hester grasped my hands in hers. 'It's all right, Doll. You can do this. Go out there and show her just how good you are.'

I would like to say that I did exactly that. Sadly, I was so beset with nerves that at best I was mediocre. Siddons was not impressed.

'Mrs Jordan had better remain where she is and not attempt the London boards,' was her verdict, brought to me by Wilkinson with a wry smile on his round, homely face. As always, he attempted to console me.

'I think it curious to note that this same advice was given to Mrs Siddons herself in her early days by William Woodfall, the critic. He thought her too weak for the large London theatres, and recommended she keep to small houses where she could be heard. But your voice is strong, my dear, and can be heard loud and clear right up in the gods.'

'What if I should fail?' I asked, my earlier confidence now rapidly evaporating.

Wilkinson patted my hand. 'There is absolutely no reason why you should. I have every faith you will be a complete success, but should that not be the case, you will always be welcome in my company, Dora dear.'

Tears brimmed in my eyes, spilling down my cheeks at the thought of leaving the safe haven this dear man had offered me in my greatest hour of need. 'You have been like a second father to me, kindness itself. I do so wish I had performed better tonight, for your sake.'

'There, there, do not take it to heart. The lady does tend to be somewhat scathing in her criticisms.'

Oh, but I did take it very much to heart, and I made a private vow to make sure that next time Mrs Siddons saw me act, she would come away with a very different view.

My last performance was in early September, and there were many fond farewells, and some very welcome ones. Mama wept at leaving George behind, but he loved working with Wilkinson, who promised to take good care of the boy as he was not yet ready for the capital.

Then we packed my precious costumes and books, and Mama, Hester and I, together with two-year-old Fanny, set out on our next adventure to London. I went with no degree of confidence. Many actresses had followed this same route to the capital, bearing the same hopes and dreams of fame and fortune in their hearts, and been obliged to return forever into obscurity, like my mother before me. Yet at least I had been granted the opportunity, and on double the wages that Wilkinson could offer, so what did I have to lose?

Mrs Smith stood watching me depart. 'Make no mistake,' she said to the coven of companions by her side. 'The Jordan will be back within twelve months.'

Nine

'She came to town with no report in her favour . . .'

We had thought that city life would be no surprise to us, coming from Dublin, but London was very different, so much larger and grander than our Irish equivalent, or certainly the part we had known by the quays. The sounds and smells of the capital hit us in full force: the rattle of carriage wheels, the clip of horses' hooves, the cries of the street sellers.

'My mop is so big, it might serve as a wig for a judge, if he had no objections,' cried one, making us all laugh.

Lamps lighted the streets, which were properly paved. There were street sweepers so less rubbish and sewage ran in the gutters, and apparently water was piped below ground to the row of fancy tall houses. Elm trees lined every street and square, with green swathes of parkland everywhere. We'd endured two long days being bumped and jostled and squashed in a public coach, till we were bruised and bone-weary, despite regular stops at inns on the Great North Road.

'At least we didn't have to walk this time,' I said in an effort to raise spirits as we trundled along.

Hester was in one of her moods, Mama weak with exhaustion and little Fanny was screaming like a banshee. But I was filled with excitement. London seemed to me a magical place, and I fell in love with it on sight.

The streets themselves were crowded with traffic: carriages, hackneys, sedan chairs hurrying by with some lady hidden inside, perhaps off on a secret tryst with her lover. There were carts and wagons and horses by the score; and fancy phaetons 'taking the dust', as Sheridan later described it, when the young bucks took their ladies for a drive.

'Turn left at the top of Drury Lane, if you're looking for somewhere cheap to stay near the theatre,' our coach driver advised us as he stopped to allow us to alight. 'It's far from salubrious but where most of the Irish immigrants live.'

I shuddered at the thought but Mama soon put him right, looking quite outraged. 'We are respectable ladies and have no intention of living in any low part of town.'

'Begging your pardon, ma'am,' he responded politely, doffing his cap. 'Then I'd recommend you choose with care, as fashionable people have moved away from the area, and criminals and prostitutes are in abundance there now.' He piled our baggage about our feet, climbed back on to his seat and with a flick of his whip drove away, far too accustomed to delivering people to the city to care greatly whether or not we ended up in a hell-hole.

But his advice indicated to me how ill-regarded the Irish were. And the closeness of the slums was an alarming reminder of where we might end up if things went wrong. I suddenly felt the pressure of responsibility for our survival weighing heavy on my young shoulders. I would shortly turn twenty-four with the burden of being the main bread winner for my family. I was fully aware that I would be but one among many, competing against the best in the business, and would need to prove myself quickly if we were not to end up in those slums.

Fortunately, thanks to Mama's memories of Thomas Sheridan, who had lived in Henrietta Street, we managed to find decent lodgings at number eight. It was a handsome four-storey terraced house which boasted a fine staircase and wood-panelled rooms, within easy walking distance of all the major theatres including Drury Lane, and quite close to Covent Garden.

We unpacked our few possessions, save for my stage costumes which we left in the basket Hester and I had carried between us all the way from Yorkshire. Our room seemed comfortable enough with three iron beds, and Mama went in search of the kitchen, shared with the other lodgers, to warm what was left of the soup she'd brought with us. I put little Fanny down for a much-needed sleep.

'So here we are,' I said, hugging my sister. 'Now what?'

She grinned at me. 'Now you sweep on to the stage at Drury Lane and charm London with your talent. Then we all become very rich.'

'Ah yes, I'd forgotten that part. And when we are "very rich" we shall all wear satin and lace, and gold slippers, and ride everywhere in a fine carriage of our own instead of the public stage.'

'And parade ourselves in our fancy clothes before the nasty Mrs Smith in Yorkshire.'

'"My, my, Dora Jordan, 'oo do you think you are lass, the Queen of Sheba?" she'll say.' I mimicked the woman to perfection.

Hester collapsed with laughter. 'You'll be the death of me, Doll, you will really.'

We were still rolling on our beds in fits of giggles when Mama returned with the hot soup and a crusty loaf she had bought from a passing baker's boy.

'What has got into the pair of you?' she asked, somewhat bewildered by our merry mood.

'Dreaming, Mama, only dreaming. Tomorrow, when I arrive at Drury Lane, I shall come face to face with reality.'

But long before I ever reached the theatre the next morning, I was filled with trepidation. 'Why do I even imagine I could be any use? Mrs Siddons is the great name at Drury Lane. The other main actresses, a Miss Farren and a Miss Pope, I am reliably informed by Gentleman Smith, play the dainty ladies to perfection.'

'Leave the tear-jerking tragedy to Siddons,' Mama said, somewhat dismissively. 'Nor are you the sort of actress to play a dainty lady. The good gentleman also said that there was no one who played farcical comedy, at which you shine.'

'But it is not in fashion, Mama, not in London. Drury Lane prefers serious drama: Shakespeare, Molière, Voltaire. What can *I* offer to compete with the likes of Siddons?'

'Yourself, dearest. Just be yourself.' And she put her arms about me and hugged me in her loving, motherly way.

Drury Lane was much shabbier than I had expected, but then theatres are never the most salubrious of places. Backstage at Leeds more often than not stank of beer, grease paint and stale sweat, although somehow I had expected better from this grand London theatre. The proprietor, Richard Brinsley Sheridan, a tall thin man with a rigid posture, offered me a bow that was not in the least foppish, despite his brightly coloured costume of blue coat and red waistcoat. I politely asked that my mother's kind regards be transmitted to his father, Thomas Sheridan.

'She has fond memories of working with him in Dublin.'

'I do not often see him,' came the cool response.

I was then shown around by the manager, Tom King, who told me that he in fact remembered my mother very well from his time in Dublin. 'I knew Mrs Bland back in the 1750s. Do give her my regards.'

'I will.' I felt as if I had found a friend.

We sat in on a rehearsal, and I listened avidly while he told me something of the history of the theatre, first built in 1662 and rebuilt following a fire ten years later.

'It is called the Theatre Royal because the first troupe of players was considered to be a part of the royal household, and as such entitled to wear the scarlet and gold of royal livery, rather like footmen do now.'

'How fascinating,' I said, smiling.

'At that time the theatre could seat seven hundred but it is twice that size today. Mr Sheridan took it over from Garrick in 1777, although he leaves the day-to-day management entirely to me.' He regarded me quite seriously for a moment. 'You must not be intimidated by him. He is a charming man, if something of a contradiction, and is himself of Irish stock, although he was raised mainly by servants after his parents returned to England.'

'Doesn't he ever tread the boards himself?' I asked, thinking of Ryder, Daly and Wilkinson, who all loved to be a part of the action on stage.

'Mr Sheridan is too occupied as a Member of Parliament to have time for such trivialities these days.' And lowering his voice, softly added, 'He suffered rather badly from bullying as a boy at Harrow, being the son of a travelling player, so now prefers not to be too closely associated with the theatre.'

'Then why own one?' I asked, astounded by this private glimpse into a very public figure.

'Money, my dear, why else? He has turned his back on both acting and writing in order to concentrate on politics, but he still has to live, and has debts to settle, so if you can pull in an audience, you will be particularly welcome here.'

I was still mulling over this information about my new employer, which seemed to add to the pressure already on me, as we returned to the office to consider how best to make my debut. Sheridan waved me to a seat with a flourish of one delicate hand.

'Our aim,' he began, 'is to dedicate the Theatre Royal to the very best in drama, as well as high moral rectitude. It is a place for intellectual culture, entertainment and enjoyment, a theatre which needs to be regarded as a national treasure. We must never allow it to slide into vulgarity and immorality. Young actresses should take particular care that they do not overstep the bounds of propriety. It is commonly agreed that they create a certain excitement in the male breast, and provoke a sense of mystery since the real woman can easily be confused with the parts they play.'

'I am aware of that,' I said, beginning to wonder where all this was leading.

'Sadly, it is an actress's lot in life that she rarely finds married joy with a respectable man.'

My heart skipped a beat at this bleak prospect for my future happiness. 'I trust you exaggerate, sir. I have every hope to marry a good man one day,' and I smiled. Sheridan's expression remained inscrutable.

'I believe, Mrs Jordan, that you have a child.'

'I do.' If he expected me to apologize for my darling Fanny, or explain her existence, then he had mistaken me badly.

Tom King looked away, clearly embarrassed. After a slight pause in which I sat rigid, Sheridan blithely continued with his lecture. 'You should ever remember that I have an instinctive abhorrence to the theatre being seen as a vehicle for vice. Nor have we any place here for smutty farce and coarse jokes.'

The manager hastily intervened. 'What Mr Sheridan means is that Drury Lane is the place where the fashionable like to come to see the great Mrs Siddons act. They are content to sit and enjoy the tragedy, but whether we could persuade them to remain in their seats long enough to view the farce after it, has yet to be proved.'

This all sounded deeply disturbing. 'Are you saying there is no room for comedy at the Lane which may be considered in the slightest risqué?'

'No, we don't mean that at all. We have no objection to a lively or bawdy comedy,' Sheridan put in, himself the writer of two amusing farces, *The School for Scandal* and *The Rivals*, and generally revered as a notorious wit. 'But the genteel will not tolerate anything too offensive or uncouth, and prefer to leave the theatre with the glow of Mrs Siddons' performance fresh in their minds.'

'Mrs Siddons is the great draw,' Tom King agreed. 'Her performances are always well attended, and she holds two benefits each season. She is very well thought of.'

'Not least by herself,' Sheridan added with a grim smile. 'But we cannot afford to offend her, you understand, by puffing up a newcomer too much. Not even one who comes so highly recommended by William Smith.'

I was beginning to appreciate the size of the challenge I faced, and the battle Gentleman Smith must have faced to get me taken on. No wonder his offer had been a long time in coming. 'May I ask what you have in mind for my debut?'

Now Sheridan actually smiled, as if he was about to offer me a rare treat. 'We have announced to the press that you are to play in a revival of *Philaster*, or *Love Lies Bleeding* as it is often called. It is a tragi-comedy and you will play Bellario, a page who turns out to be a girl.'

I thought about the disaster when first I trod the boards at Smock Alley by being forced, by Daly, to play in a tragedy. My resolve never to allow that to happen again strengthened. 'May I make an alternative suggestion?'

The two men exchanged a surprised glance but then turned to me as one, offering a polite smile. 'We are always interested to hear an actress's view,' Sheridan said, so charmingly that I warmed to him a little.

Taking a breath I mustered as much tact as I could. 'I have no wish to intrude upon Mrs Siddons' territory. She is, as you say, a great actress, the queen of tragedy. In any case, that is not my forte. Nor have I any wish to play the perfect lady parts performed so ably by Miss Farren. I do not possess either

her elegance or her dignity. I am much happier playing comedy. And if I am to succeed then I must play to my strengths, not my weakness, do you not agree?'

'I have no quarrel with what you have said thus far,' Sheridan said.

'Nor I,' agreed Tom King. 'But if *Philaster* does not appeal, then what do you suggest?'

I leaned forward in my seat, anxious to put my case as well as possible. 'While in Yorkshire I saw a performance by Mrs Brown in *The Country Girl*, the revised version, and realized the potential of the role of Peggy for myself. Consequently, I studied it with great care and feel I have a full grasp of the lines and character.'

The manager seemed to be giving my suggestion serious consideration, 'I do agree that Garrick's adaptation is less outrageous than the original. Even the most scrupulous could find no offence in it. But it is some time since it was revived. Would it work, I wonder?'

'I am prepared to take the risk if you are,' I persisted. 'And if it fails, then I will be the one to bear the greater loss. I cannot think that Mrs Siddons would have any objection to it.'

The two men put their heads together for a little private deliberation, and then Sheridan sat back and actually beamed at me. 'Very well, we are agreed. Your debut will be in *The Country Girl*. Welcome to the company, Mrs Jordan.'

First night was Tuesday, the eighteenth of October, 1785, and I was aquiver with nerves, as always. Rehearsals had gone well as I had instantly warmed to the rest of the cast, some of whom, like Tom King, remembered Mama from her days as Grace Phillips. And without exception they were all most supportive. Nevertheless, I was a trembling wreck. 'What if they do not like me?' I moaned to Hester. 'What if I am booed or hissed again, as I was at Hull?'

'That will not happen. For one thing, Mrs Smith is not here to prattle her malice, and for another you know this play inside out.'

'But my first benefit at Smock Alley was also a disaster, with hardly anyone in the house. And do you remember the riot?'

'That was because your supporters loved you and thought you'd been unfairly treated. This audience will love you too.'

'And at least the management at Drury Lane has allowed you to choose,' said Mama.

'But nobody will come to see me. Why would they bother?'

'Stop talking yourself down, Dolly, the house will be a good one this time,' Mama gently scolded. 'Now go out there and have fun. Make them laugh as only you can.'

But her optimism on this occasion was ill-founded. When I peeped through a crack in the curtain at the side of the stage it was clear the house was no more than half full. Sheridan had warned me, of course, that the fashionable did not turn out for newcomers, indeed for anyone very often, other than the great Sarah Siddons herself.

Nevertheless, as the orchestra struck up the first notes, I drew several deep breaths to steady my nerves, and when I stepped out on stage there came again that rush of excitement. My heartbeat instantly settled, I stopped feeling sick and ceased even to *be* Dora Jordan. I became Peggy, the innocent young country wife let loose in town.

I have to say that I had the most fun that night. I tripped about the stage delivering my lines with wit and humour, and had them rolling in their seats, crying with laughter. The applause at the end brought tears to my own eyes as the response of the audience seemed so genuine and heartfelt. How joyous, how uplifting it was to be so appreciated, and to give people such pleasure. I hoped they would all go home and tell their friends, so that we would have a better house for the next performance.

Tom King was beaming as he met me when I came off stage, and warmly congratulated me. 'Sheridan saw the first act before going on to Brooks's Club, and passes on his good wishes, which I assure you is a rare compliment. As for myself, while I confess to a preference for tragedy, I foresee you will bring new life and prosperity to the theatre.'

I was so grateful for this accolade I impulsively kissed his cheek. 'Thank you so much for giving me the opportunity.'

The cast and my leading man, John Bannister, plied me with congratulations and a large glass of wine to celebrate. It was all most exciting. Gentleman Smith had also been present and was generous in his praise. 'Did I not know what a treasure I had bestowed upon this great theatre, which I love? You will be a powerful magnet, my dear, bringing in a new clientele who will most readily come to see you on the nights Mrs Siddons does not perform.'

I could hardly sleep that night for happiness. I had to keep reminding myself that I had actually appeared at the Theatre Royal, Drury Lane, London, for the very first time, and the audience had loved me. Long before Mama had gathered together all the reviews she could find the next morning, I knew that I was a success.

She still insisted on reading snippets to me. 'Listen to this one: "from first to last the audience responded uniformly in an astonishment of delight." And this one, "her fertility as an actress was at its height in the letter scene . . . the very pen and ink were made to express the rustic petulance of the writer." Ah, if only your dear Aunt Maria had lived to see this day.'

'Enough, Mama, it is all rather alarming and over-exuberant.' And utterly delicious, I thought. I couldn't remember ever feeling so happy.

Hester too was combing the papers. 'This one is not in the least over-exuberant. It says "Mrs Jordan was vulgar".'

'Really, Hester,' Mama scolded. 'We have no wish to hear the bad ones.'

'I thought you wished to hear them all,' my sister sulked.

'You are quite right, Hester dear, I do need to hear all sides. But that one seems to blame me for the playwright's wit,' I consoled her.

'Here is one by our dear friend, Mrs Inchbald,' Mama said. '"She came to town with no report in her favour . . . but she at once displayed such consummate art, with such bewitching nature, such excellent sense, and such innocent simplicity, that her auditors were boundless in their plaudits."'

'I wonder what her stepson George will have to say when he reads that,' Hester quipped.

'I sincerely hope he doesn't,' Mama sternly remarked. 'That young man let our Dolly down badly. We'll hear no more about him. Some of these reviews are merely grudging, but all are most satisfactory. Let us hope they help to spread the word.'

There was no further performance for three nights as Mrs Siddons, who was expecting a child, was eager to put in as many performances as she could before taking a rest. My second night was therefore the twenty-first of October, and whether it was because of the press or word of mouth, I could not say, but the house was packed. I could hardly believe my eyes.

The third performance brought the Prince of Wales himself to the royal box, and I recalled how I had once jested with George Inchbald that I was unlikely ever to set eyes on a royal prince. Now here sat the heir to the throne right before me, far better looking than I had expected with bright blue eyes and a fine figure. Rumour had it that the Prince was at odds with the King because of his scandalous affair with Mrs Fitzherbert, also an actress. With him was his uncle, the Duke of Cumberland, the one who had married a commoner without the King's consent and prompted the Royal Marriages Act.

'The Duke of Cumberland was also once sued for criminal conversation,' Hester, always one for gossip, excitedly informed me. 'That means adultery. He was discovered *in flagrante delicto* with the Duke of Grosvenor's lady.'

Mama sighed. 'The royal family are often beset with scandal, and are reputed to be forever squabbling.'

Also present in the box was Lord North, the Prime Minister. To me it was simply astonishing that these great and powerful men should come to laugh at my antics.

'You will not long be on four pounds a week,' said Gentleman Smith, his pale lugubrious face wreathed in smiles.

And he was right. I next played Viola in *Twelfth Night*, then Miss Prue in *Love for Love*, and as audiences continued to flock in over the coming weeks, with lines of carriages queuing up at the door, Sheridan offered to double my salary to £8 a week.

'Would you consider making it twelve?' I cheekily asked, and to my astonishment he instantly agreed.

'Twelve it is. And we must begin to arrange for you to have a benefit in the spring.'

I could hardly believe my good fortune. We celebrated Fanny's third birthday, and my twenty-fourth, in fine style, all of us in high spirits. By the end of the year Sheridan was offering me a four-year contract. The usual penalties were included: no pay if I was sick, forfeits if I failed to appear at rehearsals or performances when required, but otherwise £12 week and the prospect of a benefit soon.

Our migration to the city had been a far greater success than we could ever have dreamed of.

Ten

'How I do love to hear of a protégée's triumph . . .'

In the New Year of 1786 I played Miss Hoyden in *A Trip to Scarborough*, and the King himself came to see me. I was overwhelmed, quite beside myself with shock and delight. George III might well be creating difficulties for his many sons and daughters in their respective marriages, but I felt deeply privileged that he should choose to see *me*. It was an absolute joy to perform before this grey-haired old man, or so he seemed to me, who was our monarch, and see him laughing and enjoying himself as I gave my very best performance.

I was also very slightly embarrassed.

The play, an abridged version of Sir John Vanbrugh's *The Relapse*, possessed neither dignity nor culture. One character, a Sir Tunbelly Clumsy, was as gross as his name implies. I played the part of his daughter, the kind of wayward, petulant young lady who should never have left the nursery. I wore a blue frock with red flowers that was little more than a petticoat which kept slipping from my shoulders, my hair in disarray, a jaunty little cap atop my curls. But the audience loved it, and the King roared his approval.

'You are doing well,' the manager assured me. 'But, as I have explained, the Lane prefers tragedy, so I think you should try your hand at that too. I'd like you to play Imogen in *Cymbeline*.'

My heart sank at the prospect, but I was far too new to argue. Gritting my teeth I managed a smile. 'I will do it if I must, but could I at least follow it with a farce, perhaps *The Romp*?'

Fortunately, he agreed, and having given birth to her daughter, even the great Sarah Siddons herself came to watch the performance. She was not greatly impressed by my rendition of Imogen, for which I had to agree with her. I lacked that delicate dignity necessary for the part, let alone an air of tragedy.

The reviews were no kinder, but loved *The Romp*, which saved my reputation.

'Mrs Siddons did reportedly declare herself amused by my Priscilla Tomboy, which sounds faintly condescending,' I told Mama.

'The lady is unable to tolerate competition, Dolly. You both have something entirely different to offer, but sadly, she sees you as a rival to her success.'

I worked harder over the following months than ever I had in my life, learning many new plays with barely a day off. As Drury Lane was a busy theatre and Mrs Siddons took precedence, I did not perform every night, but often appeared in both play and farce on the same night. Fans queued at the stage door to catch a glimpse of me, which I found quite astonishing.

I was also called upon to sit for a portrait, which was an amazing experience. The artist was a John Hoppner, and he painted me as the Comic Muse. I wore a pale green, flimsy gown and had to twist my body a little, to look as if I were dancing. There were other figures about me, Euphrosyne, one of the three graces, and a satyr. It was great fun and the portrait was exhibited at the Royal Academy in May, which made me feel very humble.

But I had little time to adjust to my new fame. Spring had passed by in a blur, and I could but be thankful for my own energy. My first benefit came at the end of April, making me a profit of £200. Riches beyond my wildest dreams, that allowed us to improve our lodgings at Henrietta Street. More followed in the form of a purse containing £300 from the Whig Club in St James's. Apparently I had amused the rich and they wished to show their appreciation. Mama was beside herself with delight. I was simply relieved that money was no longer a problem. Requests for assistance from my brothers were becoming a regular occurrence.

But whether I could maintain this success was yet to be proved.

'Didn't I say you would sweep on to the stage and conquer all? You seem to have London at your feet,' said my sister, with just the slightest trace of envy in her voice.

'If that is true, then it is due to the support of my wonderful family,' I replied, giving her a hug.

'So long as you don't start taking us for granted.'

'As if I would.' Our relationship was ever prickly.

Tom King continued to be a great support, but I saw little of Sheridan, save for when I signed the contract around Christmas time. He was not at all like dear old Wilkinson, who had been like a father to me. No doubt, as Secretary to the Treasury, or whatever Sheridan was, he had far more important things to do than trouble himself over a new actress. But he was businesslike and professional, and I made sure that I was the same with him. I was rapidly learning my worth, and to toughen that tender skin of mine and stand up for myself, as Wilkinson had often advised.

There was much gossip in the green room that Sheridan was involved in royal circles, and had assisted the Prince of Wales to marry his beloved Mrs Fitzherbert. The lady had fled to France in the summer of 1785, but Prince George had apparently persuaded her to return on the promise of marriage.

'But what of the Royal Marriages Act?' I asked Mama, who understood these matters better than I. 'Has he persuaded the King to give permission for him to marry?'

We were resting at our lodgings, three-year-old Fanny happily combing my curls about her tiny fingers, trying to stick in clips here and there. Hester was making herself useful backstage at a rehearsal, Mama stitching a petticoat. 'It is always best, where royalty is concerned, to ask no questions,' she warned. 'The Prince is denying such a marriage ever took place, and whether or not that is true, we must believe him.'

'But if the rumour *is* true that Sheridan arranged the ceremony then it must be right, mustn't it? Ouch, Fanny, don't tug too hard, darling.'

'Oops, sorry, Mama. Can I put lipstick on you now?'

'If you like, but only a little.'

She hurried to fetch my box of make-up and I helped her to find the stick of carmine. She began to make little dabs at my lips and I tried not to laugh.

Mama was saying, 'Fox denied in Parliament that such an event ever took place. It is said that the poor lady wept to hear it. Loving a prince must undoubtedly have its risks. As heir to the throne George is in need of a true wife, not an illegal one, and children to follow him. I doubt any offspring Mrs Fitzherbert could give him would be considered suitable.'

'But what if he stands by her? Or if he remains childless?' I asked, taking the stick of carmine from my daughter's fat little hand before she smeared it all over my face.

Mama considered. 'If he fails in that essential requirement, then I dare say it will one day fall to his brothers to follow him on the throne. And there are enough of them, so surely one could provide an heir. Let me see, after George there is Frederick, William, Edward, Ernest, Augustus and Adolphus. There are several princesses too, but they don't really count.'

I had quite lost interest by this time, my attention back with the copy of *She Would and She Would Not* I held in my hand. While Mama chattered on trying to remember all the young princesses' names, I was studying for the part of Hypolita, while Fanny was struggling to tie a bow in my hair. 'Will you hear my lines, Mama?' I asked, finally interrupting her.

'Of course, dearest, and Fanny shall help, won't you sweetheart?'

'I am busy, Nana, helping Mama dress her hair. Isn't she pretty?'

'If I am then it's thanks to you, my darling,' I told her, giving my lovely little daughter a kiss. How blessed I was, I thought. And even princes had their problems.

The theatre was more often than not packed to the doors, so crowded that some people would be squashed almost to suffo-cation in the lower passages that led to the pit. Hats would be lost, shoes drop off as toes were trodden on, and several ladies suffered from torn gowns. And these people were all coming to see *me* perform. It was a startling thought, and not a little intimidating to walk out on stage before almost two thousand people. And an audience was not always generous, or welcoming.

The throng in the pit carried cat-calls in their pockets. These were a kind of whistle, and if the young bucks did not like what they saw on stage they would most certainly use them, a cacophony of sound that would daunt any actor. They'd also hiss at the prologue, or epilogue, if it was not to their taste. I'd seen them pelt actors with food, yet another activity they used to express their displeasure. Not so uncomfortable if it was a bread roll, less fun if an orange or chewed wad of tobacco were to hit you.

Fortunately, my own performances generally proceeded without such attacks, which was a great relief and a huge joy to me. There were other risks to be wary of though. One night the audience was growing restive at the delay in starting, and some fool threw a lighted candle on to the stage, thereby almost setting fire to the curtains.

'We take our lives in our hands simply by going on,' Hester grumbled.

'At least the aristocracy are no longer allowed to sit on stage. Can you imagine having them almost within touching distance.'

She giggled. 'Or looking down the neck of your gown.'

'It makes me shudder to think of it.'

Then just as I was about to go on stage one night, she gave me a startling piece of news. 'Would you believe, Inchbald is in the audience.'

'George?'

She nodded, her eyes alight with mischief. 'He sent up his card. Go on, Doll. Show him what you can do. Give it your all tonight.'

I laughed, but perhaps my performance did go particularly well that evening as he came to my dressing room afterwards, full of praise.

'My dearest Dora, what a delight to see you again.' He pecked a kiss on each cheek, then held me by the shoulders to study me more closely. 'And you are still beautiful. Oh, how I have missed you.'

'I very much doubt that. You will have been far too busy working, I should imagine, even to remember me.'

'I have never forgotten you. How could I when you are so lovely?'

'Are you still walking around Yorkshire?'

He looked rueful. 'I am indeed, but feel I have lost a pearl beyond price in losing you. A thousand times I have asked myself why I ever allowed you to slip through my hands.'

'The past is the past, George, and we cannot alter it.'

He grasped my hands in his. 'But I still adore you. Can we not be friends again, take up where we left off?'

'No, we cannot. We left off, as you put it, because you were reluctant to commit to a poor young actress already burdened with a child. It is too late now to change your mind, now that I am a rich one. And I still have that child.' I freed myself from his hold and returned to my dressing table, where I began to unpin my hair.

He stood bereft, arms hanging limp at his sides, a look of utter bemusement upon his face. 'But you love me, and I love you. I came here especially to make you a proposal of marriage. Are you turning me down?'

I smiled up at him. 'I'm afraid I am.' And if I took some quiet satisfaction from seeing his disappointment at losing out on my new riches, I tried not to show it. 'You are always welcome to call, George, and to the use of a knife and fork at my home if you are ever again in London, but nothing more. Whatever we had is long over.'

He walked out of the door in a daze, presumably back to Yorkshire and obscurity.

Following my successful benefit I was granted the last two weeks of the season off, and Mama, Hester and I packed our bags and headed north for a short tour. I did a few nights in Manchester, then on to Liverpool and Birmingham, after which we took the post to Leeds. I simply could not resist. We sat watching the performance with the rest of the audience, which was sadly sparse, the house being half empty. I was interested to see that it was Mrs Robinson, one of Mrs Smith's cronies, who was disporting herself as Horatio in *The Roman Father*, and would later play Widow Brady in the farce of *The Irish Widow*. Having noticed our presence in the box, a ripple of applause passed through the audience, and I saw her glance across at me. I gently inclined my head by way of acknowledgement.

'This is fun,' Hester whispered, and I couldn't help but giggle.

'Mrs Robinson, and the dreadful Mrs Smith, fully expected me to return within twelve months, and so I have.'

'In triumph,' finished Mama, looking very pleased with herself.

I dare say it was very wicked of me, but it felt wonderful to come back and flaunt my success before those who had so persecuted me. Afterwards, dressed in the finest gown the London fashion houses could offer, I went backstage to see my old friends. Hester came with me, looking equally elegant, as was Mama. Fanny, for once, was not with us as she was being minded by our landlady, although she'd made a great fuss about wanting to come.

Wilkinson was eagerly waiting for us and gave me a hug in welcome. 'My dear Dora, I have followed your success with eager interest. How I do love to hear of a protégée's triumph.'

I thanked him warmly but did not ask for an engagement, and as Mrs Smith and her coven of witches stood by glowering, it was Wilkinson who was soliciting me. 'I beg you to find time in what must be a very busy schedule to perform for us again here in Leeds. Perhaps next summer, when Drury Lane closes for the season?'

'I would be delighted to play for you next week if you prefer, so long as we can agree a favourable fee, perhaps a share of the profits after house expenses?' I said, and we both laughed, each of us remembering that first meeting when I, so bedraggled and hungry and four months gone with Fanny, had not even the courage to audition for a part.

We decided on *The Country Girl*, my current favourite and new to Leeds. Also *The Romp*, which was loved by the audience even if I was growing a little weary of it. My old admirer the son of the Duke of Norfolk was in the audience, together with a crowd of his friends. Wilkinson was astonished and delighted that the House was packed to overflowing before the curtains were even drawn. Another slap in the face to the three witches, who clearly couldn't achieve one that was more than half full.

Best of all, our trip north meant that we were reunited with my dear brother, and George accompanied us on to Edinburgh, enjoying spending some time with his family. There I met with only moderate success as the Scots do rather prefer their dour tragedy to farce, but it was fun, and good to have the opportunity to introduce myself to a new audience. Then we were heading south again, eager to start rehearsals for the next season at Drury Lane.

Eleven

My fame seemed to be rapidly spreading. Artists would try to draw me while I was on stage. I could see them scribbling madly, which was very slightly off-putting. Romney, so popular in court circles that he normally charged eighty guineas, painted me later that year for no fee at all. He caught me quite delightfully, I think, in a pose I used as Peggy in *The Country Girl*.

Everywhere I went in London there were prints of my portraits, sketches and engravings. Sheet music of the songs I sang could be found for sale in the shops, and people even offered to write songs for me. Others wished to make my hats and gowns, and flowers and gifts were constantly delivered to my dressing room. It was all quite overwhelming. I was also beginning to receive invitations to rather grand social functions. I must have passed muster at the first one I attended, or at least managed not to make a complete fool of myself, as I was then asked to further events.

I loved every moment of my new fame, more than willing to work hard, never stopping to consider whether I was tired.

Nor did I regret dismissing George Inchbald from my life. He'd rather avoided me while I was visiting Leeds, tending to sulk in a corner whenever I was around. But I do not believe in looking back, only in living for the day. I certainly had no intention of pining for that selfish young man. One morning I was hurrying to a rehearsal when I bumped into Sheridan.

'I beg your pardon, sir,' I said, stepping back quickly.

'Ah, Mrs Jordan, may I present Mr Richard Ford.'

I glanced at the smiling young man by his side, and graciously offered him my hand. He was slim and rather elegant, with a boyish face, dark hair and eyes. His touch was gentle as he took my hand in his, making no attempt to kiss it but treating it with a delicate respect. My heart gave a little flip, almost of recognition.

'I seem to know your face. Have we met you before, I wonder?' I asked, feeling slightly flustered.

'I'm quite certain that I would have remembered, although I have seen you on stage, Mrs Jordan. It is a great pleasure to meet you in person, as I so loved you as Peggy in *The Country Girl*.'

'Thank you. It is most kind of you to say so.' I recalled that I had seen him about the theatre from time to time, although not with the young bucks who hovered about the green room, or the stage door, hoping for a glimpse of one of the actresses.

Sheridan explained. 'Richard is the son of my co-proprietor, Dr James Ford of Albemarle Street, part owner of the Drury Lane, and obstetrician to Queen Charlotte.'

'Ah, and are you too a doctor?' I was sufficiently intrigued by the young man to wish to linger and engage him in conversation.

He gave a little chuckle. 'I'm sure that would have pleased my father, but no. I am training for the bar, and hope one day to go into Parliament.'

I was impressed. More importantly I knew at once that I was attracted to him, and rather thought from the look in his eyes that he might be equally taken with me. He half turned, about to leave, but then again quietly addressed me. 'Perhaps we may talk more next time.'

'I should be charmed.'

As I watched him walk away I thought what a quiet, most pleasant young man he seemed to be, well educated and rather serious. And on greater acquaintance he proved to be so. He took to calling to see me regularly at the Lane, always charming and ever polite. He was the perfect gentleman, steady, and, unlike Sheridan, not a heavy drinker or womanizer. He was that rare creature, a man with good prospects and no debts or vices.

Most of all he appeared to understand my passion for the stage. I remarked upon this facet of his character, and he conceded it was true.

'My father is only interested in the theatre as an investment, but I have always been fascinated by it. Besides which, I believe a person should be encouraged to do as they wish in life, and not what is expected of them.'

'Oh, I do so agree.'

'Would you walk with me a little, Mrs Jordan?'

'If you would please call me Dora.'

He beamed. 'I would be delighted, and you must call me Richard.'

We walked over to Covent Garden to admire the flower sellers, and he bought me a single pink rose, which he said matched the colour of my cheeks. Then one afternoon he took me for a drive in his carriage. He handed me into it, did not drive too fast, and took the utmost care of me. I felt so very grand, so precious and protected, as if nothing and no one could ever harm me, quite unlike the last time I was in a private vehicle, in Daly's phaeton.

These outings soon became a regular occurrence, and it was no surprise when one day he kissed me. I had so longed for him to do so, curious to know how his mouth would taste, and how it might feel to be held in his arms. I have to say it was utterly delicious. His kiss was so tender, so gentle, so unlike Daly's that I almost could have wept with the pleasure of it. He was the sweetest, kindest man I had ever met, everything that other Richard was not.

'You know that I am falling in love with you, Dora?' he told me after only a few short weeks of walking out together. 'I cannot seem to help myself.'

'And I with you,' I admitted, feeling oddly shy.

'Were it possible I would rush you this very minute to the altar and marry you forthwith.'

Something leapt in my breast: desire, hope, happiness? How much more joy and good fortune could a girl take? 'You mustn't say such things,' I gently scolded him.

'Why not, when it is true? I love you, Dora, and if you really do feel the same then I should indeed be proud to make you my wife. It may take a little while to gain my father's approval, but I'm quite certain once he understands that my happiness depends upon it, he will come round to the idea.'

I was so glowing with happiness, shining with it, that I could barely take in the full import of what he was saying to me. 'In truth, I'm in no hurry to marry. I have a play to perform next week, and a busy season ahead.' What did a few weeks matter, I thought. Besides, I was more cautious of men now. Not only Daly, but Inchbald too had taken advantage of me in their different ways. Like all girls I longed for romance and a man to love me, a respectable marriage and a father to my children, particularly little Fanny. But I had no wish to risk disappointment again.

He peppered my cheeks and lips with his kisses. 'I perfectly understand that your work is important, and entirely support you in it. I think you are adorable, and we can at least be together.'

When I arrived home that afternoon, Mama noticed at once that something had occurred. 'Has he proposed?' she asked, excitement in her voice.

'I believe that Sheridan was wrong, that I have perhaps found myself a decent, respectable man to love me. And the prospect of marriage and more children is a deliciously enticing thought.'

'And what of his family?'

I briefly explained about needing to bring his father round to the idea, and she frowned a little.

'Will it take long, did he say?'

'He says not when his father sees how essential I am to his happiness.'

She was still looking concerned. 'But he does seem a most reliable young man, not like that Inchbald fellow. And it is good to see you so happy, dearest.'

I kissed her. 'I knew you would approve.'

The Sheridans had been away all summer at Weymouth, now they were back as the new season had begun. That autumn I played Queen Mathilda in *Richard Coeur de Lion*. As it was a musical entertainment I was disguised as a blind minstrel boy for much of the play, which allowed it to be a breeches part. Elizabeth Linley, Sheridan's wife, had arranged the music. She was a beautiful woman, and had been a professional singer until she married. Sheridan had asked her to give up her career, as he considered it unseemly for the wife of a gentleman to perform in public. She'd gladly agreed to do so, no doubt out of love for him, but was sorely missed by the public. I felt sorry for her, as she was so very talented it seemed a waste for her not to use that marvellous voice of hers.

Would Richard expect me to give up my career? I worried. Surely not. I knew in my heart that he'd never ask such a thing of me. Hadn't he made a point of saying how proud he was both of me and my profession?

And with Elizabeth Sheridan there was a fragility about her, so perhaps it was just as well she'd largely retired. I stopped worrying about such things, too entirely wrapped up in my own happiness, and then Richard startled me by suggesting we set up home together.

'That would be quite impossible,' I demurred. 'I have my child to think of, and I am responsible for providing a home for my mother and sister.'

'Then let me provide it. I have no objections to your family. So long as I have you with me every day, and night, what more could a man wish for than to be with the woman he loves?'

I kissed him most fervently. 'You are so kind, I absolutely adore you. But I will not allow you to finance my mother and sister, not on the salary of a trainee lawyer.'

In November the theatre closed for two weeks in mourning for the death of one of the King's aunts. And it was then, at Richard's insistence, that I moved my family out of Henrietta Street and into number five Gower Street in Bloomsbury. John Bannister, my leading man, also lived in the street, and there were neighbours' children of an age to be playmates for Fanny. The house was new, tall and elegant, and seemed the perfect place for a family.

'From now on you will be known as Mrs Ford,' Richard said. 'And as soon as I can bring my father round, we will make the situation legal.'

I was so in love that I trusted him implicitly. Most people assumed that we had indeed gone through a discreet little ceremony and were in fact married already. It didn't greatly trouble me that this was not the case, but then as Hester was fond of saying, I was far too trusting. Then again, why would I be tough and businesslike? This was not a theatre contract, it was my life, my happiness, not a part in a play. I was not negotiating a rise in salary with Sheridan, so why the need to be businesslike?

Or perhaps I was tired of being prudent and sensible, weary of my chaste life. When Richard took me to his bed and loved me most tenderly and sweetly, all the bad memories of those other times with Daly vanished from my mind. This was what it meant to have a man make love to you. Richard caressed and kissed me with perfect gentleness, making sure I was ready for him before he entered me. This man adored me, and cared for my pleasure as much as his own. He was a most wonderful lover, and my love for him grew with each day we spent together, each night in his arms.

Fanny was not quite so enchanted to find she was expected to knock before entering our bedroom. I couldn't help but giggle at the outrage on her little face.

'But I come into bed with you every morning, Mama,' she cried.

'I know, darling, but Richard is your new papa, and you must be polite and ask first,' I told her.

Oh, but I was supremely happy. And if I still had not met his father, my lover saw no reason for concern. 'Father will soon come round. How could he not adore you, as do I?'

'And since I am bringing good money into the theatre of which he is a part owner, I can't see any problem either,' I laughingly agreed.

'You are a most valuable asset in every way,' Richard teased me, and we would giggle and kiss, so happy to have found each other.

Richard would escort me to the theatre each day, stand back-stage to watch as I went on, and catch me in his arms when, glowing with success, I came off again. He declared it to be intoxicating to view my performance at close hand, and if it went a little less well than I'd hoped, he would console me with his kisses, then send me back on stage radiant with happiness. To me, it was utterly intoxicating to be in love. I was convinced that I could do anything I pleased, conquer the world if needed, because this wonderful man loved me.

*　　*　　*

In the spring of 1787, Mrs Siddons was planning a benefit. So entranced was she by the way the audience had taken to my comedic roles, that she'd made up her mind to play comedy herself. Although her choice was much more refined than mine, naturally. Her tall, beautiful figure, stunning good looks and deeply vibrant voice made her far more suited to the role of Lady Macbeth, which was her most famous role. It also suited her personality, in my opinion, as it was one where she could effortlessly display the vicious nature and passion of the woman who led Macbeth to his doom.

'She is to play Rosalind in *As You Like It*,' I told Mama. 'The role you said would suit me. It's as if she has decided that if an unimportant newcomer such as myself can make the world laugh, then she will demonstrate how it should be done.'

Mama was dismissive. 'None can play comedy as you, dearest.'

Hester agreed. 'More likely she will have the audience weeping as she declaims and struts about the stage, rather than rolling in the aisles with laughter.'

I confess the three of us watched her failure with a secret delight. Hester was right, the great Siddons was more used to making the grand gestures. She did not have the lightness of touch, the agility or energy, the necessary art or skill in timing to play comedy, which is far more difficult than it appears. Not only that, but she was far too much the lady to step out on stage in men's clothing, always quite revealing of the female form. She had demanded a costume be made specially for her which largely cloaked her figure. It was a disaster.

As if wishing to rub salt into my own failure, she then played Imogen in *Cymbeline*, thereby making it very clear that she still wore the crown for tragedy.

But I went on to play Rosalind in *As You Like It*. I was indeed the saucy woodlander, the handsome young buck of sprightly wit in my yellow breeches, ruffled shirt and feathered hat. My lively performance brought forth a storm of applause.

If this had been a battle then Mrs Siddons was still queen of tragedy, and I had claimed the crown of comedy.

Twelve

'Mistress Ford'

I had thought that my setting up home with Richard Ford
was a private affair, of no concern to anyone but ourselves. As
things turned out, that was not the case. Vicious comments
were made in the press. The papers said that I had taken him
as a matter of 'prudence', by which they meant, for money.
Worse, they added that I had been 'prudent' in previous amours,
and pictures of myself and Daly were printed, labelled as 'Mrs
Tomboy and the Irish manager', which filled me with horror.

'I never loved that man,' I assured Richard. 'In fact I loathe
him still with all my heart and soul.' I told him briefly of his
assault upon me, without dwelling on specifics, and he was
most sympathetic. But the scandalous reporting in the papers
was hugely embarrassing. Even George Inchbald claimed we
had been 'close friends' at one time. None of this would help
my cause with his father one bit.

'Perhaps once I am your wife in very truth, this nonsense
will stop,' I said, and Richard tenderly kissed my tears away.

'I'm sure that is the case.'

But he offered no likely date when this might come about.

And then I discovered I was pregnant.

Mama was more upset than I was by this news. 'Surely now
he must marry you,' she said, wringing her hands with motherly
anxiety.

'I really don't have time to worry about such matters right
now, Mama, not with a tour coming up.'

'You are not thinking of carrying on with the tour? Why put
yourself through all of that strain and hard work. It's not as if you
need to, not like in the bad old days when you were just starting
out. More than anything I want a respectable marriage for you.'

I sighed, struggling to make her understand. 'I have
responsibilities, Mama, which I cannot simply abandon. What

difference does it make whether we marry now, or at the end
of the tour? I shall work till my time, as I did with Fanny.'

My second daughter, Dorothy, or Dodee as she became
known, was born in August, in Edinburgh. The press had a
field day with that too.

'Homeward Bound . . . The Jordan from Edinburgh – a
small sprightly vessel – went out of London harbour laden –
dropt her cargo in Edinburgh.'

I had to laugh at the wit of it, and was back on stage at
Drury Lane by September. That winter I greatly added to my
popularity by playing Juletta to Kemble's Pedro in *The Pilgrim*.
He and I had acted together before, of course, at Smock Alley,
and it was always a pleasure to me, despite his sister attempting
to turn him against me. I also played Roxalana in *The Sultan*,
with an actor called Barrymore taking the part of the Grand
Turk. He had such difficulty keeping a straight face at my
clowning, that on quitting the stage one night he fled to the
green room and collapsed on to a sofa where he laughed till
the tears ran down his blubbery cheeks.

'By the Holy Prophet, madam, if you continue to play after
this fashion you will dispatch me in an agony of laughter
to the seventh heaven.'

'Not a bad way to go,' I chortled.

But the cast at the Lane were not always in such good humour.
Kemble and King had very different ideas on management, and
were constantly at loggerheads. In March my old sponsor, the
great actor, Gentleman Smith, had his final benefit playing
Macbeth with Mrs Siddons as his Lady, and her brother John
Kemble performing Macduff. The latter was not sorry to see his
great rival retire. I was most certainly sorry to see him go.

'I shall keep in touch, and be a regular attendee at your
performances, dearest Dora,' he assured me.

'See that you do. Friends are like gold, too precious to lose,
and I shall never forget what you did for me.'

My career seemed to be sailing along nicely, and then
I discovered I was pregnant yet again. And still unmarried,
which, despite my protests to Mama, was beginning, very
slightly, to concern me.

★   ★   ★

By spring I was performing little as I felt unwell, suffering rather more with this pregnancy than previous ones. Nor was Tom King quite so supportive as he'd once been, his passion for all things tragic still his chief delight. Comedy to him was walking with a mincing step, whereas I happily dressed as a boy without shame or vanity, which rather shocked him and offended his sensibilities.

King's real dispute was in fact with Sheridan. The manager would constantly complain that while always being in too much of a hurry to listen to his problems, Sheridan nevertheless had complete control.

'I have no power to refuse or accept a play, to appoint or discharge an actor, nor even to buy a yard of copper lace to add to a coat.'

'You could nevertheless support your actors a little more,' I told him. 'I have certainly felt somewhat ignored recently, yet my audiences are baying for me.'

'Tragedy and Mrs Siddons are still our greatest draw,' he obstinately insisted.

'I bring them flocking every bit as much as she, so deserve equal pay, would you not say?' I was becoming a tough negotiator and most certainly knew my own worth as an actress.

With Mrs Siddons determined to diminish my position, John Kemble often at odds with King, and the latter at odds with Sheridan, the Lane was not at present the happiest place in which to work. But I did my utmost to keep out of theatrical politics, as I had more personal problems to contend with.

The fact was that Richard and I were as unalike as we could possibly be. He was so logical, his legal mind planning every step as he climbed the ladder to success. While I, born with nothing, had a far less conservative outlook upon life, and preferred to take things one day at a time.

He also counted every penny, and whenever my somewhat wild elder brother, Francis, who was in the militia, wrote asking me for money, he would peevishly complain.

'Why does he always come to you with his begging bowl? Why can he not live on his army pay?'

'Because it is very small and he is a gentleman, or at least our father was, so he has that right. And I can afford to help him, Richard, so why should I not? He is my brother, and, rakehell or no, I love him.'

'Do you not have enough with your other siblings to maintain?' he snapped.

This was not the first time he'd made this accusation, as if I had no right to help my family, and it was beginning to irritate me. 'You know full well that Nathaniel is no great charge upon my purse, since Cousin Blanche has largely funded him and brought him up as her own. He went to Brasenose College, Oxford and matriculated in October 1786. Now he is taking his BA. He is a clever boy and we are all very proud of him, so I do what I can to help. As for George, I have frequently asked for him to be engaged by the Drury Lane company, but Tom King refuses to admit him.'

'It is not your place to secure his future. He is a grown man now and should take responsibility for his own life.'

'George is a quiet, gentle soul, rather a retiring young man. If he pushed himself forward more then I accept he might well do better. His skills may be limited, but he has a superb voice and still dreams of a future in opera. Who knows if he will succeed, but he is my brother, so of course I must do what I can for him.'

'And if he does not succeed, then he will continue to be a drain on your resources.'

I regarded him quite coldly. '*You* seem to expect your father to contribute to your own expenses from time to time, so why should *I* not be responsible for my family?'

'That is different. I am my father's heir. Your family depend upon your good will far too much.'

I could feel myself growing warm with anger, which unfortunately seemed to happen rather too frequently at present. 'Is my family such a great nuisance to you? Would you prefer it if Mama and Hester moved out and took up residence elsewhere?'

'I am not saying that at all,' he protested, but there was the very slightest hesitation before he spoke. I was furious.

'Hester is often given minor parts, and helps backstage. She is no drain on *your* purse, and what I do with mine is surely my business. I do, after all, contribute to the household expenses. Quite considerably. Otherwise how would we live so well?'

I had never before reminded Richard of this fact, but in this instance I deemed it necessary. I saw a flush creep up his jaw and pity rose in my heart. He was having a difficult time, struggling to make his way in the world, as well as battling against a disapproving father. 'Can we stop this squabbling? I do so hate it when we are at odds. Can we at least be friends?'

He at once took me into his arms. 'Of course, my darling. I must be in a grumpy mood today, perhaps because of the stress of our difficult situation with another new baby on the way.'

I might have said the solution to that was in his own hands, but felt I had said enough for one day.

That summer of 1788 we went to Cheltenham, where I performed again for the King. On this occasion I played Hypolita in *She Would and She Would Not*, and in *The Romp*, my naughty part. Frederick, the King's favourite son, was also in the audience. None of the other princes came although the second son, William, presently in the West Indies, did come to see me in *Richard Coeur de Lion*. I thought him rather handsome, as are all the Hanoverian brothers. They do have something of a reputation for a rackety lifestyle, but I was deeply flattered by the royal interest, never quite growing used to seeing royalty in their box.

His Majesty even sent a gift to my benefit in the form of an elegant gold locket, set with fine pearls. In the centre was a beautiful painting of the Comic Muse by Sir Joshua Reynolds. I would treasure it always.

My own dear family was with me at Cheltenham, Richard too, of course, as he hated me to be out of his sight for too long. My little ones, Fanny and baby Dodee, were enjoying some country air away from the hothouse of London. And brother George came on a visit and even trod the boards with me, which was a rare treat. We took lodgings close to the theatre and it was a most delightful summer.

John Bannister, my leading man, and I, seemed to be as popular as ever with audiences, whether playing sentimental lovers or comically at odds as misunderstood characters in disguise. It was a hugely successful tour.

I even gave a command performance, but, for once, out of respect for the King, did not play the breeches part in *The Poor Soldier*, opting instead for the heroine in a skirt. I considered this a more appropriate role, since I was pregnant. By chance I also played Mistress Ford in *The Merry Wives of Windsor*, which raised yet more hilarity and embarrassment in the press.

I can take a joke as well as anyone but was growing mightily tired of being the subject of such caustic wit. I longed for this baby to be born in wedlock, and one afternoon said as much to my beloved. 'Dearest Richard, have you spoken to your father recently? I fear this disapproval of his is lasting far longer than I had foreseen.'

'I cannot cross him at this stage, Dora my love. He is trying to sell what remains of his shares in Drury Lane, and I have no idea what his intentions are once he has achieved that. He may well retire, or he may not. But I certainly have no wish to risk being disinherited.'

'I'm sure he would do no such thing. I have borne you a daughter. What if this child were to be a boy, would you not wish him be legitimate? Would not your father?'

'We do not discuss such issues.'

'But why don't you? These are *your* children after all. We cannot go on being the subject of constant amusement and vilification in the press. They are saying that I refused to perform unless the management agreed to my being known as Mrs Ford, which is utterly ridiculous. I was forced to write and refute the lie, to explain that I was suffering a period of ill health.'

Tom King too had been far from tolerant of my absences, but then what does a sixty-year-old man know about pregnancy? Or any man, for that matter? Certainly my own husband, or would-be-husband, seemed strangely indifferent to legitimizing his children, which hurt me deeply.

'Why would I change my stage name?' I challenged him. 'It is my *real* name I wish to change and legitimize.'

'But everyone loves you, dearest, and understands our situation perfectly,' he consoled me, stroking my cheek. 'You are well received in the right circles. See how your friend Lady Lumm accepts you as my wife. She is well aware of the true nature of our alliance, and the difficulties of our situation, yet still sends invitations for you to attend her routs and parties.'

I stifled a sigh of impatience. 'Not everyone is as tolerant as Lady Lumm. She is, after all, the wife of my father's oldest friend who not only brought his dead body back to Ireland, but erected a headstone to his memory. Others are less forgiving of my position, and I am beginning to grow weary of waiting, Richard. I do wonder if your father ever will be reconciled to my presence in your life.'

'Of course he will, my love. It is simply a matter of time.'

Now I was cross. 'But we do not *have* time. This baby will not wait. The consummation of the nuptials was never supposed to be more than six months from the time we set up home together, which is *eighteen* months ago now! This is a bad business, Richard, a bad business indeed. I deserve better.' And on that note I walked away from him in something of a huff.

Mama, of course, was outraged by his recalcitrance. 'Why do you put up with it, Dolly? What if he never does marry you, what then?'

'I would certainly not tolerate such treatment,' my sister declared, getting on her high horse as she so liked to do. 'It is outrageous. The fellow is in danger of turning into a scoundrel.'

My loyalty to Richard prevented me from answering this charge. 'I am more concerned that the manager is edging me off the stage in favour of the over-sentimental Miss Farren, or the pretty nimbleness of Maria Crouch. I feel I am being neglected.'

'Only by Tom King, not by your adoring public, Dolly.'

'Crowds still gather at the stage door,' Hester reminded me. 'They are fascinated to catch a glimpse of you stepping into your carriage, or alighting for the next show.'

'They marvel at your success. Everyone loves you, Dolly, save for Richard Ford,' my mother added, rather caustically.

I sighed. 'He does love me, Mama.'

'In his way, perhaps, but if he does not love you enough to

make you his wife, then better you were alone, instead of producing yet more fatherless children.'

I was beginning to agree with her on that score. The shine on our romance had certainly dulled, my happiness blunted by disappointment. But I nurtured a small spark of hope in my breast that it might still be salvaged. Perhaps when he held his own son in his arms, he would come to the point.

Our son was born in October 1788. He was given no time at all as he died before ever I had the chance to name him, but I loved him dearly all the same. My single state continued and I was back on stage by late November.

Thirteen

'Little Pickle'

Spending the summer taking the waters in Cheltenham sadly did not save the King from a return of his malady. Soon the rumours were flying that he had fallen into a fever which had turned into madness. It was said that he wept constantly, talked continuously, and at times even barked like a dog, poor man. The desperate state of our monarch was on everyone's lips. The Prince of Wales was to be made regent and Parliament was in a state of flux. Fox hastily returned from the Continent to take charge. Sheridan too was often called upon to attend Carlton House as he remained close friends with the Prince of Wales.

By February of the following year His Majesty was showing some signs of recovery and the nation rejoiced as the royal family attended a service of thanksgiving. There were command performances, firework displays and soon the royal boxes were full again, the King smiling down upon us as before. Mrs Siddons even appeared dressed as Britannia at a celebratory ball at Brooks's.

The arguments at the Lane, however, had grown increasingly bitter. Tom King had stepped down and Kemble appointed as manager. I was now on thirty guineas a week, the equal of Siddons, although I had needed to threaten to leave and go to Covent Garden before Sheridan had stepped in to settle the matter.

And I was yet again pregnant, with still no sign of a wedding ring.

I was thankful to escape and go on tour as usual that summer, performing at Leeds, Harrogate and Edinburgh. But it was here that Mama suddenly suffered a seizure and within hours, was dead. It was so shockingly swift that I could hardly take in that she was gone from me. She was but in her mid-fifties, and had not enjoyed an easy life, having been shabbily treated by a much-loved husband and largely abandoned by her family. It was some consolation to me that in recent years she'd witnessed my success and not had any further concerns over money. Her last years had at least been comfortable.

The manager at the Edinburgh theatre protested when I took time off, but I was too overwhelmed by grief to act. Hester too was in tears, as was little Fanny, who had adored her nana. It was a sad time for us all, and I did not take kindly to the fellow's resolve to withhold payment, nor his open criticism of me in the press.

If I have learned nothing else in life, I know how to stand up for myself. I wrote a most spirited defence, pointing out that I am never anything but a consummate professional. But surely one should be allowed a little time to grieve for a much-loved mother? I received many letters of sympathy in response.

I also wrote a few couplets in Mama's memory, words from the heart, which an Edinburgh newspaper duly published.

> *A tender mother, and a patient wife;*
> *Whose firm fidelity no wrongs could shake,*
> *While curb'd resentment was forbid to spake.*
> *Thus silent anguish mark'd her for his own,*
> *And comfort coming late was barely known;*
> *It, like a shadow, smil'd and slipp'd away.*
> *For churlish Death refus'd to let it stay;*
> *A two-fold dart he levell'd, to destroy*
> *At once, both mother's life and daughter's joy.*

I was thankful to return to London, where my daughter was born later in the year. I named her after my adored and deeply mourned sister Lucy. We did have some joyous news that year when we heard that my young brother George, who had been performing at Liverpool, had suddenly taken it into his head to marry.

Hester was appalled. 'Why the rush? Marry in haste, repent at leisure, isn't that what they say?'

I had to laugh, since Hester constantly damaged her own chances of wedlock by being far too particular and critical of any likely suitor. 'His bride is Maria Romanzini, a young lady with whom I have acted at the Lane. She has good humour and a pretty singing voice, and has done well for herself despite a hard childhood and no father. Be happy for him, Hester. I shall speak again to Kemble and attempt to win George an engagement.'

It took some time but I finally did talk Kemble round, and in early February 1790 George played Sebastian to my Viola. He was not quite so polished in the role as I would have liked, but it was his first performance at Drury Lane, and I had every faith that he would improve. He was taken on at £5 a week as a beginner. Mama would have been so pleased.

From then on I was acting five nights a week, having added several new parts to my repertoire: Pretty Polly Honeycomb, Laetitia Hardy in *The Belle's Stratagem*, and Lydia Languish in *The Rivals*. And for my benefit in March I chose Little Pickle in *The Spoiled Child*. Originally by Bickerstaffe, I had myself adapted the play to suit popular taste.

On the first night, as Hester pinned up my hair and helped with my make-up, she warned me that there were princes again in the royal box.

'Oh, dear, I do wish you hadn't mentioned them. It always unnerves me if I am aware of a royal presence in the theatre.'

'Don't be foolish,' she laughed, pencilling a dark line beneath my lashes. 'They wouldn't come so often to see you if they didn't adore you. And you know how they do love the ladies. I've heard rumours that one of the younger brothers, William, I believe, was pursuing Sheridan's wife, Elizabeth. But as he is ten years younger than her, she resisted.'

I looked at my sister askance. 'How do you know all this?'

Hester laughed as she teased out the curls about my forehead. 'Don't you just love gossip? I do. Sheridan would have had only himself to blame if she'd succumbed.'

'Why?' I couldn't resist asking.

'Because he has been engaged for some time in a passionate love affair with Harriet Duncannon, sister of Georgiana, Duchess of Devonshire. There was a shocking scandal with her husband threatening divorce, and the lady was obliged to flee the country until it all died down.'

'Goodness, how dreadful. I could never cheat on a husband. How could I ever hurt dear Richard in that way?'

'Ah, but Richard isn't your husband, is he?'

I looked at her through the mirror, struggling to mask my feelings. 'But it would still be a betrayal.'

She shrugged. 'One perhaps he deserves. Unless he were to change his mind and marry you, after all.'

'There seems little sign of that,' I admitted, and putting aside my disappointment, went out on stage to meet my adoring public. From the moment I first trod the boards back at Crow Street in Dublin, the stage was always the place where I felt happiest, and could set my worries aside.

At the end of the performance, which I must say went well, I looked at my strangely naked face after Hester had removed all the grease paint, and noted a fan of lines from the corner of each eye. 'Do you realize that I shall soon be twenty-nine?'

'Really quite doddery,' she chuckled. 'Perhaps I should buy you a walking stick for your birthday? Oh dear, is that a grey hair I see?'

'Don't tease, Hester. I'm beginning to feel the passing of the years.'

'You are at the peak of your profession,' she scoffed. 'A woman in her prime with three adorable daughters, a lovely home, and money in the bank. No reason for complaint at all.'

'Now you are making me appear greedy and selfish when all I meant to say was that I feel I have failed Mama by never having married. How bitterly she resented that lack of respectability in my life, which in a way seems to echo her own precarious marriage with Papa.'

'Men are all scoundrels,' Hester scorned, as she had many times before. 'Ford might enjoy the kudos of dangling a famous actress on his arm, but I do wonder if now that he's won a seat at East Grinstead and entered Parliament, he no longer deems you worthy of him.'

I stared at her aghast. 'How can you suggest such a thing?'

'Because your dearest beloved is very much a man of ambition,' my sister persisted. 'He is where he is today thanks to Sheridan's influence, which he has carefully nurtured. He no doubt hopes to call upon it further to secure himself a post in high office. Would such a man welcome a wife who is an actress, with at least one illegitimate child?'

I could feel my cheeks growing warm with annoyance and embarrassment, yet could find no words to deny her statement. In truth I had never looked at it in quite that light until she pointed it out to me. And I did not like what I saw. I was happy for Richard's success, naturally, and we appeared, outwardly at least, quite settled. We were a couple in every way but the one that counted most, certainly to me. But if he was having second thoughts about my suitability as a wife, then our relationship was indeed doomed, my hopes of respectability forever dashed.

Richard took a little place at Richmond for us, as a weekend retreat. Was that not proof of his love? I asked myself. 'You can go there to rest and recuperate on the days you have no performance,' he suggested. 'It will be a good place to recover from the long hours you spend in rehearsal and on stage. I shall come when the House is not sitting. It can be our secret hideaway.'

'Oh, Richard, how good you are to me,' and I kissed him with joy in my heart. Perhaps he was coming round to thinking of marriage, after all, I thought.

As things turned out I was to spend more time there than he, but then the House was very often sitting, or he would have legal matters to attend to. I loved to take my children there for long periods, and indeed did a summer season at Richmond that year of 1790. Our new home was conveniently situated in Petersham, so I could easily stroll across the meadows to the theatre. On days when I wasn't playing, while Hester minded the children for me, I would escape to walk in the nearby deer park, and breathe in the fresh country air. It felt such a relief after being shut up in gloomy rehearsal rooms for hours on end.

Nor was I pregnant for once, so was feeling fit and well, bursting with energy and enjoying this time with my children.

Deciding that the house in Gower Street had too many reminders of dear Mama, I took a new house in London, at my own expense. It was a delightfully fashionable property situated in Somerset Street between Portman Square and Oxford Street. The decision was mine alone, although Richard was happy to come too, of course. He was less happy, however, when I chose not to share his bed for a while.

'I'm sorry, dearest, it is merely temporary, but I have no wish for another child just yet.'

He glowered at me, his narrow face looking more pinched than ever. 'If this is some feeble attempt at blackmail, I refuse to be bullied, Dora.'

I looked at him in all innocence. 'I really cannot think what you mean.'

It was while I was out walking in the deer park one day that autumn, that quite by chance I came across a stranger seated upon a log. He was hunched over with one of those large floppy hats pulled down over his peruke. I couldn't see his face but he was clearly a gentleman, judging by his fine suit. As the afternoon was falling to dusk, I hastily turned to leave, not wishing to disturb him, but then accidentally stepped upon a twig.

He put a finger to his lips to shush me. 'Don't make a sound. Do you see that deer, she has a fawn with her. We must take care not to startle her.'

He spoke in little more than a whisper, then patted the log beside him, indicating I should sit. I hesitated for a moment but then did so, gathering my skirts in my hands so they did not rustle the leaves. We sat together for some long moments like this, almost shoulder to shoulder in companionable silence, each of us utterly engrossed in watching the deer crop the grass, while she continued to keep a wary eye on her young.

'I love animals,' he whispered. 'Don't you?'

I said nothing to this, not wishing to risk disturbing the deer. Besides, I'd never had the opportunity to find out whether I liked them or not in the theatrical world I occupied.

He went on talking, very quietly. 'I love to sit here in peace and solitude and watch the deer. So long as I remain quite still they do not object, may not even be aware of my presence.'

Although he was still seated I could tell by the length of his legs and his powerful thighs that he was reasonably tall, with an impressive figure. I thought it unlikely the deer was entirely unaware of his presence, any more than I was, although for a different reason.

After a while mother and baby moved away into the depth of the wood, and as it was growing quite dark by this time I leapt to my feet, anxious to return home while I could still mark the path. 'I must go, but I too love the peace and solitude of this place. It really is beautiful.'

The young man likewise got to his feet and turned to me with a smile. 'As are you, Mrs Jordan.'

My eyes widened in surprise. Even though I was now supposedly famous, I still fully expected to move about without being recognized. 'You know who I am?'

'I have had the pleasure of watching you perform. I saw you as Little Pickle in the spring, and most delightful you were too,' he said. 'I can't remember ever having laughed so much.'

I smiled. 'Then you have the advantage of me, sir. Perhaps you would be so good as to introduce yourself.'

He instantly swept off the hat and sketched a deep and noble bow. 'William Henry is the name, captain in the Royal Navy, officially retired and ship paid off. Perhaps better known as the Duke of Clarence and Earl of Munster.'

I was staring at him in open astonishment, may even have gasped, my mouth dropping open most unbecomingly, for without the hat I recognized him instantly as the fresh-faced young man I'd seen occasionally occupy the royal box. I hastily sank into a deep curtsey.

Laughing, he took my hands to gently raise me up. 'No need to stand on ceremony between friends, Mrs Jordan. And I believe you and I could become great friends.'

Fourteen

'. . . her smile was like sunshine'

I met him again the following afternoon, and we talked for over an hour, seated side by side on the log. It felt rather like our own private universe, far removed from the world of the theatre, and perhaps from his own royal duties. Here in the soft green peaceful retreat of the deer park, we were simply a young man and a young woman talking quietly together, not royal prince and subject.

'I first saw you in *Richard Coeur de Lion*, but I was utterly captivated by you as Little Pickle in *The Spoiled Child*, back in March,' he said, making me blush. 'It featured the kind of boyish pranks I love. Very much the sort of nonsense we get up to on board ship.'

I laughed at that. 'The Little Pickle character is very naughty to substitute his aunt's parrot for a pheasant on a spit, not to mention removing a chair from beneath an elderly gentleman. I hope you would never stoop to such low practical jokes.'

He beamed at me, eyes twinkling. 'It has been known. But the greatest delight was in watching you, Mrs Jordan. Your perfect timing and expressive face made me roar with laughter. What was it the critic Leigh Hunt said? "Her smile was like sunshine, and her laugh did one good to hear it." I most heartily agree. You certainly lifted my heart, and set it beating rather fast.'

Yet another admirer, I thought, with some amusement. A prince, no less, who no doubt imagines he only has to crook his little finger and any woman will fall at his feet. He will soon learn I am not that sort of woman. I have never been promiscuous, having only ever been in love with one man. Certainly not with Daly, who took me by force. 'I think you confuse me with the part I was playing.'

'Not for a moment do I think of you as a young boy,

Mrs Jordan,' he quietly protested, his words heavy with meaning. 'But it does not surprise me in the least that actresses all over the country are attempting to emulate you by taking on the part. I hoped to come again to Drury Lane, and perhaps get to know you a little, but I was recalled to my ship, HMS *Valiant*, at Portsmouth in early May. I confess I did not relish returning to duty, having grown accustomed to being in dock, as it were. I spent many boring months waiting for the fleet to refit. Fortunately, the threat of war receded and the *Valiant* was paid off. I am now to be created a rear admiral.'

'Congratulations.'

'Hang me, it is but a sop, but no matter, I'm much more pleased to be back here in Richmond, with you,' he said, with a certain twinkle in his eye that made me smile. 'Joined the navy at thirteen, don't you know, and at fourteen was taken to the watchhouse at Vauxhall.'

'I had heard that you enjoy something of a reputation,' I said with a laugh. 'But goodness, fourteen is rather young to be locked up. What on earth had you done to deserve such punishment?'

William chuckled as he told his tale. 'Drat it, if I didn't go to a masquerade and was flirting with quite a pretty girl, then a Spaniard butted in, damn his soul to perdition.'

The Prince, I'd discovered, had a habit of peppering his sentences with oaths, and often took the Lord's name in vain. I gave him the kind of silent reproving glance which warned him that such language was not appropriate before a lady. He was instantly contrite.

'Pardon my French, ma'am. I was forgetting myself. Too used to the company of rough sailors, don't you know.'

I inclined my head by way of acceptance of his apology, which I thought quite charming, and found myself wondering what colour his hair was beneath the wig. Fair perhaps? His eyes were a delightful blue.

'To continue with my tale, we exchanged a few strong words which naturally ended in a fight, a drunken brawl to be precise, and were marched off by the watchmen.'

'Did that teach you a lesson?'

He grinned. 'Afraid it was but the start of a slippery slope during those rebellious boyhood years. Times best forgotten. It was all the King's idea that I go into the navy. As heir, my brother George, who is the epitome of charm and wit, naturally had to be educated for kingship. Frederick joined the army. I was selected to go to sea. Not that I had any real objection. I looked forward to a more adventurous life rather than one confined with middle-aged tutors. We'd endured a somewhat stark and over-disciplined childhood under a parsimonious father, so I was well used to hardship and regular beatings. To be fair the King did personally arrange for me to enter the navy, insisting I be treated like any other boy, which I greatly appreciated. I started as a midshipman in the normal way.'

'Goodness, I naturally assumed that royal princes led a charmed life of luxury,' I said, rather startled by this account. I could picture him as a skinny, fair-haired boy, coping alone on a great big ship. It must have been far more unnerving than he was willing to admit.

'Anything but. Our routine, set by our nurses and tutors, was a strict one. We were required to copy out endless pages of the Old Testament in our best copperplate handwriting. We also learned Latin, mathematics, French and German. All dreadfully boring, I can tell you, but then George is far brighter than me. I much preferred working on our model farm, where we were expected to grow our own vegetables. I had my toy soldiers and brass guns to play with, of course.' He laughed. 'And Papa did show affection in his bluff way. He would often get down on his knees and play with us when we were young, but not Mama. We were never allowed to sit when the Queen was present.'

'My mother was also quite strict,' I said, intrigued by this insight into royal life. 'In the nicest possible way, you understand. She had very firm ideas on etiquette and manners, and educated us herself, since she couldn't afford to send us to school, not the girls anyway. But my family was not quite as low-brow and poverty-stricken as the newspapers claim.' Here I paused to adjust this remark. 'At least not until after Papa left, and later died. My father was a gentleman, if weak and rather foolish.'

· I told him how my being taken on at Crow Street had saved the family from starvation. And he regaled me with more tales of his first year in the navy, his stamina having at least earned him his father's approval.

'Damned if he wasn't far less approving when he discovered that I had picked up the sailor's bad habits of swearing and drinking and so on. I will not offend your ears further, Mrs Jordan, with the reality of life at sea, except to say that seeking pleasure when on land is a necessary compensation for the hardship.'

'I imagine it must be.'

'The King then sent me to Germany at seventeen to learn better manners from my cousins. I was desperately bored and lonely there. It's a damnable country where there was little to do but smoke and play twopenny whist.'

He went on to speak of his time with Horatio Nelson in the West Indies, and I spoke of my move to Yorkshire, without dwelling too much upon the reason for it, and ultimate arrival at Drury Lane. He was so open and frank that there seemed little we couldn't say to each other, quite the sweetest and most understanding man I had ever met. Interesting to talk to, and genuinely interested in me.

But I sensed loneliness at the heart of him, and was beginning to see that we might have much in common. I had the urge to put my arms about him to give him a comforting hug, but it wouldn't be in the least bit motherly, so I decided it was time to leave as my thoughts were turning in quite an unseemly direction.

We met frequently after that, and he often regaled me with some of his seafaring yarns. 'If you loved the navy so much, why did you leave?'

'I'd served nearly fourteen years but in the end thought it all dashed pointless, with no hope of a proper profession for me, a king's son.'

'It must have felt strange at first, to be on dry land again,' I sympathized, noting a sadness in his eyes.

'Indeed it was. I've been rather at a loss since I left the sea. It's hard to adjust to becoming a landlubber again, and even though I was glad to leave at the time I still miss the sway of the decks beneath my feet. I also felt rather distanced from the family following my long absence. No longer felt I *belonged*! And the King and Queen were somewhat cold and disappointed in me. Is it wrong to wish to be better appreciated by one's family?'

'I wonder if one ever is,' I said with some feeling, thinking of Hester's constant moans and criticisms.

'The only person I can talk to is George. We were ever united from childhood, right through our boyhood years. I rather expected to come home and find him acting as regent, although I was heartily glad to see the King fully recovered. I was very sorry for His Majesty, very sorry indeed – no man loves the King better than I, of that you may be assured. I was horribly agitated when I first saw him, so shocked I could barely stand. I felt for the Queen too, I did faith. But the pair of them are so against George, and by association, against me too.'

'Why, for goodness sake?'

'The King sees us as rivals to his power, hovering in the background waiting for his death, or the return of his madness. There was great trouble while I was away. Pitt was for the King, supported by the Queen and the princesses, who of course can do nothing more than grumble over their embroidery. Fox hurried back from Italy when George tried to bring in the regency, but Pitt opposed him, naturally fearing a fall from power for the Tories. Pitt's plan was to form a committee, rather than a single regency. As if at twenty-eight George wasn't old enough to rule alone, were my father to be incapable. Then Fox blundered by saying it was George's *right*, as heir to the throne.'

'Why was that wrong?'

'It gave Pitt the chance to prate on about it being a constitutional government and did he not really mean "claim"? George, of course, was already irritated with Fox for having denied before all the House his marriage to Mrs Fitzherbert.'

'Ah, yes, I remember Mama saying something on the subject of the Royal Marriages Act, as Sheridan was often absent from the Lane at the time. But would not the King, and the Queen for that matter, object, if they thought it a true marriage?'

'Maria is the love of his life, but yes, it is perhaps too soon for my brother to do battle with the King over his marital status. In the end, however, the regency crisis was largely academic as before the conflict could be resolved the King thankfully recovered. Unfortunately, the dispute has left the Queen with a deeper grudge against George. In addition to her disapproval of his wild parties, his drinking and gambling, she claims he was seeking to gain power at her expense, and would have replaced Pitt with Fox.'

'And would he?'

'Possibly. I'm always filled with admiration at my brother's clever machinations. But George blames Pitt entirely for setting the Queen against him, and it will happen again, of course. The King's recovery is but temporary. There is no cure for whatever ails him.'

'That is so sad,' I said, strangely moved by his tale, as I could see how very much it troubled him, losing the affection of both his parents.

He sighed, rubbed a finger over the bridge of his nose. 'Ah, politics, what a bore! At least the King finally came round and granted me a title. After I'd objected to being ignored, of course,' he chortled. 'I had to threaten to stand as an MP for the constituency of Totnes in Devon. He was so appalled at the prospect of his son appealing to the voters that I won that battle, although he did have the final word. "I well know it is another vote added to the Opposition," he said. And we both laughed at the joke.

'His Majesty also gave me a house in Richmond, which I sadly was obliged to leave due to a fire. I now occupy Ivy Lodge, in the centre of town.'

'Ah yes, not far from where the Sheridans live,' I said with a smile, remembering my sister's gossip. 'Sheridan is acquainted with your brother the Prince, I believe, and often absent from home. How very convenient.' I was amused to see a flush creep up his throat.

'It is not for the reason you imagine, or that rumour claims,' he said, most earnestly, and I almost laughed out loud.

'I cannot think to what you refer, but having often been the victim of the scandalmongers myself, I never pay any attention to rumour, I do assure you.' I quite enjoyed teasing him, privately marvelling at how much he wished to impress me.

He took my hand then and kissed it, most tenderly, turning it over to kiss the inside of my wrist. Was it because he was a royal prince that a delicious quiver of excitement sped up my arm? He was undoubtedly an attractive man. 'You are so easy to talk to. I feel as if I have known you for ever, Dora. May I call you Dora? And you must call me William. I do so hate formality, don't you? Can we meet again tomorrow, and the day after that?'

I laughed. 'I am performing tomorrow, and for many nights following. During the day I shall be tied up with rehearsals.'

'Next week then? I shall watch your performances every night, and wait for you here each day in the hope you will come again.'

'You must not do that.'

'Why not? Would your husband object? We are only friends who enjoy talking together, are we not?'

I hesitated, wondering if I should confess that Richard was not my husband, that I was in fact still single. I also worried over what Richard would say if I told him I was meeting with the Duke of Clarence, and knew upon the instant that I wouldn't tell him, would say nothing in either case. And so I agreed to meet William again, naming the day and time so that he didn't wait around unnecessarily. I really couldn't think of a good reason to refuse his request, even as I sternly reminded myself that he was simply another admirer, one of many such. And flattering as it was to be pursued by a prince, he was not to be taken seriously.

The Duke kept his word and every evening I would see him smiling at me from the royal box, his laugh booming out as he applauded madly at the end of every scene. Seeing him there, so evidently enjoying himself, quite lifted my performance. I found I wanted to please him, to entertain him and make him happy, hear his jolly laughter. It was as if I was acting only for him.

Afterwards he would come backstage and offer to take me to supper. The first time this happened put Sheridan into quite a tizzy. Since the regency crisis had died down, he'd seemed to be more often at the theatre, perhaps keen to make money to pay off his mounting debts. He came rushing to my dressing room in a fever of excitement.

'His Highness the Duke of Clarence wishes to send his felicitations and to take you to dine, Dora. I shall bring him through and introduce him. Tidy yourself quickly and make ready to receive him.'

I was still in my robe when the Duke entered, my face bare of make-up. Nevertheless I swept low into a deep curtsey, a skill I had acquired long since for some of the parts I played.

He instantly took my hand to raise me up. 'Nay, Mrs Jordan, did we not agree to have no formality between friends?'

I could see Sheridan glance from one to the other of us, a startled expression on his face. 'You have already met Mrs Jordan, Sir?'

'I have indeed. We are neighbours, are we not, Dora?'

At this, Sheridan had the diplomacy to withdraw, suddenly discovering he had urgent business elsewhere. I apologized for the lack of seating.

'My part of the dressing room is rather cramped, not set up for visitors. And I apologize too for my dishabille.'

'No need, as always you look quite charming. May I hope to take you to supper when you are dressed?'

I shook my head, softening my refusal with a gentle smile. 'I must hurry home to my family. If you remember, I am a contented woman with a man who loves me.'

'Does he love you, I wonder? Are you truly married to him, Dora? Rumour has it that is not the case, or am I drawing the wrong conclusions?'

I sank on to my dressing stool, hands clasped tightly in my lap. 'I certainly expected to be by now. Unfortunately, Richard's father does not approve of his liaison with an actress. But we are still hoping to win him round.'

'And how long have you been together?'

I hesitated only slightly before admitting the truth. 'Very nearly five years.'

He drew in a sharp breath. 'It seems to me that if a man has not plucked up the courage to defy his father in all that time, the chances are slim that he will do so in the future.' Then, taking me quite by surprise, he came to sit beside me on the stool, where Hester usually sat when we were in a huddle over gossip. 'I could not offer you marriage either, Dora, although I already adore you beyond words. I hope we can at least be friends? Even good friends.'

I was on my feet in a second. 'Sir, I must respectfully beg you to leave. I am a respectable woman, a mother of three daughters, and must hurry home to see them.'

'Of course.' He took my hand and kissed it, his mouth tender, lingering over the moment. 'Forgive me if I have been in any way impertinent. I did not mean to be. Perhaps one day I may meet your delightful daughters, who I'm sure will be as beautiful as their mother.'

And on that note, he left me. I collapsed back on to my stool, hands to my burning cheeks, a shivering wreck of tumultuous emotion.

Fifteen

'Are you telling me that all these afternoons walking in the deer park, you have been engaged in secret assignations with the Duke of Clarence?'

I gave my disgruntled sister a shamefaced smile, having finally confessed to my meetings with the Prince. 'They weren't intended to be such, I do assure you. We met quite by chance and started chatting while we were watching the deer. He says I am the most delightful person he has ever met, that I have captured his heart and—'

I was interrupted as Fanny came bouncing in, eager to help me prepare for the theatre, as always. Hester quickly shooed my daughter out, loudly protesting, and closed the door. 'And what?'

'I seem to have a new admirer.'

'Has he captured *your* heart? Are you equally enamoured? Attracted? Besotted? Don't tell me you have fallen in love yet again?'

'Of course not, I hardly know the man, but he is sweet and kind. We are but good friends.' I gave my attention to searching in my trinket box for suitable bracelets and rings to wear on stage, not wishing her to see the betraying flush I could feel creeping up my cheeks.

'Friends!' she scoffed, then snatching up the brush began to attack my hair with unnecessary vigour, taking out her temper on my recalcitrant curls. I made no protest, realizing it would only make her worse. 'You do know he has a reputation for dalliance? What of his pursuit of Elizabeth Sheridan?'

'A delightful lady, he says, but merely a passing fancy.'

'There seem to have been any number of those.'

'Nowhere near as many as rumour would have you believe, and mainly in his youth. He is a reformed character these days.'

She snorted her derision. 'He doesn't appear to have turned chaste from what I can see. What of that Polly Finch he once had staying with him?'

I found myself flushing. 'I asked him about her and he claims that for a time he did nurse a foolish sentiment of settling down with her, but she was not that sort of girl.'

'I dare say she wasn't,' Hester scathingly remarked. 'Apparently the Duke bored her rigid by reading her his seafaring tales every night.'

'He doesn't bore me. I find him most agreeable. And a man must fill his time somehow. He has been rather at a loss since he left the sea.'

Hester tugged at a lock of hair with the brush, making me wince. 'I've seen him in the Prince's box every evening leering at you, and coming backstage afterwards to congratulate you on your performance, lingering in the hope of taking you to dine.'

'An invitation I have steadfastly refused. Although where is the sin in taking supper with a pleasant companion? I find him both amusing and entertaining.'

'He could never marry you. The King would be certain to object.'

'The subject of marriage has never come up,' I lied. 'Although it is not so important for the Duke as it is for the Prince of Wales, since he is unlikely to occupy the throne.'

'He doesn't fancy a cow-faced German princess then.'

I giggled. 'Apparently not, he prefers a woman of wit and beauty, and with a tender heart. But I doubt His Majesty expects him to live as a monk, for all he has been a faithful husband himself, or so we are led to believe. Rumour has it that the King entered a form of marriage himself before marrying the Queen, with a Quakeress called Hannah Lightfoot. But I do assure you, in our many meetings there has been no talk of marriage. Nor have I any wish to become his mistress.'

'Have you not?' She paused in her labours to study carefully my bland expression. 'Does Richard know about this new admirer?'

Ignoring her question, I continued with my tale. 'Last evening he was telling me how he used to put on performances of *The Merry Wives of Windsor* on board ship, would you believe? They'd make Falstaff fall into a coil of ropes and pelt him with rubbish. And one of the sailors would dress up as Mistress Quickly, William himself taking the Mistress Ford part.' I laughed as I recalled his amusing tales. 'We seem to have a great deal in common.'

'Except he was acting as an amateur, not a professional.'

'I mean in our shared love of the theatre.'

Hester's expression was one of disbelief as she stuck pins in my hair with more energy than was quite called for. 'I'm not so sure it's the theatre he loves, more likely your shapely legs.'

'Hester, please! We *talk*, that is all, about anything and everything. William talks as much as you and I, which is saying something,' I teased.

'William is it now? Not "the Duke", or "His Highness", then?'

'He dislikes any formality, and is, as I say, a most cheerful and friendly person.'

'I'm sure he is,' she commented drily. 'Have you not always said it would be folly to love a prince? Even if there do seem to be any number available, thanks to Queen Charlotte's fecundity.'

I couldn't help but feel affronted, and a little hurt by her disapproval. 'What is it you want me to do, Hester? I love Richard, you know I do, and would gladly become his loyal wife tomorrow, were he to ask me. But I cannot wait for ever, and possibly in vain, for him to propose. Mama would certainly not wish that for me.'

'I think you should make absolutely certain that Richard isn't going to propose, before you take this "friendship" as you call it, any further. I do not want you laying yourself open to yet more hurt, Doll.'

My expression was bleak as I looked up at her, for she was saying only what I already knew in my heart. The door flew open and an outraged Fanny stood there, hands on her skinny hips, looking extremely cross.

'May I come in now, Mama? If you do not make haste you are going to be late. When I am a famous actress I shall make a point of never keeping anyone waiting.'

'Oh, how wise you are, darling Fan. And nor must I. Do come and help.'

She ran to me and I gathered my wilful daughter in my arms for a warm hug. Even at eight years of age she was already passionate about the theatre, and would no doubt follow in my footsteps, and Daly's, by treading the boards. She was also bossy and moody, and prone to sudden impulses, quite the opposite of quiet, sensitive Dodee. I was constantly attempting to calm her down, but because of the circumstances of her conception, I loved Fanny all the more for her idiosyncrasies. With such a man for a father she deserved devotion from her mother. 'You know that I would never do anything to hurt you, my darling girls. You are ever my first concern, and I want only what is best for you.'

Kissing my cheek, she wrapped her arms about my neck to give me an affectionate hug. 'You always provide us with the best, Mama. You buy us pretty dresses and the most fashionable silk shirts and neckcloths for Papa. But I love you because you are funny and sweet, not because you buy us things, or are famous and can earn a lot of money at the theatre.'

'I love Mama best,' cried three-year-old Dodee, her small voice high with excitement as she too came bounding in to fling herself on my lap. 'Me want pretty new frock like Fanny,' and I laughed out loud.

'What was that about not loving me for my money?'

'But what of Ford?' Hester whispered in my ear, as she finished tidying my hair. 'Which does he love best? You, or the salary you bring home?'

I made no attempt to answer that question as I met her troubled gaze in the mirror. Making my children legitimate was my one and only desire, and her wise words had decided me. Before I made any decision about the Duke, I would speak again to Richard, and resolve this matter once and for all.

'Would you believe the Duke of Clarence asked me out to supper after the show the other night?' I announced to Richard a night or two later as we sat by the fire together. It was a cold evening in January and he was reading some legal documents, barely glancing up when I spoke. But then I was used to his inattention these days. 'He is a most charming man, and really quite handsome,' I added for good measure. I'd started on this conversation with all good intentions, meaning to ask Richard calmly and clearly for his final decision on our situation. Instead, I found myself attempting to arouse his jealousy. When he did not respond, I tried again. 'We enjoyed a dish of oysters at the White Swan where he regaled me with stories of his adventures at sea.'

I was filled with guilt that I had succumbed and accepted his offer of supper, despite the fact I had made sure that other cast members were present and we were not alone.

Richard looked up, a vagueness in his gaze. 'Who regaled you with what stories?'

I picked up my tapestry work, stifling a spurt of impatience. 'The Duke of Clarence. He took several of us out to supper after the performance. John Bannister, Kemble, myself, Elizabeth Fallen and one or two others. He was telling us all about his days on board ship.'

'You were not alone with him, I trust?'

'Indeed not, I guard my reputation well. However, he is far more attentive than you these days, Richard. I wonder sometimes if you would even notice my absence, were I not to be here for any reason.'

'Where else would you be but home with our children?' he snapped. 'But I cannot be listening to your chatter all day long, I have parliamentary business to attend to. And if you refuse to share my bed . . .'

He left that sentence hanging while I applied myself to my stitching, then tactfully changed the subject. 'Tate Wilkinson has written to say he hopes to come on a visit in February. It will be good to see the old rogue again, don't you think?'

'He's not staying here, I trust?'

I put down my stitching with a sigh. 'No, Richard, he is staying at an hotel in Gray's Inn Lane at the other side of town. But were I to wish for any of my friends to stay in my house, then I do not see why that would be a problem for you.'

'I would not care to have the place filled with itinerant strolling players. Goodness knows what they might do to the place.'

'How very fortunate then that you don't pay for the upkeep of this property.' I smiled, letting the silence settle for a moment around this pointed remark. Did he not realize how very pompous he had become? I wondered. 'Don't forget that I too am an itinerant strolling player.'

'You talk absolute tosh at times, Dora. *You* are a famous actress,' he corrected me.

'Is that what first attracted you to me, my sudden fame? Is that why you love me, for the thirty guineas I bring home each week? If so, then why is your father not equally impressed? I am talented, reasonably attractive, rich, bringing good money to the theatre he once part-owned. I have given you two children, and once thought I made you happy. What more need I do to make myself acceptable as a wife?'

He groaned. 'Not that again. I'm weary of it,' and quickly gathering up his mass of books and papers, he muttered something I couldn't quite catch, and abruptly left the room.

It was not an auspicious start to my quest to regulate my position.

Wilkinson's visit was sadly blighted by the weather. It rarely stopped raining throughout the few days he was in London, to the extent that the Thames overflowed its banks and we suffered considerable flooding. Battling against the mud and rain did nothing for his bad leg, poor man, but he did manage after much tribulation to bribe a coachman to take him to the theatre, where he saw me in *Twelfth Night* and as Hypolita, looking rather splendid in my plumed hat and blue braided jacket, if I do say so myself.

After the performance we took supper together, as in the old days, and he at once began begging me to come north again. 'You will do a tour in July, will you not, Dora? We miss you at Leeds, the audience often asks for you.'

'Not the cast then?'

'Some of them, of course, but as you know this is a competitive business. Nevertheless, be sure that you are loved and most needed, particularly by me,' he said, grasping my hand with warm gratitude, so that I was moved to kiss his flabby jowls.

'Not to mention your accountant,' I teased. How could I

resist such an invitation? This dear old man had given me a chance at the lowest point in my life, and for that alone I would ever hold him in deep affection.

'It is good to see you looking so well and sprightly, Dora.'

'Not increasing for once, you mean.'

He grinned. 'That is a blessing too, of course.'

It was indeed, as things stood between myself and Richard. Loyalty and the five years we had spent together as man and wife in all but name did not seem enough to sustain our happiness now.

And in March the Duke of Clarence began his pursuit of me in earnest.

'I have moved from Ivy Lodge,' he announced one afternoon as we strolled in the park. 'Which was far too small and useless for a family. I've bought Petersham Lodge, a comfortable house in its own grounds, not far from you, which I have renamed Clarence House. What think you of that, Dora? Will you join me in it, so that we can live merrily and happily together?'

I gazed at him wide-eyed, unable to find any words beyond murmuring his name, '*William*, but . . .'

He quickly stopped whatever protest I'd been about to make by putting his mouth to mine, kissing me as he never had before, stirring my senses and making my head spin with longing. I couldn't remember the last time, if ever, I had been kissed with such passion. When he finally drew away, still clasping my hands in his, I saw how his eyes were alight with love. 'Do not say anything right now. I would ask you here and now to be my wife, were it not for the Royal Marriages Act. And no one appreciates better than I the problems of loving a prince. But I couldn't bear a refusal before you have even properly considered the idea.'

'. . . I am a married woman . . .' I finished what I'd been about to say, so used to keeping up the fiction of my status that the words came out almost of their own volition.

'No, Dora, you are not. Richard Ford has had years to fulfil that promise, and has failed to do so. And you love *me*. I can see it in your eyes when you look so tenderly at me. I can feel it in the quiver of your hand when you rest it on my arm. And I've witnessed your unhappiness during these last months, know that you would not have taken supper with me, or talked with me so frankly, were you still in love with this man. You must also be aware by now how much *I* love *you*, Dora. I adore you, Little Pickle, and want nothing more than to make you happy for the rest of your life. What could I want more than to have you beside me as I make my way in the world?'

Despite my resolve not to allow this flattery to go to my head, I couldn't seem to stop the bubble of excitement that rose in my chest at these words. Perhaps because what he said bore an element of truth in it. I already felt a great fondness for him which could easily grow into love.

'You must allow me time to think. I am working so hard right now, and there are the children to consider.' I could feel myself trembling with emotion. It was right, in a way, what I had said to my sister. Never, not for a moment, had I expected it to come to this, and I couldn't for the life of me decide what my true feelings were.

'I like children, and would gladly take them too. You need have no fears on that score. You must take what time you need to decide,' he offered generously. 'Meanwhile you must write to me every week, every day we are not together. I need always to know that you are well, dearest beloved. And when you are ready to come to me, I will be waiting.'

Sixteen

'If you could think me worthy of being your wife . . .'

I meant to speak to Richard, of course I did, but I was dividing my time between the house at Somerset Street, Richmond and the theatre, and rarely saw him. When we were together there never seemed quite the right moment to speak of this delicate matter. Besides, I still loved him, didn't I? Still wanted our situation to be resolved. And then another piece of mischief appeared. Richard set the paper before me one morning at breakfast time, his thin, angular face dark as thunder.

'Is this the reason you no longer share my bed? Are you too occupied in a grander one?'

I gasped with horror as I looked at the print.

It was an Isaac Cruikshank cartoon showing the royal physician, Doctor Warren, dangling a baby over the balcony of a house in 'Sommers St'. He was shouting down to the folk in the street below: 'Damn your noise, Rascalls, you'll disturb Mrs Pickle, who has just made a faux couch of a young seagull.' Next to him the Duke, dressed as a nurse, was throwing the contents of a chamber pot over a dancing justice of the peace, who was clearly meant to be Richard. The Duke was saying: 'Well said, Doctor Warren, I will rake 'em fore and aft.'

It was labelled 'Mrs Pickle's Mistake'. And since a common word for chamber pot is a jordan, I was utterly mortified.

'I have no idea what this is meant to mean,' I cried out in horror. 'There has been nothing of that sort between us, I swear it. I am innocent of this charge. There has been no baby. You can see yourself that I am not pregnant, nor have I been since Lucy was born.'

'Yet it likens me – I take it the figure in the black suit is supposed to represent me – to Solomon. Why is that, I wonder? Am I supposed to dispute the father of our last child?'

'No, Richard, there is absolutely no doubt that Lucy is yours, as is Dodee. I do not understand this any more than you do. It is pure mischief, and entirely fabricated.'

He was glaring at me with the kind of sullen ferocity that made me shiver with foreboding. 'Are you saying that you do not harbour soft feelings for the Duke? If so, then you should stop accepting his invitations to supper.'

Determined at least to hold on to my dignity, I challenged him. 'I went just the once, as I told you, along with other members of the cast.' I made no mention of the Duke's disappointment that I had insisted upon this. 'Perhaps *you* would care to take me instead? Or even make me your wife, as I deserve to be?'

As always when this question was asked, he turned on his heel and walked away.

There were further comments in the press in the weeks following, as if they were determined to create a scandal. One claimed Little Pickle was being besieged at Richmond by an exalted youth. This presumably because at twenty-five, the Duke was four years younger than I. Another cast doubt on whether Richard and I were truly married. I longed to tell everyone the truth, but he was adamant that we keep up the pretence, for the sake of appearances.

The *Bon Ton Magazine* wittily commented: 'The Ford is too dangerous for him to cross the Jordan.'

My friend Lady Lumm advised me to stick with Richard. 'I am convinced no good will accrue from this association. These Hanoverian princes are not known for their constancy, my dear,' she warned, ignoring my protests of innocence.

Even Hester agreed with her. 'Lady Lumm is right, why would you leave Ford for yet more uncertainty? Richard is at least a gentleman.'

'He does not always behave as such,' I gently reminded her. 'Certainly he has shown little sign of honour, or care for my respectability. You yourself have dubbed him a scoundrel.'

My sister frowned, as if personally affronted by the scandal. I might well have laughed at her cross expression were it not all so terribly serious. 'I will admit his failings have disappointed me, but what of the children? You might lose them.'

She had, of course, touched upon my greatest fear, and the real reason I had held back so long from telling Richard of the Duke's earnest pursuit of me. My children were everything to me, and I could not envisage a life without them.

When my sister saw that raw terror in my face, all her temper melted away and she gathered me in her arms, as she always did in moments of crisis. 'We will make absolutely certain that whatever you decide, the children are safe. I would be happy to care for them myself, as I do now when you are at the theatre.'

Tears rolling down my cheeks, I could scarcely speak for the emotion choking my throat. 'What would I do without you, sister dear?'

Richard himself settled the matter. 'The scandal will die down, as these things generally do. We are perfectly content, as are the children, so we will speak no more of this unfortunate business. We will stop buying newspapers, and ignore these scurrilous gossip sheets.'

Riddled with indecision, I readily agreed.

But it was less easy to ignore the Duke. In the following weeks he was at the theatre at every opportunity, coming to see me backstage, sending me flowers and gifts which I absolutely refused to accept.

'Please,' I begged him. 'You must allow me time, some breathing space to decide. It is only fair to both Richard and myself.'

He gallantly agreed to do so, and went away to patiently await my answer.

On the fourth of June, 1791, I played the lead in the last production at Drury Lane, as the theatre was about to be demolished and rebuilt on a much grander scale. Henry Holland, the architect the Prince of Wales had used for Carlton House, was heading the project. In the meantime, the entire company was to move to the old opera house at Haymarket. On this final night I played Peggy in *The Country Girl* to a packed house of two thousand.

The Duke was not present on this occasion, which I secretly regretted despite my request to him to allow me some space to think. He was attending a celebration of the King's official birthday, the first time, he explained, that he'd been able to take part, usually having been away at sea. He'd also taken delivery of a new carriage and was in high spirits. I wished I could feel the same.

I was sad to say goodbye to the old theatre, and even sadder over the gulf that was developing between myself and Richard.

That summer the revolution in France was causing considerable unease. There were riots in Birmingham and surrounding towns, in sympathy with their compatriots across the Channel. Yet it didn't seem to put people off going to the theatre, or enjoying their card parties and soirees. Life for some continued to be a veritable merry-go-round of pleasure.

The Duke was present at my next benefit, which took place at the Haymarket in August, and again the following evening when I played at Richmond to a full house. As always he came backstage.

I was expecting Richard, who had suddenly become most attentive, insisting on escorting me to the theatre each and every day, waiting for me in the Green Room and seeing me home in my carriage afterwards, rarely letting me out of his sight. I was therefore brusque almost to the point of rudeness to the Duke.

'You really shouldn't be here. You agreed to stay away and give me time to think.'

'I came to invite you to a fête at my home. There will be many friends there, and I thought you might enjoy it.'

'You have surely not done this for me?'

'You are the guest of honour,' and he beamed at me.

'I'm truly sorry, but I cannot accept. It wouldn't be right, Sir.'

'William, you must call me William.' He took my hand and kissed the tips of each finger. 'I keep rushing you, don't I? Unfortunately, I can't seem to help behaving like a besotted schoolboy.'

'It is quite endearing,' I confessed, melting a little. 'And I promise you will have your answer soon.'

I later learned that the fête had been cancelled, since I had declined the invitation. By then Richard and I were on our way to York, rather later than Wilkinson had hoped. But I was desperate to escape and this seemed the only way.

The weather in York was unusually hot with occasional thunderstorms, which seemed to shorten tempers. Perhaps this was the reason the house was a poor one, or else fears of further riots had finally taken root. For when I walked out on stage in *The Country Girl*, I felt no friendly warmth emanating from those who had bothered to turn out. The cool reception reminded me very much of that time in Hull many years ago, when Mrs Smith and her coven of witches had spread their malice. I was just getting into my stride when, to my utter horror, someone in the audience shouted out, 'Strumpet! Whore! Caught your prince yet?'

So they had been reading the gossip sheets too, or someone had circulated the scandal.

'Is this the same tribe who hissed and booed me before?' I asked Wilkinson, the moment I came off stage. How I had managed to struggle through, I couldn't rightly say. Sheer professionalism, I dare say.

'It is common knowledge, Dora, that you are not married to Ford as everyone had thought, and that you are now being pursued by the Duke of Clarence.' He grinned good-naturedly at me, but then Tate Wilkinson had never been one to presume to pass judgement. 'They are calling you the Duchess of Drury Lane.'

I was not amused.

In short, I would say that apart from that best-forgotten night at Hull, this was the worst performance of my entire career. I did not shine or sparkle, my lines were delivered flat and without conviction. I longed only for the play to end, and when it finally did, the audience gave lukewarm applause laced with a few muted hisses.

Wilkinson was waiting for me offstage. 'Make haste and change and go straight back on and sing. They can never resist your singing, Dora.'

I did as he suggested, and this time they softened a little, even joined in with the familiar melodies, and the applause was warmer as the curtain fell for the last time.

'Saved,' Wilkinson said. 'What a star you are.'

I fled to my dressing room and burst into tears. 'This is all your fault,' I snapped at Richard. 'Had you not destroyed my reputation, I would still be a respectable woman, a respectable *married* woman!' I thought of how much Mama had longed for that happy state for me, which made me cry all the more. 'What have I ever done to deserve this sort of vilification? All I did was to love you and believe in your promise of marriage.'

'Don't blame me for their behaviour,' Richard caustically remarked. 'If you are losing the loyalty of your audience, the fault may well be yours, not mine.'

Wilkinson attempted to lift our spirits by entertaining Richard and me to a splendid dinner party, inviting many old friends: John Kemble, Michael Kelly, Maria Crouch and others, all of whom happened to be in Yorkshire too, no doubt working the circuit. Poor Richard, obliged to lower his dignity sufficiently to dine with a bunch of itinerant strolling players.

'It will be better tomorrow,' Wilkinson assured me. 'We've certainly sold more tickets. Perhaps the play was a little risqué for Yorkshire folk. And I'll make sure the stage door is locked so that no pranks are played there either.'

If anything, the following night was worse. I was playing one of my favourite parts, Hypolita in *She Would and She Would Not*. But instead of laughing when I dressed up as a man, pretending to be the rival to my own lover – the outcome being the usual tangle – the audience booed and hissed, again calling out insults regarding my personal life.

At the end of the show I took my revenge. Instead of bowing towards the audience, as I normally did, I turned my back upon them and bowed showing them my rear end. Let them salute my backside, I thought, telling them very plainly what I thought of their disapproval.

I could hear Tate Wilkinson's roars of laughter from the wings. 'Dashed if I don't admire your fighting spirit, girl.'

I left the theatre without even bothering to take off my stage costume and make-up, and refused to return the next day. Instead, Richard took me to Castle Howard, but I was so upset I simply couldn't relax and enjoy the beauty of the countryside. Later, back in our hotel room, I took out my ill temper on him, not unnaturally in the circumstances. It seemed that the moment to settle our differences had finally arrived.

'Had you made good on your promise of marriage the scandalmongers would not have printed such scurrilous rumours about me, and the audience would have had no reason to call me vile names. They are punishing *me* for *your* neglect.'

He looked at me with disdain. 'If the moralists disapprove of your association with a prince, you have only yourself to blame for encouraging him.'

'I did not encourage him! Five years I have waited for you. Five long years of listening to excuses and procrastination, yet still you refuse to make me your wife. You have deprived me of a proper legal status.' I was pacing back and forth, brimming over with rage, while he sat calmly smoking a cigar, feigning absorption in a newspaper, but I knew he heard every word. 'Before I met you I was still considered respectable, save perhaps by Siddons, who likes to look down her long nose at everyone.' Thinking of my old rival only made me angrier than ever, as, unlike me, she was respectably married, her children legitimate. And didn't she just love to crow about this difference in our status.

He heaved a weary sigh. 'I cannot see that it makes the slightest difference whether we are married or not. You are an actress, therefore you are fooling yourself if you imagine anyone would even consider you to be respectable. I am not the one to ruin your reputation. You never had one to lose in the first place.'

Flashes of fire seemed to dart before my eyes, such was my fury at this cruelly heartless remark. 'How dare you say such a thing? What is it about the acting profession that makes everyone assume an actress is a whore? We tread the boards and entertain people in all honesty. I do not walk the streets and offer services of a less salubrious nature.'

He actually laughed at that. 'You know full well audiences imagine you lead the same life as the characters you play.'

'Then people are more stupid, or cruel, than I took them for. But, my reputation aside, what of our children?'

He gave a careless shrug as he turned a page, as if the news sheet were far more interesting than his family. 'Why would our lack of marriage lines trouble them?'

'It may not now, while they are young, but what when they are older? How will they feel to be constantly accused of being illegitimate? And there are worse words to describe the condition. I suffered many such flung at me as a child. My own father's family treated Grace and all of us children with shameless derision, all because the marriage was not legal. Is that what you wish for your own two precious daughters?'

'Better than risking the loss of a fortune from my father. Names never hurt anyone, being poor does.'

'Money, is that all you think of? Does the happiness and honour of your children not count for more than your own greed?' I could hardly contain my anger, wanting to fly at him, to scratch his arrogant face as a wild cat might. In that moment I truly hated this man I'd once professed to love.

Exhausted with emotion I collapsed on to the bed and ordered him to leave. 'Go! I have no wish for dinner tonight. I need to be alone, to think.' I was still sobbing into my pillow when I heard the door bang shut behind him.

After the tears finally subsided I lay on my bed for some time thinking of how the Bland family had actively encouraged their son in his ultimate betrayal, yet condemned to near starvation the innocent woman he had so callously abandoned. And all because his children, my brothers and sisters and I, were illegitimate. My poor mother must be turning in her grave to see me faced with a similar dilemma.

Were Richard Ford to do as my father had done and marry another woman of whom his parent did approve, there was no law to make him support our children. He too could leave them to starve if he chose to ignore them, and if I were not around to protect them. Or take them from me, if he so wished, as once they were seven I would have no rights over them at all, being only an unmarried mother.

I felt humiliated, violated, not only by the audience influenced by the lampoons and scandalmongers, but by Richard Ford, the man in whom I had placed my trust.

Hester once said that I was far too affectionate and trusting for my own good, and she was right.

$$\star \quad \star \quad \star$$

The next day, aware of my distress, Kemble came to see me. 'I'm sorry you've suffered this fracas, Dora. The reason I was in York was that I was on my way to Newcastle. I suggest that you go in my stead with my brother Stephen, and I will take your place in York. I'm staying with the Mayor here, as he is a friend of mine. I could easily do Othello. I've already suggested this to Wilkinson, and he has agreed.'

'That is most generous of you.' I was touched, as there still remained some of the old rivalry between myself and his sister.

'Wilkinson, however, is less so. Money is tight, so he demands the payment of an indemnity of thirty pounds since you walked out of the theatre before the conclusion of your agreement.'

Taking a breath, I nodded. 'I accept your offer with gratitude, and will gladly pay the sum he asks. Anything rather than perform in that miserable theatre ever again.'

I at once wrote to Wilkinson.

> Sir,
>   I agree with pleasure to your proposal of giving you thirty pounds rather than ever perform in York again. I shall return tomorrow and settle the balance of the account.
> I am, dear sir,
> Your obliged, humble servant,
> D Ford

Even writing that name which I had once used so proudly, made me feel sick to my stomach.

Kemble agreed to deliver the note and I returned to York on the Monday to pay Wilkinson the money he requested. 'I would risk being ruined as an actress were I to play to such a milk-and-water audience,' I told him.

'You are the lucky child of fortune, caressed and nursed in the lap of Mother Nature, the reigning Thalia of our age. To your comic talent, archness, whim and fancy, I submissively bow. And I trust that you and I will remain friends, Dora?'

I softened and gave him an affectionate hug. 'For ever. Did you not save my family from starvation, and me from Daly by introducing me to Cornelius Swan who paid off all my debts and penalties? I have done well, thanks to his, and your, tuition and guidance. Unfortunately, my life is in turmoil at present.'

'You were ever a good daughter, but Grace would be most distressed to see you in danger of losing all decency.'

'I know, and it is a situation only I can resolve.'

As we again dined with him that evening, John Kemble suddenly changed his mind. He decided that the agreed thirty guineas he'd asked for to play Othello was insufficient and demanded a share of the profits, something he knew I often received.

'Stab me if I'll not agree to such blackmail,' Wilkinson cried, although I heard later that when the evening in question arrived, he backed down at the last moment rather than risk a riot in disappointing his audience. Kemble came out of the deal with a pocketful of cash.

Richard and I went on to Newcastle, barely speaking, but that engagement too fell through as Kemble had failed to inform his brother of the change in plan. I might have sued Kemble myself, but was wearied by it all, and only too thankful to return home. I had far more important matters on my mind.

By the time we arrived back in London I was convinced that Richard never would marry me, so I asked him outright. 'I have fought you long and hard over this matter for my children's sake, and for the security of their future. But you have made it perfectly clear these last weeks that any hope of marriage between us is virtually nil. Am I correct in this surmise?'

He gave one of his exasperated sighs. 'Dora, I will not tolerate constantly going over this old ground.'

'Thank you, that tells me all I need to know.'

'That you should have so little faith in me is despicable.'

'What faith can I have after you have treated me so reprehensibly?'

'I refuse to be bound at your say so. And it is equally iniquitous that you should consider yourself free to leave if I do not fall in with your demands.'

'I have no wish to leave. If you could think me worthy of being your wife, no temptation would be strong enough to detach me from you and my duties. But if I am doomed to be a gentleman's mistress and never a wife, let it be with one who treats me more fairly.'

On the twenty-second of September I opened the new season at the Haymarket, and the very next evening the Duke and the Prince of Wales came to see me. As William was not alone he did not come backstage, merely sent a note with flowers, and yet another request to take me out to supper the next evening. This time I meant to accept, for my decision was made. I would become the Prince's mistress.

Three weeks later, on the thirteenth of October, the Duke drove me in his yellow carriage to Petersham Lodge in Richmond, now renamed as Clarence House. My new life had begun.

Seventeen

'. . . the best feather you have in your cap'

'The question of a settlement still needs to be resolved,' the Duke announced one day, quite taking me by surprise. 'I may not be able to offer to make you my wife, but I am anxious to protect you in every other way.'

'I am no Mrs Robinson, or Mrs Crouch, who would give her favours casually and then argue over the spoils,' I tartly responded.

'I do not suggest otherwise, but I mean our relationship to be a lifetime commitment. Therefore you deserve the very best consideration and to be properly provided for. I have told my brother all about you in this letter. Here, I will read to you what I said:

> You may safely congratulate me on my success: everything is arranged. They never were married. I have all the proofs requisite and even legal ones . . . On your way to Windsor come here Sunday . . . I am sure I am too well acquainted with your friendship to doubt for a moment you will, my dear brother, behave kindly to a woman who possesses so deservedly my heart and confidence . . . Mrs Jordan through a course of eleven months endless difficulty, has behaved like an angel.

It was more than I had hoped for, although I was aware that the Duke's involvement with his elder brothers was a costly exercise, as they were both seriously profligate. Yet how could he resist their charms when he so enjoyed their company, even if it did lead him into sharing their bad habits? 'Can you afford to do so?' I tentatively enquired, and his smile was reassuring.

'My brother is the one with debts, not me. George believes that princes should not concern themselves with money.'

'An interesting philosophy,' I wryly remarked.

'For my part, I do not entirely disagree as we are surely entitled to a little pleasure as well as public duty. And we have fine houses to maintain, are required to dress in the height of fashion, so is it not proper for us to have expensive, sophisticated tastes? But I could not begin to compete with the Prince of Wales in his spendthrift ways. I find costs and expenses do tend to rise at an alarming rate, but whenever I express concern over George's gambling, or the size of his liquor bill, he simply laughs.'

I frowned. Hating debts as I did I could only hope it was not a trait that William would follow. 'Does the Prince make no attempt to resolve the problem?'

'Shortly after we left the navy, I agreed to join my two brothers in the Antwerp loan, which was meant to provide us with 3,600,000 guilders on the security of George's Duchy of Cornwall and Frederick's Bishopric of Osnaburg. The King got wind of this extraordinary, and I admit possibly scandalous, transaction and put a stop to it. The result was a loss to those bondholders who had already paid, a most disappointing outcome for all concerned. The King soundly scolded us, in particular me, since I didn't even have the excuse of huge debts, as did the other two.'

'And now the King has granted you an income of your own.'

'Indeed he has, and I sincerely believe that I can live within it. I am certainly determined to do the right thing by you, Dora. You shall have an allowance of one thousand pounds a year.'

I was stunned by this generosity. 'Goodness, that is far too much. I do not need such a sum, not if I'm earning money from my career. You have no objection to my continuing with that, have you? Sheridan has already urged me to do so, otherwise people would soon forget all about me, and it would be lost.'

'No objections at all. I should think you would be as lost without the theatre, as the theatre would be without you, dearest Dora. And I shall be there with you to share the fun. But if you do not need all the allowance for your own use, then secure a portion of it on your children. You cannot depend upon Ford to maintain them. I have already discovered that the fellow thinks only of himself, and his career in the law.'

It crossed my mind that Richard might have written to the Duke demanding recompense for having been deprived of his domestic bliss. Had I been traded like horse flesh? I wondered. Would Ford suddenly rise in his chosen profession? I thought it best not to ask, and instead merely thanked the Duke for his thoughtfulness.

'How kind you are to me, William, that is exactly what I shall do. The children shall have five hundred and fifty pounds a year, and I shall also set up a trust fund in their names, giving them all of my savings. More than anything I want my daughters to have substantial dowries to offset the disadvantages of their birth.'

William beamed. 'Splendid! Although with their beauty, and you for a mother, I doubt they will be greatly hindered by that.'

Leaning close, I kissed him on each cheek. 'You are the sweetest man. I shall make certain that the children are properly provided for. In addition I intend to assign Hester a small personal allowance of fifty pounds. We thought it best that they live with her, and for the present they will remain at Somerset Street. But I intend to find them a more convenient house, with fewer memories. Richard seems to have no wish for the responsibility, and Fanny isn't even his.'

The Duke had, of course, by now learned the full story of how Daly treated me, and had been appalled by it. He fully understood that Ford, being the selfish man he was, would not give Fanny the care she deserved. This concern showed in his face.

'Are you sure that is what you want, dearest? They can come here, if you wish. I love children and would not oppose such a plan.'

'Hester has made the offer, and, forgive me, William, but I think it more fitting for them to stay with her. You are a prince of the realm, and I hope we will have children of our own one day. I would not dream of asking you to take on the responsibility for my other children as well.'

'Whatever you say, Dora dear. As their mother it is for you to decide. I am content to go along with whatever you wish.'

I could only smile at his generosity. 'Besides, in view of the long hours I spend in the theatre my sister has been their main carer since they were born, so they love her dearly. You would not object to my spending time with them, would you, William?'

'Indeed not, my dear, I shall come with you. We will have a great fun together.'

'Look at him, sailing boats in the bath as if he were a boy still,' I laughed. 'But then he had such a stark childhood himself he fully intends to provide all the love and happiness to his own children that he never received.'

'He is clearly a good man, Doll, to be showing such kindness and consideration to these children who are not his own. I too promise to care for them as you would yourself.'

Tears sprang to my eyes as I thought of how many times in the past I had sacrificed spending time with my darling children simply in order to earn a living for us all. A part of me longed to devote myself to motherhood, and yet I dare not relinquish my independence in order to do so. Everything might be fine right now, but who knew what lay ahead on the stony path of life? I shook away any sense of regret and thanked God for a loving, generous-hearted sister. Despite her failings, her criticisms and petty jealousies and sharp tongue, Hester was always on my side. 'Dodee and Lucy are too young to notice the change in their lives, but how has Fanny taken to the idea?'

Hester pulled a wry face. 'You know little Fan, she ever has an opinion on everything, and feels deeply affronted to be left out of what she deems to be an exciting change in your life.'

My heart sank. Had Richard Ford kept his word, my girls would not now be in this delicate situation. Hearing her name mentioned, Fanny left the game of soldiers which was now engaging them, and came to lean against me, putting on her most wheedling tone.

'Mama, may I come and live with you and the Duke at Clarence House? You told me that Richard Ford was not my real papa, that he is far away across the sea, so can I have the Duke, instead? I like him, he's funny and kind.'

'Now that you are a big girl, are you too big for a cuddle?'
I asked, and with a little smile she shook her head. I lifted her
on to my lap and gave her a hug, as my own mother would
do with me whenever I was upset. 'I was hoping that you
would help Aunt Hester to look after the two little ones here.
You can understand what a great responsibility that is for her,
and they will need a big sister to look up to and show them
how things should be done.'

Fanny thought about this quite seriously for a moment.
'Lucy can be very difficult when she is hungry and cross. And
Dodee had a shocking tantrum the other day, but I was able
to calm her with a kiss.'

'Well, there you are then, you are needed here, to help
Hester. And I shall call in every day, of course, to see you all,
and play with you.'

'Every single day?'

'Every single day.'

'And you'll read us a story or sing us a song before you go
to the theatre?'

'I will, sweetheart. And you can come and stay at Clarence
House sometimes, for little holidays. How would that be?'

'Ooh, that would be lovely.' Satisfied, she wrapped her arms
about my neck and kissed me, then ran back to the game. I
turned to Hester with a small sigh of relief. 'She will be fine
now. Has Richard asked to have the children, or visited perhaps?'

'He came to see Dodee and Lucy, but refused to see Fanny,
which again upset her.'

'Does that man have no heart?'

'I should say not. He is too relieved to be free of the expense
of raising them, more than ready to leave it all to you and the
Duke.'

'We will change their names back to Jordan, I think. I
certainly have no wish for them to bear Ford's any longer. So
long as we keep further scandalous comments out of the press,
all will be well.'

'Too late, *The Times* had great fun at the end of October.
Listen, I kept it for you.' She pulled a cutting from her sewing
bag and began to read. "A certain Duke held a private party,
and the names of the guests were Priscilla Tomboy, Miss

Prue, Master Pickle, Miss Viola, Signora Hypolita, a country girl, a Virgin unmasked and Miss Hoyden. Although the porter swears he only admitted one lady!" What think you of that?'

She giggled, and even I, the subject of this pillory, could not resist a smile at the wit. 'They have at least advertised all my best roles.'

'They did miss out Harry Wildaire in *The Constant Couple*. Not as good as Farquhar's other plays, *The Recruiting Officer* or *Beaux' Stratagem* admittedly, but you always play that part well, I think. I particularly enjoy your expression of complete shock and embarrassment when you discover that Angelica is not the prostitute you were led to believe.'

I shared her laughter, my own bubbling up as it so often did on stage. 'The Duke enjoys seeing me in all my cross-dressing roles.'

She was suddenly serious. 'What of the King, what does he think of all this?'

'Apparently, His Majesty is entirely sympathetic. He appreciates that as the Duke is unlikely to reach the throne, and yet cannot choose a wife freely because of the Royal Marriages Act, he deserves a comfortable domestic life. He wishes us both well and many years of happiness.' I clutched her arm as I tried to restrain a fresh onslaught of giggles. 'When William wrote to tell me this, he said that the King's response went something like this . . .' and I perfectly mimicked the King's tone of voice, or how I imagined it would sound. '. . . You keep an actress, keep an actress, they say.

"'Yes, Sire,'" William replied.

"'Ah, how much do you give her, eh?"

"'A thousand a year, Sire."

"'A thousand? A thousand? Too much, too much! Five hundred quite enough, quite enough!'"

Hester was bent double with laughter by this time, but then sobered quickly. 'We really shouldn't mock the King. And what did you say?'

'I tore a strip from the bottom of a playbill where it says: "No money returned after the rising of the curtain", and sent it back to William. He says he laughed till he cried.'

Hester hugged me close. 'Oh, Doll, you seem so much happier, so relaxed.'

I felt as if I were glowing with happiness as I looked again at where the Duke was now crawling about the drawing room on his hands and knees, firing miniature brass cannons at my little daughters, who, in fits of giggles and excitement, were happily firing back. It was a magical, family scene, and I loved him for it.

'I am the happiest woman in the world. It took me no more than a matter of days for the affection I felt for him to turn to love. He is the dearest man.'

'Let us hope this time you are lucky, and it lasts.'

'Amen to that, sister dear.'

There were still arrangements to be made, as William and I had had little time thus far even to discuss the fine details of our coming life together. 'I fear that I find myself in need of a carriage,' I was obliged to say to him one day, hating to be put in a position that I had to ask anything more of him. 'Since the one I shared with Mr Ford I have left to his use entirely.'

'Whatever possessed you to be so generous with the cad?'

'I wished not to deprive him, and to make our break as civilized as possible.'

'What a delightful Little Pickle you are.' He kissed me and stroked my cheek. 'Then you shall have a new one, all of your own. What colour shall you choose?'

I looked up at him, wide-eyed with delighted surprise. 'There is really no need. I thought I could perhaps borrow yours from time to time.'

'There is every need, you must have your own independence, and security,' he assured me. 'How shall you style it?'

'Your kindness and attention to detail is both exciting and flattering. What love you must have for me.'

'I love you with all my heart and soul, and shall never tire of telling you so.'

'And you must know how dearly I love you.'

'Then do me the honour of accepting my gift and decide upon the colour.'

I couldn't help myself, I just gave that delicious surge of laughter that ripples up right from the heart of me when I'm happy. 'Very well, it shall be yellow. The interior of my own carriage was dark green turned up with buff and bound with silver, so perhaps it could be the same. And if it is not improper, an anchor on the panels. I love everything that has the least reference to you.'

He considered the matter in mock seriousness. 'It might well be mistaken for a passing ship,' he teased. 'I think we will keep to a plainer style.' And we kissed again, as lovers do, William loving the warm pressure of my soft full breasts against his hard chest, and me the sensation of melting in his arms, both of us dreaming of all the joys which lay in store for our shared life together.

The Duke was ill. He'd been forced to take to his bed with a feverish cold and was confined to quarters, as he described it. He was no doubt lying there fretting about all that still needed to be done, while I was staying, temporarily, at the house in Somerset Street until I'd found a new home for the dear children. Mr Ford, as I now referred to him, remained at the house in Richmond, with the apparent intention of relinquishing the lease once he too had found alternative accommodation.

Oh, but the Duke claimed daily in his letters to me that he'd never been so passionately in love. I was his darling Dora who had given meaning to his life, brought a new purpose to it, and he was so very anxious to do everything right by me.

And having banned me from his side in case I too should fall ill, we had to be content with exchanging letters several times a day. In these he poured out his love for me, how his anxieties were increasing with every hour we were apart in case I should tire of him and change my mind. I did what I could to reassure him but he worried too whenever he thought of me unprotected, with Mr Ford still protesting loudly about being publicly humiliated and embarrassed. As if the arrogant fellow hadn't had ample opportunity to do right by me in the past. After all, he was not bound by the Royal Marriages Act.

The Duke would write to me at length on practical matters,

discussing the settlement on the children which Coutts and his lawyers were arranging. I had signed over to my sister all my savings in the form of a trust fund for the children, but there was much still to decide.

'The house I am now in I must let, for many reasons,' I wrote. 'First, it is too far from the theatre. Second, I have gone through so many cruel scenes in it that there is a constant gloom hangs over my mind whenever I am in it.'

He would write back the most supportive, fondest letters, always signed with love, and I would respond in kind, as well as gently scolding him not to venture out as he might suffer a relapse.

'If I may judge of your love by my own, I am sure I may with truth say never two people loved so well. It is impossible to tell you how happy, how more than happy your dear enchanting professions of love make me.'

There was much more in this vein, and the Duke at last confessed himself content, that he was the most fortunate of men. As one wit wrote:

> *She's in truth the best feather you have in your cap.*
> *How you got her, to me, I must own, is a wonder!*
> *When I think of your natural aptness to blunder.*

The Duke and I both giggled at the wit, and he did not disagree with the sentiment. Then the lampoons started.

Eighteen

'Her Grace bearing her new dignities . . .'

The Duke was shocked and appalled by the vilification to which I was subjected by the press. There were pointed references to my wantonness in taking a royal lover, to my preferring the superior attractions of a Royal Lodge to the domestic bliss I apparently enjoyed with Richard Ford.

'That is as inaccurate as it is outrageous!' he roared, helpless in his sick room.

But the clamorous press continued long after he'd made a full recovery, becoming so intrusive that it quite affected my own heath and I missed several performances.

The *Bon Ton* displayed a frontispiece of the Duke kneeling upon one knee while I was sitting on the other, my arm about his neck and his arm around my waist. He was cooling me with a fan, and I was giving him a roguish smile. The Duke thought it in the lowest taste possible as it made me look like a common harlot, which infuriated him beyond measure.

There was one cartoon of me in bed, sitting up proudly declaring my prowess, his jacket casually hung upon a chair at the foot. In another the satirists dared to show me with my breasts bared, and in the cruellest of all by James Gillray a male figure in striped sailor trousers was depicted climbing through the crack in a chamber pot, my dainty slippers peeping out below the pot. Vulgar was to put too fine a word on it. Walking past the print shops in town became an absolute nightmare for the Duke.

But if the cartoons were bad, the comments were worse.

A favourite comic actress, if Goody Rumour can be trusted, had thought proper to put herself under the protection of a distinguished sailor who dropped anchor before her last summer at Richmond.

There were many such. 'Public jordan open to all parties,' wrote one cruel wit, again using the chamber pot connotation, while another accused Little Pickle of receiving her weekly salary from the Treasurer.

'Damn me, if they aren't bringing politics into it now.'

To add insult to injury, this little ditty began to circulate:

> *As Jordan's high and mighty squire*
> *Her playhouse profits deigns to skim;*
> *Some folks audaciously inquire*
> *If he keeps her or she keeps him.*

William valiantly dismissed this as a joke he must live with, but it was one in the *Morning Post* which caused me the greatest distress:

> *To be mistress of the King's son Little Pickle thinks respectable,*
> *and so away go all tender ties to children!*

'As if I would abandon my own children for any man, even if you are the son of a king. It is unspeakably cruel. I believe Mr Ford's friends and relatives are responsible for these cruel calumnies. They are saying that I callously and unnaturally deserted my children for grandeur. I beg you, William, to intercede and make them put a stop to this mischief.'

The Duke wrote at once to his lawyer, William Adam, who in turn corresponded with the *Morning Post* expressing his concern at the severity of the attacks, insisting the paper desist as the accusations were entirely false and damaging to the good lady's health.

I begged my former lover to complain too, and to his credit, Ford did so. He sent me a most reasonable letter which I instantly had published in the paper concerned:

> *Lest any insinuations be circulated to the prejudice of Mrs Jordan*
> *in respect to her having behaved improperly towards her children*
> *in regard to pecuniary matters, I hereby declare that her conduct*
> *in this particular has been as laudable, generous and as like a*
> *fond mother as in her present situation it was possible to be.*
> *She has indeed given up for their use every sixpence she has*

been able to save from her theatrical profits, she has also engaged
herself to allow them £550 per annum, and at the same time
settled £50 a year on her sister. It is but bare justice to her for
me to assert this, as the father of those children.
Signed,
Richard Ford,
October, 1791

He followed it up with a second letter:

In gratitude for the care Mrs Jordan has ever bestowed on my
children, it is my consent and wish that she, whenever she
pleases, see and be with them, provided her visits are not attended
by any circumstances which may be improper to them or unpleasant
to me.
Signed
Richard Ford.
October, 1791

Unfortunately, although Ford did not deny that these letters
were written by his own hand, he complained that they had
been published without his knowledge or consent.

'I rather thought that was the whole point of his writing
them, in order to publicly protect me, and his children,' I said,
and William agreed.

'He is concerned only with his own damaged reputation,
not yours, dearest, nor his own children's.'

'I never could understand how that man's mind works.'

The papers continued to claim that Mrs Jordan was often seen
walking westwards, away from the house, which was surely proof
of her desertion. The truth was that I had found a house at
Brompton Road where the children were now living with Hester.

When the *Gazetteer* discovered this fact, and informed the
world that the lady had taken a house at Brompton, 'not in
the Row, but in the town, which is more private', the Duke
breathed a sigh of relief. 'Things should quieten down now,
my love, as they can see you are spending time with your dear
little ones every day.'

★   ★   ★

Thinking the fracas was behind us, I thankfully returned to the theatre. But then Mr Ford began making a nuisance of himself by constantly turning up backstage whenever I was performing at the Haymarket.

'Have you yet seen sense?' he would ask. 'I shall continue to come every day until you do.' And there he would sit, just as he always did, while I stood behind the screen to change. His constant attendance made me feel like some sort of peep-show.

One evening, when the Duke found me weeping in my dressing room, distressed by his presence at every turn, he asked Sheridan to demand he leave.

'Pray, make it very plain to the gentleman who infests this theatre with his presence backstage, that he is not welcome. Mrs Jordan has every right to her privacy. I wish him to desist from constantly calling upon her, or I shall be obliged to demand that he be forcibly removed.'

Sheridan, for once, did not kowtow to royalty, appearing unmoved by the request. 'With all due respect, Sir, Mr Ford's standing as a gentleman precludes such a prohibition. In point of fact, he has as much right to be here as yourself.'

The Duke reacted angrily to this but Sheridan remained adamant that he could do nothing to assist. He was equally frustrated with William's own presence in the green room. Most evenings the Duke would come backstage, laughing and talking with me before I went on. He loved to listen to me recite my lines as I put on my make-up, join in the chat and general horse-play, laughing as George mimicked Signora Storace, a young lady who had achieved brilliant success as an opera singer in Vienna, and whose rough-sounding voice my brother could take off to perfection. Or he would happily watch the dancers practising their steps.

Sheridan, however, was never particularly welcoming to visitors during a performance, for which I could not entirely blame him. Nor did he feel much sympathy for a man who had once attempted to seduce his own wife, even if the Duke was blind to such sentiments. For my part, I was so upset by Ford's presence and the resulting fracas, that I cried off performing the next night, quite unable to face going on.

Hester came to see how I was faring and even she castigated me for my lack of sensitivity towards Ford. 'You are not the only one being tormented by the press. Richard too is suffering public humiliation, and considerable embarrassment from those friends to whom he introduced you as his wedded wife.'

I frowned at that, irritated by her support of him. 'You know full well that those hints about a secret marriage between us were all lies, entirely of *his* making. He could have rectified the embarrassment of our situation at any time during this last five years.'

'He was protecting *you*.'

'He was protecting *himself*. I am aware of his friends' animosity towards me. Lady Lumm and her husband have already made it clear that, however painful it might be to their personal feelings, they can no longer tolerate me as a visitor to their mansion,' I said, mimicking the lady's cut-glass accent. 'I am sorry to lose such old and loyal friends, Hester, but I never for a moment thought they believed the fiction of our marriage. Lady Lumm has chosen the side she wishes to be on, and it is not mine.'

'Can you blame her? You brought this scandal entirely upon yourself.'

I gasped. My sister had been my constant support throughout my life, now she appeared to be taking Mr Ford's part. 'I admit I never claimed it to be a love match with the Duke, not in the beginning, but I had little choice but to take his offer seriously, if my children were to be protected.'

'You've virtually turned yourself into a courtesan,' she snapped.

'*Hester!* What a dreadful thing to say.'

'It is no less than the truth. What would Mama say, were she to see you now?'

Tears filled my eyes. 'It is unfair to bring our dear mother into this. I'm sure she would understand that Mr Ford never had any intention of making good on his promise. Did she not suffer a similar fate? So what did I have to lose?'

Hester had the grace to look contrite, instantly enfolding me in her arms as she always did when ashamed of her quick temper. 'I'm sorry, Doll, but I do worry about what you are getting into.'

'I'm more concerned with what I am getting *out* of. My relationship with Ford was going nowhere.' Tears were rolling down my cheeks, my heart sore that we should quarrel like this.

'But you have to feel sorry for the man, as these friends of his are now apparently demanding explanations which he is finding hard to supply.'

I can't say I shared her sympathy, and was mightily relieved when Ford decided to go on a visit to France. But if I thought my troubles would disappear with his departure I was soon to be disenchanted. His friends, after all, remained behind.

One morning at breakfast I saw the Duke tear up a letter in obvious irritation as he tossed it aside, but I could not resist asking from whom it came.

'From a Mrs Crouch, apparently, but I read no more than a dozen words in which she feels the need to warn me against you.' He smiled. 'Clearly such a project is doomed from the start.'

Maria Crouch, a fellow actress, had never counted herself among my friends, as she hated to take second billing. Nor was she in any position to pass judgement on my own conduct when she had set up a *ménage à trois* with the musician Michael Kelly and her own husband, although the poor man did not remain long with his wife after that. There was much I could say on the subject of Mrs Crouch but I refrained from doing so, determined to maintain my dignity for William's sake.

We made a pact to ignore, as best we could, all the malicious gossip and enjoy life regardless. We were happy, and I knew in my heart that I had made the right decision. We appeared in public together for the first time at his box at the Haymarket. I had just finished playing Peggy in *The Country Girl*, and instead of him coming backstage to my dressing room as he usually did, he asked me to sit with him for the second piece, *The Cave of Trophonius*, as I was not in it.

We sat holding hands, teasing and kissing each other in a fond way, cocooned in our own private world of happiness. Unfortunately, our laughter and badinage attracted some attention in the pit, and from a *Morning Post* critic who, unbeknown to us, was present. The following morning we read a full description of our flirtatious behaviour in the paper.

Her Grace tapt his chin, he seized her by the muff. For the play was all nonsense, the singing all stuff.

'Stuff and nonsense to him too,' said the Duke. 'Can they not allow us to be simply happy together, as other couples are?'

'They will grow tired, if we ignore them,' I assured him, hoping it was true.

We would walk through Bond Street and St James's arm in arm, determinedly oblivious to passing stares. And then we would read in the press the next day:

The conduct of a certain pair, in their journey to and from the neighbourhood of Richmond, is the daily occasion of a blush in everything on that road except the mile-stones. Her Grace bearing her new dignities with becoming indifference.

I hated them calling me such names, to which I had no pretensions whatsoever. But such titles as '*Her Grace*' and 'the new *Duchess*' fell into common use. And the tales fabricated about me now included the fiction that messages must only be brought to me by my own servants, that they were expected to dip a curtsey and say: 'Your Grace's carriage is ready,' or 'Will Your Grace have your bed warmed tonight?' And even, 'Your Grace's tailor waits below to take the measure of a pair of breeches for Little Pickle.'

Despite their wit they were deeply hurtful. 'Surely it is common knowledge that I do not preen and flatter myself. I have always lived a quiet, modest life, content to work hard and bring up my children.'

'Pay no attention, dearest, they are but names,' the Duke comforted me. 'I am constantly referred to as the royal tar, warned to buffet the storm, give a broadside, or close the hatches, not to mention apparently skimming your profits. But what does it signify? Am I not the happiest of men?'

And I kissed him, assuring him that I was likewise the happiest of women. 'I will listen no more to their scurrilous gossip.'

The next morning came this, which was hard to ignore:

Mrs Jordan's family will present a curious assemblage of infants. Irish, Scotch, and English, and probably Princes and Princesses.

'And look at this,' I said at breakfast one morning. 'They say my carriage, for which I apparently requested the crest of a seagull for the panels, is attended by three footmen, and, as I couldn't have scarlet and gold, I opted for green and silver in abundance.'

The Duke considered. 'Would the crest of a seagull have been preferable to your proposal for an anchor, I wonder? Perhaps not,' and I really couldn't help but laugh out loud, which brought a fond smile to his face.

'That's the ticket, don't lose that wonderful ability of yours to laugh at yourself.'

'I won't, my love. I just wish they would leave us alone.'

It all came to a head one night at the end of November. I had recently missed a performance of *Richard Coeur de Lion*, being too indisposed to appear, and Sheridan had apparently gone on stage to announce that the show would be cancelled, an alternative to be put on in its place.

'Return the money!' the audience had cried.

'Why did you not put a notice on the doors?'

Then no doubt some specially placed plant in the pit cried, 'Mrs Crouch! we will have Mrs Crouch!'

The *Gazetteer* joyfully reported the entire story and the ensuing disturbance, as of course Mrs Crouch eagerly took my place as Mathilda, ready with lines learned and costume in place for just such an opportunity. Pretty as she was, she had always thought well of herself and been jealous of my success, even as she consistently failed to enchant the audience. She also gave lavish parties to which she invited all those she thought might be of use to her, and would then be the worse for drink and fall about, which no doubt had an effect upon the quality of her performances.

There were further criticisms of my absence in the press in the days following. No longer were they complimenting me upon my sweet smile and frank, intelligent gaze. Rather they were seeking every bit of salacious gossip they could find to damage me, and stories of actresses studying all of Little Pickle's parts were rife. It felt like a witch-hunt of the worst kind, and I knew the source. I suspected that Mrs Crouch was in league with Ford's friends, and in addition to accusing me of abandoning my children, they were now attacking my career, to her benefit.

I attempted to refute these charges by writing a letter myself.

> *Nothing can be more cruel and unfounded than the insinuation that I absented myself from the theatre on Saturday last from any other cause than inability, from illness, to sustain my part in the entertainment . . . There can be no impropriety in my answering those who have so ungenerously attacked me, that if they could drive me from that profession they would take from me the only income I have, or mean to possess, the whole earnings of which, upon the past, and one-half for the future, I have already settled upon my children.*

It felt good to fight back, although what benefit it would bring I wasn't at all sure.

The very next time I appeared on stage I could feel the hostility of the audience like a physical presence in the auditorium. It was early December and I was to play Roxalana in *The Sultan*. As I went on stage, instead of the joyous, enthusiastic welcome I was used to, there was a smattering of applause mingled with boos and hisses and whistles, even some shouted profanities.

My heart felt as if it were breaking in two. As I struggled to continue, desperately attempting to carry on acting despite the noise of a baying audience, the anger and unfairness of it all began to build inside me. Ford had brought this upon me. He had robbed me of respectability and a legal status for my children. I would not allow him to destroy my career as well.

This wasn't Hull or Leeds with Mrs Smith and her coven of witches spreading their jealous malice. This was my home territory, the theatre where I appeared regularly before my adoring audience, where people queued at the stage door to catch a glimpse of me. This hostility was the result of vilification in the press led by Ford's friends, and Mrs Crouch, out of jealousy, had sided with them. Her moralistic judgement was entirely hypocritical as, being something of a beauty, she had herself once flirted quite outrageously with the Prince of Wales, but failed to catch him. And, of course, she'd recently written to the Duke to try to turn him against me.

Now she'd convinced the audience that I was a wicked mother who would not only sell myself, body and soul for a thousand a year, but also my children. She had fired their virtuous censure to such a point they were ready to inflict their wrath upon my head.

As the hissing continued I stopped speaking in mid-sentence, stood stock still for a moment, then walked calmly to the front of the stage. My sympathetic fellow cast members drew back, silently offering me their support.

'Ladies and gentlemen, I should conceive myself utterly unworthy of your favour if the slightest mark of public disapprobation did not affect me very sensibly. Since I have had the honour and the happiness to please you, it has been my constant endeavour by unremitting assiduity to merit your approbation. I beg leave to assure you, upon my honour, that I have never absented myself one minute from the duties of my profession but from real indisposition. Thus having invariably acted, I do consider myself under the public protection.'

The response to this heartfelt statement was a profound silence, and then came the first ripple of genuine applause which grew louder by the second, punctuated by a few cheers and hoorahs.

I knew in that moment that I had won them over, and I smiled. It was, without doubt, the most moving moment of my career.

Nineteen

'. . . but would never have invited the Duke of
Clarence had I known whom he might choose to
bring with him'

The comments in the press rumbled on for a while longer,
although at least one paper, *The Secret History of the Green Room*,
put up a spirited defence for me:

> *No Actress has been more harassed by them (the press) than
> Mrs Jordan. They did all in their power to drive her from the
> stage on account of her connection with the Duke of C, and
> now that she does not perform they accuse her of ingratitude, of
> refusing to amuse that public which a little month ago they
> pretended would never suffer her again to appear before them!
> Can anything be more insulting to common justice, or to common
> sense.*

I was thankful to get back to work, but the disputes over the
girls sadly continued, Mr Ford demanding at one point to have
Dodee, his favourite, live with him and relinquish Lucy
altogether. She was but four years old and I found this most
upsetting, first that he would attempt to steal my child from
me, and second that he cared so little for his other daughter.
The Duke finally intervened in the quarrel, insisting that
Somerset Street, where I still lived when I was working, was
now her true home. He meant only to help, but this infuriated
Hester who fiercely objected, since she considered Brompton
to be Dodee's home now.

'Tell the Duke from me that I will not be considered as his
nurse or housekeeper, nor will I continue in a house of which
he is master.'

We had given up the house at Richmond, and I'd handed
over all the furniture to Hester, and the lease at Brompton to

Ford, so neither of them could accuse me of neglecting their needs. But she threatened to quit Brompton and disappear without telling me where she went, if she suffered any more interference. While admiring her fiery spirit and ability to stand up to royalty so stoutly, I found it all most distressing. She refused even to see me or speak to me on the matter, which made negotiations particularly difficult. But then Hester had always been quick to take offence, with an impulsive way of jumping to the wrong conclusions, not to mention overstating her case. It took some time but I calmed her down, Ford dropped his ridiculous claim over Dodee, and gradually the press lost interest. Life settled into some degree of normality.

Actors are not known for rising early and the mornings became our time to be alone together. The Duke's gentle teasing and kind manner soon helped me to overcome the sense of shyness I at first felt in his company. He was sweet and loveable, but also a vigorous and passionate lover, such a contrast from the bland indifference of Mr Ford, and the crude violence of Daly. We would lie abed and make love, teasing and flirting, kissing and caressing; talk endlessly about anything and everything. He was not, he readily informed me, as sharp and witty as the Prince of Wales, but I found him utterly delightful, a man of enthusiasms and interests, and one who was always ready to listen to the views of others. In truth I had never been happier.

It had taken no more than a few days of living with him before I'd fallen headlong in love. It seemed like a miracle to find a love so rich and fulfilling after all I had been through. And that a prince of the blood should be the one to love me so devotedly and unselfishly, was utterly astounding.

At dinner he would take but a few glasses of wine, as I tactfully encouraged him not to over-imbibe. Afterwards he would walk for miles, and on occasion I would accompany him for a part of the way, though not the entire ten or twelve miles he liked to do. Then on the days I was home he would sit and read his seafaring yarns while I studied my lines. And each night before we retired he would be the one to lock up, insisting that the servants were not required to stay up late, which was so typical of his consideration for others.

We were fast becoming a most harmonious couple, if somewhat staid as we liked nothing better than spending our time quietly together at home. It felt as if we had found in each other what we had long sought.

But I was no Mrs Crouch, nor Mary Robinson. I had protected myself with the best settlement possible, which meant that even if it all came to an end, I would still receive an allowance.

And by the following March I was delighted to discover that I was pregnant.

My condition did not, of course, prevent me from working, which was in any case essential as there were many calls upon my purse, and my career was important to me. Although those mornings I was able to spend with my dear Billy at the Petersham house, and not be rushing to the theatre or staying at Somerset Street because of rehearsals, continued to be precious.

I would also call at Brompton most days to spend an hour or two with my three daughters and listen to Hester's grumbles. She still helped me to prepare for a performance when she could, but rarely accompanied me to the theatre these days. She was utterly devoted to Fanny, Dodee and Lucy, and caring for them took up her entire time. Even so, I would have my girls come to stay with me in Petersham just as often as I could. Hester would protest that I didn't have time.

'They are my children, I will make time.'

These days too were precious with the Duke playing games with them, or marching them off on one of his long walks, just like a proper family.

I took my benefit on the sixteenth of April that year, 1792, in *The Country Girl* and a farce called *The Village Coquette*. It was met with general approval from an adoring public, far removed from those dreadful performances at the end of the previous year. Even the critics found a few kind words, saying 'the new entertainment was received with loud and reiterated peals of applause.'

It was interesting to note that despite the recent furore my benefit raised £540, second only to Bannister at £545, and far more than Kemble, Mrs Siddons or the dreadful Crouch woman. There was some small satisfaction in that, certainly.

However, such success engendered no love between the Kembles and myself, and I was granted a part in a new play on only two occasions throughout the entire season. In the main I was confined to old favourites, including *The Spoiled Child*, *The Romp* and similar pieces, and given no new characters to learn. It was frustrating, even infuriating, as I was certainly not the first actress to take up with a prince. But the seeds of jealousy and moral disapproval still lingered, as if I had become a pariah overnight.

William never complained once about my working, save to remind me every now and then of my condition. 'Put your feet up, my love. You do not take nearly enough rest. Let me bring you a chair and you can sit in the garden for a while, and later perhaps pay a call or take tea.'

I would think of the society ladies of Richmond who would spend their days paying calls and taking tea, and their evenings playing cards. I was not one of their number, never having touched a card in my life, and I rather thought that fitting in and being accepted by local society would not be easy. I tried to say as much to the Duke, but he pooh-poohed the idea.

'Nonsense, they'll be delighted to make the acquaintance of a famous actress such as yourself.'

I shook my head in despair. 'You don't think that you might be just a little prejudiced? The ladies of Richmond will be scandalized by my living here at Clarence House as your mistress.'

He frowned, not much caring for that comment. 'Mrs Fitzherbert takes a full part in society, why shouldn't you?'

I couldn't help but wonder how true that was, since the lady insisted on being considered the Prince of Wales's true wife.

When, at the end of May, William received an invitation from a neighbour to a rural breakfast, he politely requested if he might bring a lady.

'There, you see, she has no objection,' he assured me when his appeal was granted.

I very much doubted my darling Billy would actually have named me. Communicating detail of any sort was not one of his strengths, no doubt because he was accustomed to leaving such trivialities to his secretary, Barton. And some less trivial matters too. Barton it was who had arranged an annual payment of 100 guineas to the mother of a child whom William readily accepted to be his. Not that this was any concern of mine. We were both anxious to put the past behind us and concentrate upon our future together. There was a careless ease about him that I rather liked.

'Who is this neighbour?' I asked, feeling nervous at the thought of entering a room with all the moralistic society ladies of Richmond. Far worse even than Hull, I should think. They would be certain to turn their backs and snub me, no doubt consider me quite beyond the pale, a fallen woman no less.

'She is a Mrs Hobart, dubbed by the gossips as Mrs Circumference as, not to put too fine a point on it, she is rather large.'

I couldn't help but giggle. The Duke had a lovely way of appearing to be completely oblivious to gossip and yet being in full possession of it. 'Ah yes, I've heard that she and her husband share a passion for all things connected with the theatre and acting.'

'Indeed they do. The good lady is noted for her theatricals, as well as her faro parties when in town, and her garden parties when staying in the country. I am sure they will be most delighted to meet an actress in the flesh, as it were, if deliciously more slender than her own.' Then he was kissing me again and we were falling into bed, eager for love.

However, on the morning of the event in question there was a downpour of rain which seemed set to last the entire day and the Duke changed his mind, adamant that we did not go. 'Standing about in the rain all day will do you no good at all in your condition, my dear.'

With some relief I sent a polite note excusing ourselves on the grounds of a previous engagement. 'Should Mrs Hobart's fête be put off on account of the badness of the weather till Monday or any other day, His Royal Highness will be extremely happy to wait on her.'

The event did indeed take place, even though the heavens

opened and it must surely have been spoiled. But we learned later that she had enjoyed herself at our expense, passing my letter among her guests and saying how relieved she was that she'd been spared from receiving me.

'I am quite used to entertaining the royal princes at my functions, but would never have invited the Duke of Clarence had I known whom he might choose to bring with him.'

Her friends were naturally most eager to warn her of the impropriety of our situation and how inappropriate it would be for her ever to make the same mistake again. So it was that when Mrs Hobart held her second party in July, we were not invited. Even a prince, it seemed, could not bestow respectability upon a mistress, not if she was an actress.

Nevertheless, I continued to pursue my profession and acted at the Haymarket until the end of the season. I closed it on the seventh of June with my portrayal of Rosalind in *As You Like It*. Even then I was asked to perform in a benefit at the end of July. For once, my dear patient Billy did object. 'Have you not done enough for one season, my love? It is surely time for you to put your feet up and rest.'

'But it is only one night, and I should like to perform, for it is my old friend, Mrs Bannister. She has perhaps more sense than me as she is retiring to devote herself to her family, something I cannot quite bring myself to do.'

'I should think not. You are far too talented to rusticate. It is not my place to stop you, and as you say, my love, it is but one night.'

So I performed with my dear friend, then just a few days later in early August, I suffered a miscarriage.

I have little recollection of the event beyond the pain, and the sad expression of the Duke as I faded in and out of consciousness. The royal physician was called and for a time I seriously feared that my life was in danger. I was devastated by the loss of this child, a girl, as I had so wanted to give the Duke the family he so longed for.

Yet as I slowly recovered in the days following, returning to the theatre in September for the new season, he uttered not one word of blame. All he said to me was, 'The doctor says you are perfectly healthy and there will be other babies, so you are not to worry.'

Come the New Year of 1793, I was again complaining to Kemble that I was never allowed to act in any new plays, only revivals, while he and Sheridan continued at loggerheads over money as well as the programme.

'Why may I not play in anything new? I am often given no part at all, yet you still pay me at the top rate.'

'We will let you know when there is a suitable new part for you,' came the predictably cool reply.

Perhaps out of desperation I wrote a play myself, albeit in collaboration with a Miss Cuthbertson, which we called *Anna*. Kemble and I quarrelled furiously over whether or not to put it on. In the end he agreed but sadly it was not a success. It would have been better had I not pressed him.

Meanwhile, in the real world, England and France were fast moving towards war. French émigrés were constantly arriving with tales of horror. More alarming still, the French King and his Queen had been taken prisoner and were on trial. The Duke naturally offered his services to the navy, but then fell on an icy step and broke his arm, which prevented him from doing anything.

'Now it is you who must rest, my darling,' I told him, enjoying fussing over him for a change.

Pitt, however, was firmly against the Duke taking part, even after he was fit, and despite the fact that several of his brothers were given roles. William was incensed.

'The Prime Minister has objected to the criticisms I made about the war in the House of Lords, simply because I said we should negotiate peace at the earliest opportunity. I strongly believe that the war effort should be confined as far as possible to naval operations. In response Pitt said that he could not have a political admiral. Yet I wish to serve my country. What is so wrong in that?'

I looked at his outraged expression, thinking how well meaning he was, how passionate and caring, yet also perhaps a little naïve. 'But as you don't agree with the war, you can surely see Pitt's point of view.'

'I do see his point of view, but I distrust Pitt's policy of military intervention on the Continent. Events will prove me right, I'm sure of it. I tell you, Dora, if ever, unfortunately for this country, I should by providence be commanded to wear the crown, my greatest desire would be to be considered a peaceful monarch, and to study the true interests of Great Britain by attending to the extension of its commerce and consequently to the increase of the navy.'

I made no response to this comment, for were that occasion ever to arise, it would be the end of our relationship. Mistresses did not become queens, even if they were not an actress with three children by two different fathers.

I was also pregnant again, but he gave no thought either to the implication of that outcome for his unborn child.

Events did, however, as William had predicted, prove him right when the British army under the leadership of the Duke of York were defeated at Hondschoote, and a few weeks later the allied army was beaten at Wattignies. Worse news came when we received word that the French King and his Queen, Marie Antoinette, had both been executed, their heads cut from their bodies.

I was quite beside myself with horror. 'I never imagined such a thing could happen,' I cried.

'It is indeed a barbarous and inhuman murder, but it could not possibly happen here, my love.'

'How can you be sure?'

'The British are not like the French, we are far too pragmatic to start a revolution. Fate, I am sorry to say, seems unfavourable to us on the Continent, and every day convinces me more and more of the propriety of my objections to the war in that quarter.'

Out of respect for the French royal family, Kemble closed the Haymarket for the day, but Sheridan reacted badly to the gesture. 'Am I not struggling enough over financing the building of the new theatre at Drury Lane? It's costing me a small fortune. I cannot afford to miss a single day's trade, and certainly not for the French.'

Their disputes rumbled on, as always, but I was too busy with rehearsals, and taking extreme care over the child I was carrying, to concern myself too much with theatre politics. I was, however, aware that Sheridan was heavily involved in calls for parliamentary reform, determined to avoid a similar threat here to that in France. And, like William, hard-pressed as he was for cash, yet he could not resist putting on a bet that reform would pass into law within two years. I feared he would lose his money.

His long face with its downward sloping eyes and small pinched mouth looked more mournful than ever, and I did feel most dreadfully sorry for him as Elizabeth, his wife, had recently died of consumption. To everyone's astonishment this much-betrayed and once innocent woman had given birth to a daughter that was not her husband's, only shortly before her death. Nevertheless, the guilt-ridden, grief-stricken Sheridan had taken the child to his heart, only to lose her too within a twelvemonth. He did find himself a new love, but she flagrantly married his late wife's ex-lover.

Poor Sheridan, finally being paid in kind for all his own adulterous betrayals in the past. A lesson to us all.

The war continued but William took no part in it. The King would not permit him to go to sea, and the government refused to give him a job at the Admiralty, for which I was deeply thankful, despite his very real sense of frustration. But I wept for those two lost souls. Whatever the French King and Queen's faults and flaws, they surely did not deserve such an end.

And looking at my own royal prince, I silently prayed nothing of the sort would happen here, should he ever wear the crown, whether or not I was at his side.

Twenty

'. . . a young Admiral or a Pickle Duchess'

In January of 1794 I at last gave the Duke the son he craved. We named him George FitzClarence, and had him baptized in May. The birth was long drawn out but he was a fine healthy baby. As always I recovered quite quickly and fed him myself, which I'm quite sure the society ladies of Richmond would never do. I also took some much-needed rest from the theatre, enjoying a few months' peace to devote myself entirely to my child. I loved to walk out through the park pushing the perambulator, calling at the shops in Richmond, one of my favourites being a milliner's shop. I liked to remember the days when I had worked in one myself as a girl of fourteen. I loved to try on hats, and they would laugh when, having done a fair imitation of a society lady admiring myself before the looking glass, I would then put baby George on my lap and change his linen.

'I have never seen the like,' marvelled the proprietor. 'You are a mother to those children in the truest sense of the word.'

Mother, mistress, actress, manager, sister, financier, supporter and help-meet. All things to all people, except a wife. I stifled a sigh of nostalgia for what might have been. Perhaps Sheridan had been right after all, respectable marriage for an actress was never on the cards, but I loved my Billy and had no regrets.

In April he was made a vice-admiral, more by way of compensation as it was but an honorary position with no role attached to it. He seemed reasonably content and was often at the House of Lords, and visited his brother for hard duty drinking sessions perhaps a mite too often. He seemed content, yet I worried about his lack of purpose in life.

'Are you sure you won't grow bored when I return to work?' I asked him.

'I shall find plenty to amuse myself. Do not fret, dearest.'

'Perhaps you will grow tired of my frequent absences in the end?'

He drew me into his arms and kissed me. 'I would never grow tired of you. So long as you come home every weekend, I am content.'

Later that summer we enjoyed a short holiday in Brighton at Mrs Fitzherbert's house with William and baby George, and it was here that I was privy to a conversation between the brothers.

'I fear if I don't do something, I may well lose Petersham,' William confessed to the Prince of Wales. 'As you know, I have it on a mortgage and I never know from one month to the next whether I can continue to maintain it.'

'The King will surely never allow that to happen,' the Prince replied, somewhat dismissively.

'I think it highly likely that he will, since he refuses to settle my debts.'

Possibly out of a sense of guilt for helping to create those debts, George later went to the King and suggested that His Majesty might ask Parliament to purchase the property, and allow William to remain as tenant. Apparently Pitt did not approve of the plan, pointing out that there were far more important matters upon which to spend the public purse.

The King also declined to relieve his son of the mortgage, and my Billy was obliged to seek a loan elsewhere to help pay off at least some of his debts.

'Robbing Peter to pay Paul, that's all I seem to do these days,' he mourned. 'I've written to Coutts stating that seven thousand pounds will settle my difficulties, and then by economy I hope to be once more free.'

Coutts was sympathetic if not particularly optimistic, but then William had given no indication of any real understanding of the word economy, bless his dear heart.

I returned to the stage in September when baby George was eight months old, thinking it important to keep some money coming in. I signed a new contract to appear at the new Drury Lane Theatre, which was at last open. It was utterly magnificent, if with a vast auditorium that was far too high, with poor sight-lines and difficulties with sound. Sheridan was still struggling over finances and wages were not being paid, resulting in strikes by dissatisfied staff and actors alike.

In the time-honoured fashion of all actors I took my baby with me, sending his devoted father constant little notes that 'your dear little boy is perfectly well. He is now very much a theatre baby.'

By then I was already pregnant again. The Duke was, as I say, a most vigorous and passionate lover.

The *Bon Ton Magazine* announced:

> *Mrs Jordan is shortly expecting to produce something, whether a young Admiral or a Pickle Duchess it is impossible yet to tell.*

I continued with my career as before, staying at Somerset Street during the week and going home to Richmond every Saturday. Sheridan arranged for Elizabeth Inchbald to write a play for me. It was entitled *The Wedding Day* and was a great success.

The one that followed, however, was a most dreadful flop. This was a satirical play about gambling, titled *Nobody*. It was written by Mary Robinson, who was most condemnatory on the subject of the nation's favourite pastime. She had begged me to persuade Sheridan to put it on, and, perhaps foolishly, I did so, not only because she had once been mistress to the Prince of Wales, but was also a writer of some renown.

It was a bad mistake and most of the cast cried off. Bannister and I struggled through as best we could, despite the society ladies hissing behind their fans, and the young bucks in the pits blowing their cat-calls. It was also slated by the critics and finally Mrs Robinson had the good sense to withdraw the play. It was particularly sad considering the many literary achievements this fine lady had to her credit, most of which commented on the shortcomings of high society.

But seeing how pitiful this one-time adored and beautiful mistress of royalty had become, now suffering ridicule, ill health and neglect, brought a shiver to my spine almost as if someone had walked on my grave.

Such worries had little time to linger, as I soon had concerns of a more personal nature when Hester sent me a frantic message to say that Fanny was ill. She was twelve by this time, and normally such a healthy child, but I went at once to Brompton to nurse her. I found her fretful and feverish, but glad to have her mother there.

'I will stay with her,' I told Hester. 'You keep the other children away so that they don't catch whatever it is.'

'I can cope perfectly well,' my sister snapped, in that impatient way she had. 'Are you not in a production? We cannot risk you catching it either.'

'She is *my* daughter. Do as I ask without argument for once, please, Hester.'

But our efforts were in vain as Dodee did catch it. Both my girls were soon very ill indeed, although thankfully Lucy was spared, having been kept well clear. Doctor Turton, one of the royal physicians, quickly arrived on the scene, the Duke having kindly called him out.

'I would say it is either putrid or scarlet fever. Either one can be extremely dangerous.'

I felt weak with fear. 'What must I do to make her better? Is there something you can give her?'

'If she can take this bark, and keep it down, there is hope.'

He very generously stayed with me all through that first night, which seemed endless, one which Hester and I spent wringing out cold cloths in an effort to bring down the girls' fever. I stayed for a further three nights, so fearful for my daughters that I grew quite demented. The Duke wrote regularly, asking to meet me, but I was nervous of using the coach in case I should infect it. I offered to walk out to meet him, although not too far as I was utterly exhausted. But then I was advised by Doctor Turton not to do even that in case of spreading the contagion.

'I should never forgive myself,' I wrote to him, 'if I was the cause of giving you any pain either of body or mind. Poor Fanny is very ill – her life depends on her being able to keep the bark on her stomach. Love and kiss my dear little boy . . . Yours ever, Dora.'

Praise the lord, my darling Fanny slowly began to recover, as did little Dodee.

'All thanks to your good nursing,' Doctor Turton told me.

'My daughter owes her life to your bark, doctor, whatever it may be.'

In March 1795, I gave birth to another child, this time a daughter. The Duke chose to name her Sophia after his sister, a beautiful name for a beautiful girl. Within the month I was back at work, taking baby with me as I was still feeding her: a necessity as money had begun to be something of a problem.

As if I didn't have enough to contend with, the Duke and I were sitting peacefully at home at Clarence House one afternoon when we heard a great commotion at the door.

'What on earth is going on?' he cried, jumping up.

At that moment a footman appeared, looking somewhat harassed. 'I tried to send him away, but the fellow says he is Mrs Jordan's brother, Your Highness.'

And there stood George, looking very much the worse for drink, his clothes in a most disgusting state. I was utterly mortified. 'George, what on earth are you doing here, and in such a condition?'

The Duke very tactfully left the room while I drew George on to the couch beside me. I recoiled a little as he stank strongly of gin. 'Please bring coffee, and a bowl of hot water,' I asked the footman.

'My lovely Maria has left me,' George cried, his words slurred. Never had I seen him so inebriated, as he'd rarely touched a drop of drink in his life. 'She says we have drifted apart and has taken up residence with Caulfield, the comedian.' And my poor brother began to sob.

'Oh, George, I am truly sorry.' It was quite common in our profession for actors working in different parts of the country to see each other but rarely, and marriages frequently broke down as a result. 'Is there no hope?'

He shook his head in despair. 'None. She has turned me out of the house, so I have nowhere even to live. She says I am useless, which is certainly true. I am not the actor she is, or you are, Dolly,' he mourned, maudlin in his self-pity.

'You do not have to be, George. You need only be yourself. Our mother once told me the very same thing when I was feeling low.'

'I cannot. Without her, I am finished. I shall never act again.'

'Nonsense, you will recover. We all must after heartbreak.'

I was devastated to hear this news, as the last thing I wanted was to take my brother in. But despite my sisterly scolding, copious amounts of coffee, and helping him to clean the vomit from his clothes, it was clear he was a broken man. I had no alternative but to send him to Cousin Blanche in Trelethyn to recover, and agree to give him an allowance of fifty pounds a year. What else could I do? He was ever weak, like his father, yet he is my dear brother.

I apologized profusely to the Duke, but unlike Ford, when he learned of my generosity, he uttered not one word of condemnation.

Oh, but it was an extra burden I could have done without.

'It is the most vexing thing, but I am to be obliged to marry,' The Prince of Wales mourned to us one day. 'Parliament has agreed to pay off my debts, which confound it have now topped six hundred thousand pounds, so long as I agree to marry a German princess.'

'But I thought you were married already, to Mrs Fitzherbert?' William said, looking puzzled. I never took part in these brotherly discussions as it did not seem to be my place. I sat silent, my head bowed over my embroidery, an occupation that kept my fingers busy when waiting backstage, or as now when I wished not to appear to be listening.

'My marriage to Maria is not considered to be legal, since I never received the King's permission. I am to be sold off to Caroline of Brunswick. How I shall face another woman in my bed after my darling Maria, I cannot imagine.'

William laughed out loud. 'But you never were faithful to your darling Maria. What of Lady Jersey? Is she not your mistress also?'

'But Maria is the wife of my heart and soul.'

'I understand,' William softly agreed. 'As Mrs Jordan is to me,' and he cast me a fond look which I smilingly returned.

'I am told that Caroline is very like our dear sister Mary. If so, then she will be all I could wish for in a wife.'

The Duke naturally attended his brother's wedding on the

eighth of April, 1795, and witnessed George's revulsion at sight
of his bride, who turned out to be not at all like Mary. I, of
course, was not present, but he told me that the poor girl had
been trussed up in a most unflattering gown at Lady Jersey's
instigation. She was presented to the Prince almost the moment
she stepped ashore without even being allowed time for proper
ablutions, over which the Prince was most fastidious. She was
also loud and somewhat vulgar, certainly in her husband's opinion.
He went to her bed drunk and left it swearing never to return.

The wedding celebrations continued with a ball, and I was
not invited to that either, which was only to be expected, this
being a family occasion, but hurtful all the same. William,
however, was unaware that I watched the proceedings from
the gallery where the band was playing.

I found it excruciatingly painful to witness how closely he
paid attention to the court ladies. I fear he rather enjoyed
himself dancing with all the young beauties in their enchanting
gowns, no doubt telling them his seafaring yarns, and basking
in their enticing little smiles.

'You were flirting with that woman,' I accused him later,
eyes hot with tears.

He looked quite shocked. 'Dearest, I did no such thing.'

'I saw you with my own eyes. While I was considered
unworthy of attending such a magnificent event, thereby being
humiliated before everyone, you can put yourself about as you
choose.'

He looked rather annoyed by this charge, although I was
quite certain he'd thoroughly enjoyed the attention. 'How
could you be humiliated when you were not even present?'
he said.

'Because I am your *wife*, in all but name. I am beginning
to think that perhaps this was all a terrible mistake and we
should separate.'

He looked utterly mortified. 'Why would you wish such a
terrible thing? Do I not love you with all my heart and soul?'
I could see him struggling to damp down his quick temper,
but I was too far gone in my own to care that he felt hurt by
my accusation.

'Oh, I dare say you do, just as the Prince of Wales loves

Mrs Fitzherbert. But yet you are both free spirits and can love more than one woman without fear or favour, it seems,' and I burst into tears.

William instantly drew me into his arms. 'Never could I love any woman more than I love you, Little Pickle. You are my *life*, my *All*.'

I looked up into his blue eyes, warm with love, and was filled with shame. How could I have doubted him, even for a moment? 'Oh, and I love you too, dearest Billy.'

He beamed. 'Well, there you are then. Are we not the happiest, most devoted couple? Do we not have a domestic bliss that most would envy? Dora, my love, you have nothing to fear from anyone, I swear it on my honour.' And somehow his sincerity was so genuine, so heartfelt, that I was convinced, and all ill feeling between us was dispelled with a night of passionate lovemaking.

Fortunately for the Prince of Wales, Caroline of Brunswick almost instantly fell pregnant, so he was further spared her bed. But I sensed that William felt sorry that his brother did not share our good fortune on the domestic front. That summer George came to Clarence House to bemoan the misery of his marriage and stayed for two long weeks.

'I refuse to live with that woman,' he declared over his fourth glass of claret.

'But you must,' William chided him. 'If this child is a girl you will have to try again for a boy.'

George grimaced in horror. 'Never!'

I made a great fuss of him, sitting at the head of the table and playing the perfect hostess, even though I was feeling far from well myself, having suffered a miscarriage in July, no doubt caused by pressure of work and one or two falls and sprains onstage. In January of the following year I sadly suffered yet another. By then Caroline was safely delivered of a girl, christened Charlotte after her grandmother. George was delighted and declared himself most satisfied. Three months later the Prince and Princess of Wales separated.

The Duke celebrated his brother's success, even if the new Princess Charlotte did put him one step further from the throne.

*   *   *

To my complete horror, Daly suddenly presented himself at my dressing room one night at Drury Lane, turning up at my door like the proverbial bad penny. It took all my strength and resolve to see him, but I was curious to know what he wanted from me. I feared it might concern Fanny, and I was right, at least partially.

He stood before me with that squint-eyed look and my stomach curdled with loathing. 'I have come to see my daughter. It was naughty of you to run away like that without even telling me about her. But I shall forgive you, Dolly, as I always do whenever you make a mistake.'

Anger rose hot and fierce in my breast; even the mere sight of him filled me with loathing. 'The biggest mistake I ever made was to trust *you*. Fanny is *my* daughter and no concern of yours. And my name is Dora.'

He held out his hands in a familiar placatory gesture. 'You cannot deny the child a father.'

'She has no need of a father. She has a doting mother and an adoring aunt, not to mention the Duke to protect her.'

'I can offer you one hundred guineas a week if you would come back to Dublin and perform at the theatre. What do you say to that?'

I laughed out loud. 'So that is what this is all about! You wish to cash in on my fame. Either you are desperate, or a liar, or maybe both, but were you to offer me ten times that sum I would not come. Get out of my dressing room this minute. I also recommend you leave the country before I have you arrested for what you did to me.'

'You would never dare,' he scoffed, and straightening my spine I took a step closer, so that he did not mistake my sincerity.

'Do not test me too much, Daly. If you come anywhere near Fanny you will live to regret it. The Duke is a powerful man with friends who could make life extremely difficult for you. Go home to Ireland in one piece, while you still can.'

He swore loudly, spun on his heel and strode away. I found that I had to sit down as I was actually shaking. But the bluff, for that is exactly what it was, had worked. At last, I thought, Daly is gone from my life for good, and from dear Fanny's.

*   *   *

There were times during the long, cold winter that followed when I would think of that offer of one hundred guineas as Sheridan continued to struggle with his finances and paid me only in dribs and drabs. But never would I trust Daly again, so I dismissed him from my mind, proud that I had found the courage to stand up to him at last. But at times I felt worn out by the struggle to fit everything in, to constantly move from house to house, being at Somerset Street when in town, then home to Richmond at the weekends, minding my children and keeping the Duke happy.

Yet we were happy, deliciously so. Busy but content. Sheridan naturally disapproved of my frequent pregnancies, for all I kept on working, often to the very week I went into labour.

This season I was playing Nell in *The Devil to Pay*, and even Ophelia, would you believe? And my fame continued to blossom. Admirers would come to my dressing room simply to talk to me. I became friendly with a young Cambridge undergraduate by the name of Samuel Taylor Coleridge, who fancied himself as a poet and playwright, and sought my critical appraisal of his work. Seeing that he had merit, I gave him every encouragement, as I am rather fond of poetry myself.

There were others too who came to me for support and advice: a William Hazlitt, and a young clerk by the name of Charles Lamb who liked my rendition of Shakespeare.

In the months that followed exhaustion would often get the better of me, and I sometimes longed for a more settled life and a home in one place, able to devote myself entirely to my family. But then I would remind myself what a very fortunate woman I was to have such a beautiful family and also a wonderful career which brought me so much pleasure, and not a little in the way of financial reward.

On one occasion I was offered twenty guineas for three more nights, which is hard to resist, particularly if the house is a good one. And with a rapidly growing family, money was ever a cause of concern. Yet I was careful not to trespass upon the Duke's good will too much. I always made a point, if I was to be away longer than intended, of seeking his agreement before I accepted.

Twenty-One

'Mrs Jordan never has been to me the least cause of
expense'

'Would you believe the King has offered me a post as ranger
of Bushy Park?' William said to me at the end of a particularly
tiring week. I smiled at him fondly, thinking this would be a
new enthusiasm, which always did his spirits good, particularly
since he still had been given no proper role in the war. 'I am
delighted for you, my love. What does that involve, exactly?'

'Dearest, you do not understand. Seeing how cramped we
are here at Clarence House, particularly when the older girls
come to stay, and how contented you and I are together, the
King has offered us a fine new home.' He was grinning from
ear to ear, and I found a broad smile of delight breaking out
on my own face.

'Oh, how very kind of His Majesty. What kind of home?'

'It is a beautiful mansion in Teddington, set in more than a
thousand acres. It's part of the Hampton Court estate, on the
opposite side of the bank from Richmond. No more than two
hours by coach from St James's, and would not lengthen your
own journey to Drury Lane.'

'Oh, my love, can this be true?'

'The King seems to think that I have presented myself well,
serving as an example of domestic decorum by comparison
with the way George has behaved with Mrs Fitzherbert, Lady
Jersey and the Princess Caroline. Better one established mistress
than two unsuitable wives, eh?' he said with a laugh.

It didn't seem appropriate for me to comment so I kept on
smiling, waiting for more.

'I wish you all to see the house and tell me if you like it.
Then if you do, we shall arrange to move in as quickly as
possible.'

Like the proud family man he had become, the very next

day he took us all, myself, three-year-old George and two-year-old Sophy, to view the property, as if their opinions too were of value. It was a cold January day, the lime and chestnut trees stark and bare of leaf, the ground hard with frost, an ornamental pond frozen over, but I loved it on sight. How could I not?

'It is beautiful, my love. Can it really be ours? Can we afford such splendour?' I was already beginning to estimate the cost of maintaining such a grand mansion.

'Most certainly we can, the King has decreed it,' William said, with perhaps more confidence than certainty. He began to expound his plans for developing the estate. 'I shall become a farmer. There are deer and pheasant in the woods, and I shall increase the flock of sheep, grow vegetables, plant peach trees and perhaps install an orangery.'

'May we have a pleasure garden?' I asked, beginning to catch his enthusiasm.

'But of course. Absolutely essential. And ponies for the children. Dogs and lots of animals for them to grow up with.'

'I have some savings, were you to be in need of a loan to get you started,' I offered. This was meant for my older girls as they would each require a dowry, and once I left the stage I would also need a pension for myself, but I did some rapid calculations and decided I could afford to offer some assistance.

'I would pay you back,' William assured me.

'Of course you would, dearest, but there is really no hurry to do so. It will, after all, be my home too.' And was he not the love of my life?

The Duke trotted us briskly along a seemingly endless array of open colonnades, taking little account of the fact I was again pregnant, seven months in my estimation, and this time progressing well. 'The perfect place for entertaining, do you not think?'

'And for children to run,' I said with a smile, not quite seeing myself playing hostess for the society ladies here, any more than I did at Clarence House.

'It was once the home of George Montagu, Earl of Halifax. And more recently the late Lord North, Earl of Guildford and erstwhile Prime Minister. His lady wife sadly has also recently died, and so the post of ranger fell vacant. I have offered my condolences to her daughter, and use of the Keeper's Lodge on the estate. Now do come and see the bedrooms, of which there are more than enough for a growing family, dearest Dora.'

I laughed, for this was exactly what he needed, a new role and purpose in his life. And who was I to question his dream? For my part, I would welcome any change which was good for the children, so long as we truly could cope with the expense of such a fine property. The Duke set about resolving that problem by writing numerous letters to Coutts about his plans, and his need for a loan on the basis that it could easily be repaid when the farms and woodland began to pay their way. 'There is equipment to buy, and farm stock, cattle and sheep.' I, of course, insisted on lending him £2,400, which I told him to repay when he thought proper.

'It is most generous of her,' he told Coutts, and much to my amusement went on, 'I freely admit Mrs Jordan never has been to me the least cause of expense.'

I sincerely hoped I never would be.

Coutts agreed to lend him £2,000, but, like the Prince of Wales, he could not resist making considerable changes to the property, although he fully intended them to be both practical and suited to a family, not at all like the pavilion at Brighton. The Duke, believing himself to be far more sensible than his brother, began to make comprehensive plans for refurbishment, holding no fears about financing it.

'After all, the mansion belongs to the nation,' he said. 'So why should not the public purse help fund it?'

'I doubt Pitt can supply all the money you'll need, as the country's finances must already be stretched to the limit by having to pay for this seemingly endless war. And I'm afraid there is also the question of a number of accounts having been sent in by the shopkeepers of Richmond, my love, once they learned of our proposed move.'

'I have no wish for you to fret about such matters, dearest, not in your condition. All will be attended to,' William promised, the very slightest edge to his tone.

'Forgive me for fussing but following my experience with

Daly, I determined never to allow myself to fall into debt again. Nor must you, dearest. But I shall certainly do my part to earn what I can to help.'

'What a fine woman you are,' William said. 'Ever practical, loyal and generous-hearted.'

In March, I presented him with a second fine healthy son, named Henry, a joy to behold after our recent disappointments. 'Perhaps I took more care with this one,' I ruefully remarked as I lovingly cradled my child to my breast. 'Finding the right balance between my career and motherhood is not always easy.'

'You need more assistance, my love, and I shall provide it.'

William took on more nursemaids, including a Miss Sketchley, who would be something between nurse and governess. And also the Reverend Thomas Lloyd, as chaplain and general mentor and assistant for me and the children. He was a tactful, amiable man, willing and able to assist us in any way. This included taking the daily prayers, baptizing the dear children and somehow managing to maintain the requirements of his faith with a pragmatic realism. The Duke was determined that his own offspring would be provided with a loving home, doting parents, and yet be instilled with the necessary manners and education.

'Can we afford all these wages?' I asked. Lloyd alone was to be paid £400 per annum, and the costs of the refurbishment seemed to be escalating by the day.

'We can and we must. I will not have you overtaxed.'

'Yet we must watch our expenditure carefully.'

'I *do* watch it,' the Duke snapped, and I said no more, knowing when to hold my tongue.

'These builders will send in their account twice if you don't watch out,' the Prince of Wales warned him, no doubt speaking from experience. 'You must keep a close eye on your debts, Billy boy.'

Irritated that not only I, but his own brother should be nagging him, the Duke's reply was somewhat tetchy. 'It is all very well for you to talk, having had your debts settled.'

George smoothed the silk of his new neckcloth, looking momentarily glum. 'Sadly, they are rising yet again, like the phoenix.'

* * *

It was May and William had recently attended the marriage of the Princess Royal to the Prince of Wurttemberg at St James's. All the family were present, for once including the four princesses, but again I was excluded. Afterwards the Duke told me how he'd boasted of my being an excellent manager, and that he meant to hire an architect to assist with the building project.

'Would you believe George remarked how fortunate I was to have your capacity to add to the coffers.' His expression darkened, clearly hating the inference behind this remark. 'I told him quite bluntly that I do not view you in those terms.'

'I am glad to hear it,' I said, not sure whether to be amused or insulted by this charge. 'And what else did you say?'

'That I may be permitted to be partial but cannot help thinking you are one of the most perfect women in this world. "Is she not a champion for the independent woman?" I said. "I dare say she is, Billy Boy," George replied. "And no one can deny the good lady is a worker." He has apparently seen you most days being driven in and out of London in your new carriage, or in mine on occasion with its royal crest. "And a most excellent mother," I replied, with some pride. "Our children will grow up cheerful, independent and happy. What more can a father ask?" "A win on the state lottery?" my brother quipped, and even suggested that I might feel unmanned by you.'

'And are you?' I asked, holding my breath.

'Of course not! What utter tosh! Why should I? I told George in no uncertain terms that I like minding my children, and supervising the work at Bushy, and shall enjoy running my farm. Although it's true I would still relish serving my country.'

Soon after being made ranger William had heard of Nelson's arrival in the country, and having once been instrumental in procuring him HMS *Agamemnon* back in 1793, he at once abandoned supervising the work at Bushy House to hurry to his old friend's side. Nelson's arm had been shattered by a cannon ball at the Battle of Santa Cruz de Tenerife, necessitating amputation. William was only too happy to welcome him home and offer sympathy. 'I envy Nelson's adventurous life, and long to be more involved in the war. Failing that, the wish dearest to my heart is to be Marine Minister.'

'You would make a good one,' I agreed, my heart going out to him, knowing how he ached for a more active role.

'My sister, the Princess Augusta, however, doubts my capability. She claims that I have many good parts, but am far too indolent to do any role justice.'

'Did she indeed?' I asked, hiding a smile.

'"You are a man so fond of his ease you let everything take its course," she said. What think you of that?'

He sounded so infuriated that I felt bound to console him, even though I thought the Princess might well have a point. 'I'm quite sure that given a position of proper merit and importance, you would exert yourself to the utmost.'

'That is exactly what *I* said. Augusta's response was that I try *too* hard, and the long worthy speeches in the Lords count against me. How can that be?' he protested. 'Did I not speak up against the fragile position of women following a divorce, and oppose efforts to bar them from remarriage? I also helped abolish laws against dissenting Christians.'

'Of course you did, dearest,' I concurred, and refrained from saying how he did not always see the hypocrisy in such a stand, and even if he did, I should think most of the Lords would be asleep by the time he'd made his point. But I felt sorry for him. Despite his regular attendance at the House of Lords, and keeping himself in touch by corresponding with Nelson and other officer friends, I knew my dear Billy felt deeply frustrated at being so overlooked and denied any opportunity to serve his country. Now it seemed even his own family could not recognize this important need in him.

'I say only what needs to be said,' he went on, growing ever more heated over this sense of injustice. 'Otherwise Pitt would have it all his own way. I am not simply a family man, and a man of economy, I do have considerable experience in naval affairs. But of course George must always have the final word. "And how long did you say your good lady has been acting in London? Five years is it, or ten?"'

'Did you tell him that I came in 1785?'

'I most certainly did, but he wouldn't have it. "I'll stake five hundred pounds it was long before that," he insisted. Done, said I, seeing an easy profit, and the Prince at once burst out laughing, so full of arrogance he couldn't contemplate losing.'

I groaned. 'Will you two never learn? Where is the point in transferring five hundred pounds from the Prince of Wales's debt to your own? Man of economy indeed!'

'What is it, what have I said?'

'I believe the Prince has proved his point, that you are not a man of economy at all.'

William flushed, realizing he'd been duped by his clever brother yet again. Sadly, his siblings had too often proved how much sharper their brains were.

Shamed by my scorn, and conceding that I made a fair point, William withdrew his bet. But economy remained a problem for him. The architect was not always present to superintend the work, and neither was I, so this task was left largely to William's steward and the builders' own discretion. Nor did he ever question the price of materials and labour on any of the accounts he forwarded to Coutts. Budgets, after all, were not generally the concern of princes.

Walls were taken down, new rooms formed, doors and windows moved, the stables extended and the gardens redesigned. While work progressed, he chose to rent a house in Dover, being intolerant of the mess and disorder created, and quite unthinking of the extra expense. I joined him for a while after Drury Lane closed for the season, but then moved into Bushy with the children in order to hurry things along and make the house presentable as quickly as possible. This proved to be an excellent plan, as I was by then performing in a short season in Richmond.

Hester was with me, and Fanny and Dodee too. They were to live nearby at Gifford Lodge, so that I could visit them more easily, and already they were keen to help with the harvest and the gardening.

'The children are going to love living here, and it will make *my* life so much easier.'

'And considerably more expensive,' Hester said. It was ever her wont to see the worst in things.

'You really have no call to criticize the Duke on that score. Are you and the children not amply provided for?'

'But who supplies the funds?'

I flushed angrily. Why did my dear sister always manage to spot the flaws, and raise my hackles with her complaining? 'The Duke is most generous, but we share many of the expenses, as we do everything else, whether it be caring for the children or working on this house. As should all couples, I might add.' Hester seemed to be rapidly turning into a crabby old maid.

I had intended to keep a better eye myself on the legions of workmen who milled about the place, but in reality I was far too busy. Even when William finally joined me, he too was often occupied elsewhere.

When not at the Lords he consoled himself for his lack of a proper role by forming a guard of yeomanry. This comprised local farmers and other worthies in Spelthorne, and he was nothing if not rigorous with their drills. Young as they were, he declared he would have been happy to take them into action, and I know he longed to do so. At least putting these men through their paces gave him a purpose.

After Richmond I moved on to Margate, an engagement that could not be declined as it was particularly well paid at £50 a night. I regularly dispatched what money I could to the Duke, as promised, and of course took the youngest children with me.

'Why not put a kiss in this note to Papa,' I suggested to little George, when writing one of my many letters to him. Giggling with excitement he put his mouth to the paper and spat on it. I laughed out loud, for he was such an imp, and felt obliged to add a sentence or two to explain the wet marks on the page to his father. I expect William would laugh too, for he adores his children, and they could do no wrong in his eyes.

At the start of the new season at Drury Lane in September I played Miranda in *The Tempest*, and Beatrice in *Much Ado About Nothing*, the latter very much a part which suited me, and surprisingly easy to learn. We also performed *The Count of Narbonne*, and *The Castle Spectre*, very gothic and hugely popular.

I became very involved in charity work, not only providing layettes for poor mothers, but also performing in many benefits to support lying-in hospitals. Did I not understand what it was to be poor and not to be able to afford to pay a doctor to attend at this most dangerous time in a woman's life? I endowed a free school for girls locally in Richmond because a good education, my mother always said, is so very important. Like all parents she did what she could for her children, and naturally gave preference to the boys. But girls need educating too, and I was determined to help in this respect, since I could afford to do so.

My own eldest daughters were by this time very nearly full grown, then in December 1798 I gave birth to Mary, followed almost exactly a year later with another boy, Frederick, who kept me from work until the following April. This resulted in my not being paid for the entire winter. I was compelled to have strong words with Sheridan on the subject.

'Perhaps if you could reduce your pregnancies,' was his caustic reply, which infuriated me all the more.

The money was most definitely owed to me and I had no wish to be a burden to the Duke, since he had enough to contend with refurbishing our beloved Bushy. I was obliged to write to Coutts to explain the delay in payment of their allowance to Hester and my older girls, and asked for him to subsidize me until the money came through.

'I shall get my money from Mr Sheridan, make no doubt, but not time enough to prevent the distress and discredit that must be the result of his remissness.'

These minor irritations aside I had never been happier in my life. My dear Billy and I were the most contented of couples. The papers published a cartoon of the Duke wheeling a perambulator packed with children in the park, which he so loved to do. It showed him with a doll hanging from his pocket, and me walking alongside, book in hand, learning my lines. I think he was rather flattered by it. But then he was the very best of fathers.

Twenty-Two

'. . . the lady who has so captured my heart'

In the years following, our lives at Bushy continued in the most pleasant manner imaginable. I would often find myself overseeing work still going on; dear Billy was never short of plans for improvement, yet nor did he stint on the requirement for him to attend the House of Lords, so how could he always be present? I would speak to the builders then take my daughters to their dance class, attend rehearsals for my latest production, or enjoy afternoon tea with my neighbour, Mrs Garrick. Somehow I managed to divide my time between family and stage, able to pursue a career I loved while living with a man who meant everything to me, a man who adored me in return and who frequently sought my advice and counsel.

On one occasion I was able tactfully to persuade him against erecting a building which would have been to the detriment of old Mrs Garrick's estate.

'If you continue the building you will have all the old cats at Hampton Court on your back,' I warned him. The plan was cancelled. Mostly though, I was careful to defer to the Duke's wishes. He was, after all, a royal prince.

'Shall we have green or crimson drapes in the dining room, Dora?' he would ask.

'My love, let us call in the upholsterer to bring us some swatches and advise,' I would cautiously reply.

Never in my life had I lived in a house of this magnitude, and it felt at times overwhelming. But to me it was more than a mansion, it was our home. The colonnades were closed in to form curving corridors along which the children did indeed love to run, each leading to a pavilion. The entire house bristled with activity, with nursemaids and servants, but also with dogs and muddy boots, with toys left scattered about, with fishing rods and sporting guns. There was noise too, and plenty of it, perhaps the discordant notes of a child hitting the wrong keys in a piano lesson, a boy tooting on a trumpet, the squawk of a pet parrot, or simply endless happy laughter.

In the summer there would be the crack of leather ball on willow as cricket became a passion for all my boys. There would be jolly picnics and swimming in the lake, boating on the Thames, tug-of-war and team games with the village boys. Oh, what fun we had. Even helping in the gardens and on the farm was regarded as a pleasure. The children loved to join in, whether it be the gathering and stacking of hay, helping with the lambing, or picking the ripe peaches, plums, strawberries or raspberries when in season. They might have tangles in their hair, their clothes be stained with dried mud or blackberry juice, but they were carefree and happy. What better childhood could they have?

We also had staying with us the Duke's eldest son, William, a dear boy of whom I was most fond, and naturally destined for the navy. I would see him to school and write to him every week, sending him presents as I did all the children when their time came. Sometimes the Duke of Cumberland's son, FitzErnest, also came to stay at Bushy. His father took little interest in the boy, but he was very much loved by me and he too came to regard Bushy as his home.

No child would ever lose out on love and attention from me, no matter what his background.

I loved to plan birthday celebrations. I might bring in a conjurer from a local fair to entertain the children, or a band so that they could dance. And there were indeed ponies and donkeys for them to ride. Dogs and cats, rabbits and hamsters, not forgetting Polly, our pet parrot.

Christmas was always a joy with a full and merry house, in which the Duke delighted. I was more shy in company, preferring not to put myself forward.

Of course children are sick sometimes; then I would sit up with them at night, rub embrocation on their chests if they had a cough, nurse their colds or dose of measles. I would read them stories and every night visit each child's bedroom before retiring to my own. They were, and still are, the world to me.

As was my custom I took Freddles, as we came to call him, with me to Drury Lane when I returned to work in the spring of 1800. And to my joy, in May, the Duke informed me that the King himself was to attend a performance.

'He wishes to see *She Would and She Would Not*. Can you do that for him, dearest?'

'With pleasure.' I believed I was yet again in the family way, but would not be showing for some months, and my health was very much improved.

'For once His Majesty will be accompanied by the Queen and the princesses,' William said, giving me one of his most tender kisses. 'I think they wish to view more closely the lady who has so captured my heart.'

My stomach lurched in a conflict of excitement and trepidation. The royal family might be tolerant of my presence in the Duke's life, but no attempt had been made to meet either me or our children. Would this be the moment when they did? I wondered. 'Hypolita is one of my most famous roles so I will do my utmost not to let you down, although pleasing Her Majesty will not be easy.'

As things turned out, pleasing either one of them was the least of our concerns. The Duke himself led the royal party into their box. Sheridan was supervising backstage and I was watching from the wings, waiting to go on. As the King entered there came the loud crack of a pistol. To my horror a man in the pit had fired a shot, narrowly missing the King. A great gasp went up from the terrified audience and perhaps, in the midst of considerable confusion, the Queen thought the noise came from backstage, for she carried on walking into the box. I saw the King frantically signal to her not to enter, then heard him say: 'They are letting off squibs and perhaps there may be more.' As if trying to stop her.

But Queen Charlotte was no fool and quickly realized what had occurred. 'My dear, is it safe to remain? Should the show not be cancelled?'

'Certainly it must continue,' said the King, and bravely stepped forward to show that he was unharmed. More gasps from the audience, followed by rousing cheers.

While this was going on, William had leapt over the edge of the royal box and flung himself at the would-be assailant, manhandling the fellow to the ground, along with one or two other noble gentlemen who came to assist. It was the bravest thing I had ever seen him do.

The audience were in near pandemonium by this time. 'Put him up on stage,' someone cried.

'Aye, let's see him properly bound.'

Fearing the bucks in the pit might turn nasty and call for the man to be strung up there and then, I walked to the front of the stage and put up my hands to quieten them. 'My friends, do not fear, all is well. The miscreant has been secured, and will be properly dealt with. As you see the King is safe, and the evening's performance will shortly recommence.'

The prisoner was then frog-marched from the theatre by the constabulary, and dispatched to the prison in Cold Bath Fields. He was later identified as James Hadfield, a dragoon with the Duke of York's company, and duly incarcerated in Bedlam on the grounds of insanity.

But that was still to come. On the night in question the audience were responding to my calming words and beginning to settle. To my astonishment Sheridan handed me the words of a new verse for 'God Save the King', which he had that very moment scribbled down.

'Sing it, Dora,' he instructed, but I did not feel I was the right person for such a task.

I handed the verse to Michael Kelly, who stepped forward and led the entire company with his amazing voice, the audience joining in with gusto. They sang the verse, 'Our father, prince and friend', three times, savouring the words, before Kelly finally brought the rendition to a close.

The King and Queen stood proudly smiling throughout, but as they settled themselves to watch the performance I could see that the princesses were far from happy. What a terrible shock for them, poor creatures: so rarely allowed out in public, and on an evening which should have brought them nothing but pleasure, they instead saw their father almost assassinated before their eyes.

*   *   *

I was joined the next day at Somerset Street by an old friend, James Boaden, who wished to ease his mind that I was quite well after the fracas. We enjoyed a dish of tea and a little light refreshment while discussing the horror of seeing our monarch so attacked, remarking upon his equable composure. 'I dare say His Majesty must live in fear of revolution reaching our own shores. Fortunately, no real harm was done and the man quickly restrained, thanks to the Duke's quick action. He spent the night at the palace, anxious to calm his sisters after their fright.' I strummed my fingers lightly over my lute, smiling at young George who had decided to engage in a play fight with our visitor. Boaden also liked to bring me the latest gossip. Not necessarily good, as in this case.

'All the papers are full of it this morning, expressing admiration for the bravery of the Duke of Clarence, and great relief at the safety of the King. Unfortunately, some are saying that it was not appropriate for your good self to address the house as you did, Dora, in the presence of the Queen and the princesses.'

My fingers stilled. 'What nonsense! I did nothing much at all, and certainly nothing wrong. *I* was not the one who attempted to kill the King, and someone needed to calm the audience. Since it was I who would be facing them first onstage, the task surely fell to me. Why would I refuse simply because the Queen was present? What difference did that make?'

'They claim that you are not fit to be in Her Majesty's company at all,' Boaden said, avoiding my eyes by feigning to field my son's attacks while actively encouraging him to continue the game.

I could feel the warmth and colour slip from my cheeks, as if the spring sunshine was not shining into my drawing room and my beautiful children were not playing about my feet. 'Is that because I am not considered to be a decent, respectable citizen, but one who should be kept locked away, unfit for public viewing?'

Boaden sadly shook his head. 'Do not take these things to heart, Dora. There are always moralists who will loudly prate their opinions. It is but a storm in a teacup. All that matters is the King is safe, as are the princesses, although Princess

Amelia will take some time to recover, I believe. My dear, this boy is a veritable Hercules.'

I looked at my six-year-old son pummelling poor Boaden with his small fists as if in a boxing ring, while eighteen-month-old Mary had her arms clasped about one of my old friend's knees, hanging on like the grinning monkey she surely was. I couldn't help but laugh. What cared I for gossip? Had I not put all that scandal and mischief behind me and was at the peak of my career and happiness? I had no intention of allowing them to sully my life again. My fame was stronger than ever, and all was going well for me. More importantly, I was blessed with the most wonderful family, and a brave lover who did not hesitate to overpower a would-be assassin. I was indeed the most fortunate of women.

'Listen to this,' I said, changing the subject. 'I have written a song, "The Bluebell of Scotland", all about a brave young man going to war, which is to be published. Let me sing it for you.

Oh where, tell me where is your highland laddie gone?
Oh where, tell me where is your highland laddie gone?
He's gone with streaming banners where noble deeds are done
And it's oh! in my heart I wish him safe at home.

By the time I had finished my soldier song the children were dancing, Boaden was singing with me, and we had quite forgotten the unpleasant criticisms from the press.

The country was at last enjoying a period of peace, the Treaty of Amiens finally coming to fruition in March 1802. How long it would last no one could say, but it came as a great relief to all. By then I had added Elizabeth, born in January 1801, and Adolphus, born in February 1802, to our growing family. Mrs Siddons was apparently threatening to retire while I was working harder than ever.

Every August the Duke would go to Brighton, and he would often take the three older boys with him where they could enjoy the sea bathing. I was touring in Kent, dreaming every night of my new son, now known as Molpuss, the most melancholy and dissatisfied woman in Margate. As it turned out it was just as well the children were not with me, as I had a scare of my own while on my way to Canterbury from Margate, quite late one Sunday evening. I rarely slept well when I was away from home so it seemed to make sense to save time by setting out after the show, which turned out to be a bad mistake.

Thomas was with me, of course, and my maid. Turner was driving the coach. Thankfully Lloyd was with me also, and it was he who first noticed that something was amiss. The summer night was warm and wet, and we were all tired. I cushioned my head on the squabs, the sound of the wheels swishing in the mud soon lulling me to sleep. After a time, Lloyd shook me gently awake.

'I have no wish to alarm you, madam, but I fear we are being followed by what appear to be two black-coated highwaymen. They have been behind us for some miles, ever since we left Sittingbourne.'

I felt my heart quake a little, but moments later came the sound of galloping hooves as one of the horses approached the carriage. The brigand must have set about the post boy as I heard Turner call out to him to leave the lad alone. His bravery won him a beating, and I cried out in fear as Lloyd attempted to calm me and the poor maid, who was by now in hysterics. The second highwayman brought the carriage to a halt while the first again struck Turner, this time across his face so that he fell from where he sat atop the leading horse. I saw my valiant driver at once scramble to his feet, determined to protect us. Thomas too attempted to retaliate and was likewise struck for his pains.

'Leave us be, we are nought but poor strolling players,' shouted Lloyd.

They must have seen that we had nothing of value, or else thought themselves out-numbered, for the pair suddenly turned tail and rode off. I collapsed with relief, and it was some time before I could stop shaking. We drove the last three miles to Canterbury at top speed and I vowed never to travel at night again, no matter what hours it might save me.

As if this were not bad enough, I then experienced a further disaster when at Margate a week later my gown caught fire, with flames up to the waist, while playing in *The Country Girl*.

'Notwithstanding all these disasters,' I wrote to the Duke, 'I shall come home safe to you and the dear children.'

Twenty-Three

'I am perfectly satisfied with Mrs Jordan . . .'

By 1803 the older boys were at school at Sunbury, George being almost ten and Henry a year younger. The Duke's son William was in the navy, and I gave birth to another daughter, Augusta, in November. The year following Fanny came to me demanding a home of her own. 'I am twenty-two years old,' she reminded me, 'and surely deserve my own establishment. I refuse to live any longer with Aunt Hester. Her temper grows shorter by the day and I will take no more of it.'

'It is true that while we were at Trelethyn we found it so much more peaceful to be without her,' Lucy added.

I had been quietly reading my copy of *Lyrical Ballads*, very much a favourite since my friend Coleridge sent it to me some months ago, proving my faith in the young man's talent had not been misplaced. Now I took off my spectacles and set it down with a sigh, for I had to agree. Sadly, my sister had allowed herself to become overwhelmed by bitterness and envy, the very worst kind of spinster, and nothing I did could alter that fact.

'If she has led you the life she did me for many years, I do not wonder at your resolution.'

'Why do you always pander to Fanny's demands?' the Duke said when I told him that I intended to buy them a house in Golden Square.

'Because there is no one else to provide for her, and she feels very much the odd one out. Dodee and Lucy did at least know that Ford loved them, although he neglects them now he has a new family.'

'She is using you,' he snapped. He too was sometimes short of temper and could roar like a bull if the mood took him, but I only smiled, privately wondering why he never thought to apply that charge to his own demands upon my money.

In fact all three girls moved in together. Mrs Sinclair, an aunt on my father's side who had been with them in Wales, was to act as companion. Hester would remain for the moment at Gifford Lodge.

'I may move to Trelethyn permanently,' she sulkily remarked, when these plans were made known to her. 'I certainly have no wish to be a burden to you.'

'You are never that, dearest. How would I have managed without you?' It could be said that my entire family was a burden to me, but I preferred not to think of them in those terms. The responsibility for their comfort and security was surely mine, and I was glad to be in a position to help, if perhaps they stretched my finances more than they might appreciate. 'It is simply that my girls are growing up. Even Lucy is fifteen now, and Dodee seventeen. How did the years pass so quickly?'

I did not tell Hester that I had taken out a mortgage on Gifford Lodge some time ago, the interest paid quarterly out of my allowance.

'If the money could be £700 instead of £550 it would serve me still more, as I have no prospect of any immediate assistance from Drury Lane,' I had written to Coutts at the time. More recently I had felt obliged to lend dear Billy a further £450 to pay the upholsterer. Balancing my books took up an unreasonable amount of my time and energy. And soon I would again have to stop work as this latest baby was almost due.

The Duke sat holding my hand as I lay thrashing in my bed, sweating with fever. It had come upon me within twenty-four hours of giving birth and, increasingly anxious, he kept on stroking and patting my hand, murmuring loving words, praying for the fever to abate, as was I in my muddled state. The house was silent, the only sound that of my own small gasping breaths. The door knocker had been tied up, straw laid upon the courtyard outside, or so I was told, the floors covered with cloths so that nothing could disturb me. The entire household crept about holding their breaths as I lay close to death.

The fever had begun on the Saturday evening and as the hours slipped slowly by, the night seemed endless. Cold cloths were constantly wrung out to ease my aching head, but did nothing to ease my pain, and William became increasingly fearful.

'You must try to rally, my darling. How would I manage without my Little Pickle?'

By Monday morning I was barely sensible but vaguely aware of the doctor's presence, for I could discern some conversation about a fine healthy son, but the mother needing to be bloodied and blistered to balance the humours.

I knew full well that the cure was often worse than the affliction, but clearly there was no alternative. Child-bed fever was notoriously dangerous and I knew my life was in danger, before even the doctor leaned close to whisper that he would do his very best for me.

'I cannot abide the thought of her being cut,' I heard the Duke say.

'I will not cut her, your Grace, but use only leeches.'

My beloved's face held a horrified fascination as the worms were put on my pale, milk-white skin. I cried out, wanting to rip them off to stop their biting jaws, but that would have been folly. I must trust the doctor. I saw agony in my Billy's eyes, as if he were sharing my pain, and I loved him for that. A tear formed and slid down my cheek.

'Do they hurt her?' he asked the doctor, his voice coming as if from a far distance, seeping through the heat that pounded in my skull.

'Not excessively so, but they will hopefully help to bring down the fever.'

'Is she aware of what is happening to her? Can she even hear me?'

'I very much doubt it.'

I can, I cried silently, my fevered mind filled with images of a young girl fleeing from the stage on her first night, of the malicious jealousy of her rivals, and her adoring public running after her carriage to catch a glimpse of her. That must be me, I thought, and I saw the leering grin of Daly as he ravaged me, the faces of my dear children, and that of my beloved Billy. Was he real or a dream? I felt the grip of his hand on mine and knew instinctively that he was with me still, giving me strength.

'She generally has little difficulty with child bearing, save for one or two occasions,' the Duke was saying. 'I need not inform you that with nine children a mother is absolutely necessary, not forgetting an intercourse of uninterrupted happiness for more than thirteen years.'

I could have cried at those words, realizing just how very much he loved me.

When Doctor Nixon was satisfied that sufficient blood had been drawn off, he gently turned me on to my stomach, heated some cups and set them at intervals upon my bare back. As they cooled, a vacuum formed which raised blisters. These were then pricked to let out the foulness within. The pain was so horrendous I wasn't sure how much longer I could tolerate it.

'They must be kept open, the scum periodically drawn off,' he informed Miss Sketchley, who was acting as my nurse. 'She must have someone with her day and night, kept cool and rested. I will call again tomorrow.'

'For more of the same?' asked William in some distress, remembering my whimpers during the cupping.

There was pity in the doctor's face as he looked upon the Duke. 'If necessary. But Mrs Jordan is healthy and strong, and, as you say, has largely dealt with childbirth easily in the past. I see no reason why she should not make a full recovery.'

I could think of a thousand reasons, all of them related to the terrible pain that consumed me. Why did they not simply let me die?

And yet, miraculously, I did not die. When Nixon called the following morning he expressed his delight to find me much improved.

'My head aches as if a clapper bell were ringing in it,' I complained, and the doctor smiled and patted my hand.

'It will pass, your strong constitution is serving you well.'

'And my baby, is he well?' I asked, tense with anxiety.

'He is hale and hearty, as will be his mother ere long.' He leaned closer to whisper in my ear. 'Although she may consider making this one her last.'

I gazed at him, wide-eyed. 'If only I knew how, doctor.'

And as my child was put into my arms I quite forgot the

pain in my head, the difficulties of the birth, and even the fever and the painful suck of the leeches. Here was my son, and here was my dear Billy beside me, as always.

'I think we shall call this one Augustus,' the Duke decreed, 'since the last one was Augusta,' and he beamed at me in that jolly way he had.

'As you wish, my dear,' I agreed, as always.

'I've been put in charge of the Teddington Volunteers,' the Duke complained to the Prince when he came to supper at Bushy one evening. The two brothers had discussed how long Pitt was likely to remain in power, considering that his second term of office was not going so well as the first. Now they were back to their favourite topic of war and the escalation of further trouble with France. 'Stab me if they aren't a confounded nuisance. Surely there are more important matters upon which to spend my time and energy?'

'No doubt you did too good a job with the local yeomanry. And what does Mrs Jordan think?' the Prince enquired, turning to me where I sat at the head of the table.

I smiled. 'That if he cannot make them serviceable then let them go to the devil.'

The Prince of Wales roared with laughter. 'You ever have a way with words.'

'She has indeed,' William agreed with a grin.

'I'm delighted to see that you have made such a good recovery, dear lady, from your recent lying in.'

'Thank you, I shall be returning to the stage by the first week of May.'

'Then I shall raise a glass to your continued success. I'm quite sure you will be wonderfully received, as ever.'

William frowned. 'Did I tell you that I am having a new portrait of her done by Beechey? He always captures her well, I think, only this time I want a more sedate, regal look.'

'Quite right. As mistress of Bushy Park rather than simply your mistress, eh?' the Prince said, casting me such a teasing glance that I blushed and hastily excused myself.

'Forgive me if I retire, Sir, but I am still not quite myself.'

The Prince rose, bowing over my hand as he kissed it and

bid me good night. He was ever kind to me. But once outside the supper room I stood with my back to the door, listening, curious to know where this conversation was leading and why my Billy was frowning so.

'I have also commissioned a young painter, a George Harlow, to paint the children,' the Duke went on. 'The fellow has done one or two sketches already for me to see. I think he'll do rather well by them. I particularly like the one of Freddles, Eliza and three-year-old Molpuss, or Lolly as we tend to call him now. I want the boy to be painted holding a crimson banner with the royal coat of arms emblazoned upon it. What think you of that?'

'Very patriotic,' the Prince drily remarked.

'I may be prejudiced but I think them most handsome, charming children.'

'Of course you are prejudiced, and why not, for goodness sake? I too confess young George is a great favourite of mine, as you well know. Would I'd been blessed with such a fine boy, although I adore my darling Charlotte. And they are indeed most handsome, and exceeding well-mannered children, as is our entire family. But can you afford all this extravagance? What of your debts, brother?'

'The day will come when Parliament will be obliged to clear our debts,' was William's response, carefully avoiding answering the question.

'You take the words from my mouth. You could always choose to marry, then Pitt would be obliged to settle them as he did mine. Did I not once suggest the daughter of the Landgrave of Hesse-Cassel as a wife?'

My heart seemed to turn over and I pressed myself close against the door, anxious to hear my Billy's reply.

'I am perfectly satisfied with Mrs Jordan, and nothing has changed since then except that she has given me five more children.'

I closed my eyes on a breath of relief, a small smile playing at my lips. How this man did love me.

'But she is not your wife, and never can be,' the Prince gently reminded him. 'Although I can see that having almost lost the love of your life, you may wish it to be otherwise.'

'But would the King allow it? Would Parliament agree? Could I legitimize my children? I rather think George and Sophy are beginning to suffer from the irregularity of their parents' position.'

'So what do you intend to do about that?' his brother softly enquired.

Silence followed this remark, lasting for some moments, and then the Duke said: 'What think you of the recent proclamation of Napoleon as King of Italy? Will he attempt to invade Britain?'

Whereupon I hurried away, deeply puzzled and slightly unnerved. They said eavesdroppers never did hear good of themselves, yet the Duke had declared his love for me in no uncertain terms. But was that enough to keep me safe?

I was staring at him in a state somewhere between disappointment and shock. 'Leave the stage? But you have never asked such a thing of me before, why would you do so now?'

'With nine children I think it perhaps time you devoted your attention entirely to them. You have said yourself that other actresses have done so, Elizabeth Farren for instance. Mrs Siddons even has now retired.'

'I shall believe that when I see it. Siddons has carried out her very last performance four times to my certain knowledge.' I felt quite sick inside. How could I give up what made me who I am? Never again to experience the joy of stepping on stage, which was like home to me: not as Bushy is, but as vitally important to my wellbeing. And there were more practical considerations. William had given me no reason to suppose that he would grow tired of me but I must always keep in mind that I was not, and never could be, his wife, as that overheard conversation with the Prince illustrated only too clearly. Therefore, much as I loved my children, it was essential that I hold on to my independence and an income.

'It is not seemly for a mother of so many children to work.' His tone carried that note of stubborn authority which the Duke always adopted when he wanted his own way.

'It is quite unfair of you to ask this of me, William. Did we not agree that if I retired the public would soon forget me?' I said, feeling the need to remind him of our arrangement from the start.

'The situation has changed.'

'In what way?'

'You are more famous now. You could return at any time to the stage and they would welcome you with open arms.'

'I would be finished!' I protested. Unfortunately, the Duke could be most desperately obstinate.

'Are you refusing to obey me?' he challenged, his temper quickly rising as it did on occasion.

'A *wife* promises to obey, William. I am not a wife so have taken no such vow.'

A crimson flush crept up his throat and his jaw tightened. 'Is that meant as some sort of criticism? Because if so . . .'

'No, dearest Billy, it is not at all. I knew from the start how things would be, but you ask too great a sacrifice.' Keeping my tone reasonable and a smile firmly fixed in place, I put out my hands, anxious to placate him. 'As you know I have responsibilities that I cannot simply abandon. My girls, my public. You always said that my being absent during the week when performing in London was not a problem, nor even when I was on tour, because you were often attending the Lords or various committees and charities with which you're involved.'

He scowled, looking rather like a sullen schoolboy caught out in a lie. 'Perhaps I would now prefer you to be less in the public eye.'

I stifled a sigh, battling with the irritation that was growing inside. This request was like a bolt from the blue, totally unexpected, and I had no intention of giving up my career without a fight. 'You have always expressed pride in my talent and fame, said you were delighted that I am adored by so many.'

'That may be so,' he conceded. 'Nevertheless, for the moment at least, I would prefer it if you gave up the stage. It would be more fitting.'

'But we desperately need the money I earn,' I cried. The moment I said these words I regretted them, but could not snatch them back.

'Hang it, I have an income now of eighteen thousand pounds a year,' he roared. 'I need no help from you!'

'Well, you've had plenty in the past,' I snapped right back.

We gazed upon each other in complete horror. This was, without question, the worst quarrel we'd ever had. It was quite dreadful. We did not often disagree, largely because I was careful never to overstep the mark, or to expect more than I was entitled to. But the Duke had always been subject to sudden fits of rage. They would rise fast and furious, although as quickly vanish, never lasting long for he was generally the kindest of men. And we always made up afterwards most delightfully.

Now the silence between us was profound as he simmered with rage.

I wanted to ask how we would afford to maintain Bushy, to pay school fees and servants' wages, live as well as we did if I were to stop working. His allowance, though substantial, never went as far as he would like, not when all the social activities and responsibilities expected of a royal prince were taken into account. And he could never resist being led into gambling debts by the Prince of Wales. Yet my influence was severely limited by my lack of status.

Having reminded myself of this fact, I gracefully gave in. 'Very well, I shall do as you ask and take a break. It is clearly important to you and I ask nothing more from life than to please you.' I was trembling, close to tears as we hugged and made up, but not for the world would I risk losing him.

Twenty-Four

'I dreamed of everyone at Bushy, my heart crying out
to be home'

Following this request, or rather demand, I informed Drury Lane
that I was taking a sabbatical and resisted all attempts by Bannister,
my leading man, to entice me back with new plays. Throughout
that spring and summer of 1806 I no longer needed to dash off
in the carriage every day for rehearsals. Nor did I need the
expense of the house in Somerset Street, which I let go. And
instead of fussing over costumes and make-up I was able to relax
in a simple gown and fichu. We lived a modest, quiet life, so
quiet I would sometimes joke that we could be dead and buried
without anyone knowing we had even been ill.

The poor Duke grieved over the death of his friend Nelson
and attended his funeral in January. But then we were beset with
family problems. George was sent home from Great Marlow,
the military college, in February in disgrace for not paying proper
attention to his studies. His misery wrung out my heart, but I
feared the reason for such neglect on his part may well have a
deeper cause. I said as much to William, suspecting he thought
the same.

'Do you think he was bullied or ridiculed because of me?'

'Nonsense,' he said, although his eyes did not meet mine.
'The boy is clearly bored with lessons and seeks adventure, as
his father did before him.'

He was certainly a high-spirited, intelligent boy, and not
insensitive to the world around him. In our hearts we both
knew that George's unhappiness was due to the irregularity of
his parents' relationship, his illegitimacy, rather than ineptitude
with his studies. But neither the Duke nor I made any further
comment on the subject, either to George himself or to each
other. Where was the point, since a situation that could not
be cured must be endured?

Worse news came in March when we learned that the Duke's son William had been drowned at sea when the *Blenheim* became caught up in a cyclone and foundered off Madagascar. How we grieved for that fine boy. I had loved him as if he were my own, and he was but seventeen. What a terrible waste of a young life. The poor Duke was utterly heartbroken. Nothing meant more to him than his dear children.

But happy relations between our two selves were thankfully restored and by August he was sufficiently recovered to celebrate his forty-first birthday in fine style. We held it in the new dining room, which everyone admired, as they did the newly painted clouds on the ceiling of the hall, the bronze pilasters and lamps suspended from an eagle. The grounds, where music was played, were open to the public, and in the evening four of the Duke's brothers came. The Prince of Wales himself led me to the head of the table where I was to preside over dinner. I was deeply flattered, and foolish enough to believe that abandoning my career was beginning to pay off, so that I might be fully welcomed into the royal family after all.

But yet again I was attacked by the press. William Cobbett branded my children bastards, accused me of vice and immorality, and their father of being guilty of a crime both in law and religion. He claimed the whole birthday celebration to be a lie on my part, as the royal family were far too pious and moral to involve themselves in such an occasion. By this he meant *be seen in my company*!

It near broke my heart to see William's reaction. 'How dare the fellow defile us in that way,' he roared, more angry than I had ever seen him. I certainly felt that my sacrifice had been in vain.

I did enjoy having more time to spend with my children, and in March 1807 Amelia was born; as I was by then forty-five, I sincerely hoped she would be my last child. There were yet again builders working at Bushy and for a while I feared my bedroom would not be ready in time. The Duke was away, as he so often was, and I wrote a mild complaint of the stress I was under.

'I really don't know how to manage the bricklayers.'

Fortunately he returned at once, and assured me the room would be ready by March.

'Good, as that is when I shall need it,' was my patient response. But by the time little Mely was six months old I knew I needed to earn some money, that the question of my returning to work could be ignored no longer.

I approached the Duke with caution, casually mentioning a pressing tax bill as I put forward my request. 'In addition, dearest, my older girls are coming up to a time in their lives when they are likely to marry and will require dowries. I must do right by them, make sure they marry well and are properly set up. And you know full well that I have no wish to be a burden to you.'

Perhaps because of all the trauma we had suffered, he made no objections.

Drury Lane welcomed me back, if at reduced fees, with jubilant applause and packed houses despite my long absence. Sheridan seemed relieved to see me, perhaps because his debts were greater than ever. This time I took a house in Mortimer Street where I was able to have the children with me, although we naturally returned to Bushy each weekend.

Oh, but it was good to be back on stage, to feel again that moment of pure exhilaration when an audience falls about with laughter at something I have said or done, or simply at the expression on my face. It is always an honour and a pleasure to bring people such delight.

The Duke was able to gain young George a commission in the 10th Hussars as a cornet, which made the boy proud to carry the colours of his regiment. He faithfully promised his father that he would mend his ways. William himself took him to Portsmouth to see him embark with his regiment for Portugal, as his own father had once taken him. I could hardly bear even to think of my fourteen-year-old son at war, yet like all mothers I must learn to let him go.

As for dear Henry, I had been obliged to swallow my fears and make no protest as he went as a midshipman at the tender age of eleven with Admiral Keats to the Baltic.

The poor Duke, however, was still suffering from a severe lack of purpose. And having supplied the nation with three recruits already in William, George and Henry, and with three more boys to follow, he begged yet again to be given a command at sea. This time he had every hope of having his wish fulfilled.

He wrote to me from Portsmouth to explain his coming absence in one of the many letters he sent me while I was in London.

> *Through your excellence and kindness in private life I am the happiest man possible and look forward only to a temporary separation to make that happiness more complete from having provided for our dear children. My love and best and tenderest wishes attend you all at Bushy . . . Adieu till we meet and ever believe me, dearest Dora, Yours most affectionately . . .*

I fully sympathized with this need in him, for all it filled me with terror at the thought of his actually going, but of course nothing of the sort actually happened. The Duke's request, as always, was refused.

His brother the Duke of York was then involved in a most dreadful scandal where his mistress, Mary Anne Clarke, was found to be using his position as commander-in-chief to sell commissions. The scandalmongers once again did their worst and then like hungry wolves turned upon us, accusing the Duke of having seduced one of my older girls.

'So far as I am aware neither one of my daughters is pregnant, and they look upon the Duke as a father figure, not a lover,' was my sharp response to anyone who repeated these cruel and infamous reports to me. But, much as we might try to ignore them, they were deeply hurtful and offensive. Were we never to be left in peace?

'The Duke is an example for half the fathers and husbands in the world,' I protested, which is most certainly true.

And then, to add insult to injury, Drury Lane burned down in February of 1809. I was mortified. What ill luck to have enjoyed but a few short months back on stage, only to lose it again.

But however inconvenient for me, to Sheridan it was a disaster of mammoth proportions. He and I had often been at odds during the twenty-four years I'd worked for him, but I felt nothing but sympathy for him now.

'We have at least managed to salvage the theatre's charter,' I said, striving to offer some sort of consolation.

'But not much else. And I doubt I can recoup my losses this time.'

'The company will be able to "borrow" other theatres, so surely you can continue? You have rebuilt before, why not again?'

'I need backers, Dora, and so far there is little sign of my ever finding one.'

He was not the man he had been, certainly no longer the clever wit who had written those two marvellous plays.

I threw myself into performing in several benefits to support stage hands who had lost their jobs. But then the Duke, for reasons best known to himself, again requested that I withdraw from the stage.

This time I was prepared. Remembering how he'd used the words 'more fitting' were I not to appear, as if the King or Queen objected to seeing my handbills all over town, I tactfully put my suggestion to him.

'Would it perhaps be more appropriate if I were not to appear on the *London* stage? Would you prefer it if I were to confine myself to touring?'

His face seemed to light up with relief. 'Ah, what a very sensitive and understanding person you are, Little Pickle. That is a splendid notion. Yes, let us agree that you will take no more engagements in London, but simply tour.'

The prospect of spending my entire time on tour filled me with dismay: the cold, flea-bitten lodgings, the dreadful food, the endless travelling, being constantly beset by people from dawn to dusk, with twenty hands to help me out of my carriage. And very often the most amusing entertainment to be found to fill the long hours when I was not on stage was only to read, read, read. But touring was better than nothing, and allowed me to continue earning.

And if I were never seen in London the royal family would not be constantly reminded of my presence, I thought, although I refrained from saying as much.

And so I returned to endlessly touring the provinces. It might be Margate and Canterbury, then there was the northern circuit from York as far as Edinburgh, and on occasion Manchester or Birmingham, neither of which town I cared much for, although the houses were always good, and the people most respectful and friendly. The West Country was ever my favourite. I rather think that if I did not have Bushy I could live in Bath. It is a most delightful town.

But my next engagement was in Ireland. What on earth had possessed me to agree to go there?

The sea was rougher than I remembered, but then I had only ever done this crossing once in my life before when I was running away from Daly, so how was I to judge? The Irish Sea is well known for strong currents that pull you this way and that. As we heaved and tossed in our misery, the prospect of returning to my native land depressing me even more than the weather, I couldn't help but think of young William, his dear life cut short in such a terrible way. His death made me fear for my own sons: George in Corunna caught up in the war, Henry still somewhere in the Baltic. I worried about them constantly and was a constant correspondent to both my boys. As was their father, advising them against gambling and drink, and not to waste money.

While we were in Bath on this current tour, we all walked to the stagecoach and expressed universal joy to find letters from dear George. In my reply I urged him to write often, and to use a dictionary for his spelling which was quite atrocious.

I also gave my eldest son advice on how to address the Duke.

'. . . as you are now a Lieutenant and employed on actual service it would be more appropriate if in future when you mention the Duke, that you should say my father, or the Duke. It may prevent any little ridicule that might be excited by your saying Papa.'

It was, I believe, important to do what I could to protect my children from the derision I had suffered in the past for my own lack of legitimacy. Sophy too was causing concern as she frequently refused to stir from her bedroom.

'What is wrong with the girl?' her father would fret, and I would offer what reassurance I could.

'She is but suffering from a headache as her constitution will shortly undergo a change. She is fourteen, and we must be as understanding as we can.'

But I think the problem was more troubling than simple biology. Both my older daughters had recently married: Fanny to Thomas Alsop, a young clerk from the ordnance office, whose temper I feared very much. Dear quiet Dodee had wed his friend, Frederick March, also a clerk, only two months ago. I believed the pair to be very happy, a complete Darby and Joan. He too was illegitimate and I provided both girls with a substantial dowry of £2,000, of which in Dodee's case I paid half up front. The Duke had agreed to pay the rest as interest on several loans I'd made him over the years. I also agreed to provide an allowance of £200 per year.

How I longed for a respectable happy marriage for each of my younger daughters. But is that possible with me for a mother?

'Will this journey never end?' poor dear Lucy moaned as she retched into the bowl I held for her. She had been a welcome companion throughout this most successful tour, although by now she might well be regretting having offered to come at all.

It certainly seemed a lifetime since we had left Holyhead. Even our beds were soaking wet and there was no comfort to be found anywhere. We were all mightily relieved when, after ten long hours at sea, the ship finally docked and I could see the customs house at last. We were taken straight to our lodgings in St James's Street.

I saw at once that they were not so clean as the ones we had in Bath, although at least they were not devoured by bugs as were the beds at the Bush Inn at Bristol. And the weather had improved, the June day warm and pleasant, most welcome after the cold spring we'd endured with snow as late as April, and a sea of mud and water all around Bath.

'The managers, Mr Crampton and Mr Atkinson, have called to see you, Mama,' Lucy said, her own pallor as white as the sheets – whiter perhaps, looking at this particular linen.

'Tell them I am too much fatigued and unwell to see anybody.'
Had I nursed the hope that a good dinner would restore
me, I was soon disenchanted. When the food finally appeared
at eight o'clock it was quite inedible. We were obliged to eat
some cold soup that we'd brought with us.

'Do I not deserve every penny of the money I earn, with
what I have to suffer?' I asked of my daughter.

'Indeed you do,' she agreed. 'And the first thing we must
do is to clean up our quarters.'

'If we can do so with tact. The Irish easily take offence
from the interfering English.'

After a moderately comfortable night in which the bed was
at least dry and did not rock from side to side, we were woken
early by a noisy commotion downstairs. I sent Thomas to
investigate and he returned within minutes with disturbing
news.

'The place is heaving with people anxious to see you. They
have brought you fish and fowl, flowers and sweetmeats, gifts
galore to lay at your feet.'

My heart sank, as of all things I do like to guard my privacy.
I had learned that in my particular station of life it was wise
to keep one's head down and avoid company. Had I not suffered
enough from the scandalmongers? 'Pray thank them kindly,
Thomas, and explain that I never go out when from home.'

'Very good, madam.'

He had, of course, delivered this message countless times
before on any number of occasions. Apart from any other
consideration, I'd learned to my cost that if I was not careful
I could find myself on public view from the moment I
breakfasted to long after the fall of the curtain at midnight.

Lucy returned from a trip to the bakery to purchase bread
with sorrier news. 'It seems that we have arrived far too soon
and you will not be needed for several days yet. Kemble has
still not completed his own engagement, and is in a rage at
your even being here, his wife claiming you did it deliberately
in order to injure him.'

I was utterly devastated, and rightly angry. 'Goodness
gracious, the fault was not mine, more likely a piece of bad
management.' I found it quite distressing to think of the extra

time I could have enjoyed at home had I known. Lucy slumped
in misery on the bed and I wrapped my arms about her as my
mother had used to do with me.

'I assure you, dearest, we are not staying here. I would pay
ten guineas to be allowed to quit this place.'

I sent Thomas to fetch us dinner from a local tavern that
night, and the next day, having no wish to go out, I returned
the hired carriage as I regretted the expense. We did not find
better quarters but at least employed a cook, although I was
startled when she served us in her bare feet.

'I beg you to put on your shoes and stockings,' I said, but
she only laughed at my fussing.

'Sure and I can't be bothered with them. I think meself
much cleaner without them. It's a nadeless custom, to sure,'
she concluded, as if that settled the matter.

'Well, I suppose you will not be dressing the dinner with
your toes, so I must endeavour to be content,' I replied with
a sigh of resignation. There really is no telling the Irish anything.

'Mr Jones, the proprietor, has invited you to dinner on
Friday,' Lucy informed me later that day.

'Then you must politely decline. Say that I am unwell.'

She looked alarmed. 'But he may cancel your engagement,
Mama, if he thinks you ill.' She was such a gentle, unassuming
child, I thought.

'Then ask him to postpone the occasion until I am fully
recovered from the journey.'

As it turned out we dined instead that Friday with an old
friend, Mrs Lefanu, Sheridan's sister, a *huge* woman, and no
wonder judging by the lavish hospitality she offered. I swear
I have never seen so much food, nor a salmon so large. Its tail
rested on my plate and the head almost in the lap of my
neighbour opposite, an Englishman who was, I believe, as
astonished as myself.

'Would you take a little salmon?' he was asked.

'I think I have quite enough on my plate already,' he drily
remarked, and I dared not catch his eye for fear of laughing
out loud.

Both Lucy and I ate our fill, but declined a sip of the very
large cup of porter that was passed around. The prospect of

putting my mouth to the same place as others, even if the cup was silver, made my stomach heave even more than the rough crossing.

'I always hated my native land, if that is what it is, but now I detest it,' I told my daughter on our journey back to our lodgings in the chair we had hired in place of the carriage. And that night I dreamed of everyone at Bushy, my heart crying out to be home.

I hated to be absent for too long. The King could not maintain his fragile state of health for ever, and with only the Princess Charlotte as heir following the Prince of Wales, pressure would surely be brought to bear upon the other brothers to marry. Aware as I was of this risk, I could not bear to think of it. As I tossed and turned in yet another strange bed, I brought to mind a comment of the Duke's in a recent letter to me in Bath, where he said that I had been more punctual this time. He appeared just to have found out that we 'go on together very well'.

In my reply I wrote, 'It was fortunate that you concluded the sentence with the hope that it would never be otherwise. *You* may have your doubts about it, I have none. Mind, I only answer for myself.'

I spoke in jest, as is my wont, yet I was beginning to worry, very slightly, that he was perhaps growing accustomed to my absences. Did he need me as much as he used to?

'I have read somewhere of a man that was very much in love, who left his mistress for the sake of receiving letters from her. This was great refinement certainly,' I wrote. 'For my part I like a little personal intercourse a great deal better . . .'

Not something that can be enjoyed when there is the cold Irish Sea dividing us.

Twenty-Five

'I really feel myself lost when in the world, and not fit
to live out of my own family'

Kemble was gone and rehearsals began at last, for which I was
truly thankful. We worked for some hours, then as we took a
welcome break Atkinson brought forward an old man whom
I'd seen watching from the wings.

'Do you remember me, I wonder?' he asked. 'I was the one
who dragged you on stage that first night when you ran away
to hide in the dressing room.'

I stared at him in amazement. 'Ryder? Can it really be you?'

'It is to be sure. I'm astonished myself that I'm still alive, but
filled with pride that I was the one to have instigated your career,
Dolly. May I call you Dolly? I shall always think of you as such.'

'Oh, Mr Ryder, what a pleasure it is to meet you again
after all this time,' I said, hugging the old man tight. 'And to
say thank you, for had you not dragged me back by force,
who knows what would have happened to me.' I smiled at
him, feeling a rush of gratitude at this rare meeting. 'You
offered me a kindness I did not find at . . .' I paused, not
wishing to dwell on what happened to me at Smock Alley. 'I
did not find the like again until I reached Yorkshire.'

He gave me a knowing look. 'I can well believe it. My
grandchildren are tired of my bragging about how I discovered
the famous Mrs Jordan,' he added with a chuckle. 'But you've
changed beyond recognition since those early days, Dolly, a
fine lady now indeed. The theatre, you'll see, hasn't changed
at all.' And we both laughed at that.

Echoes of my past came before me in a less pleasant manner
when I was presented with bills amounting to £394 for debts
contracted by two of my brothers! I examined them in dismay
but agreed to give the matter all due consideration, dismissing
the fellow who brought them as politely as I could.

'I know the law and am not responsible for their debts,' I vigorously protested to Lucy. 'No one can force me to pay them.'

'Yet it places you in a most awkward position, Mama, if you do not,' she very sensibly pointed out.

'I dare say you are right, but you see what a victim I have been all my life, since I was fourteen, to my ungrateful family.'

'I could call upon Sir Jonah Barrington. He is kindness itself, and may well be able to advise.'

I took her wise advice, and he came at once, although his words brought little comfort. 'It is a cruel thing your brothers have done to you, but I recommend you pay the sum immediately. Though the law may not enforce it, yet for your own sake you must submit. Whatever the cost it is not worth thinking of when compared with what those rascals could make you suffer. They would insult you both in private and in public.'

But when I continued to protest, Sir Jonah explained how Mrs Siddons once came to Ireland, and her brother Stephen managed to get himself arrested for a debt of £300 which she refused to pay. 'The consequence was that she was grossly insulted on the first night she played, and was obliged to pay it before she could appear again.'

I quaked to think of it. 'But I do not have such a sum.'

'I have,' he most generously replied. He took my hand and kissed it, as the true gentleman he was. 'Allow me to settle this unpleasant business for you, as a friend.'

'I accept only on the grounds that I will repay you as soon as I am able.' I hated to be in debt, yet responsibilities to my family, the cost of the work on Bushy, and the Duke's lifestyle seemed ever to overwhelm me.

He smiled. 'Consider the matter done.'

I was in fact able to repay his generosity once Atkinson settled with me; nevertheless the sum had come as a huge blow.

'Although I had some vague fears such a thing might happen when I came here,' I confessed to Lucy. 'You can see for yourself how my family continually endeavours to harass and use me. But let us bury all this in oblivion. I will never mention, nor if I can help it, think of the matter again. I conclude here on the second of July and shall set out on the third should the sea be afire.'

* * *

Many in Dublin must have been pleased to see me as the manager opened the doors early on the first night, nervous of an accident because of the crowds.

'I don't think I ever played *The Country Girl* so ill,' I mourned to Lucy when it was done, but she dismissed my worries as nonsense.

'You are being overly critical because of the long wait. The audience loved it.'

The next night I played Lady Teazle, and Widow Cheerly in *The Soldier's Daughter*, after that Beatrice in *Much Ado About Nothing*, with more of my repertoire following. 'Yet there is hardly a night passes but there is a fight in the gallery,' I complained.

'It is a savage sort of place,' Lucy agreed, as eager for the engagement to be over as was I.

Each morning I was beset with people, as if I were holding a levee. It was all Thomas could do to attend the door.

'Why do they come?' I asked in despair.

'It is quite the fashion, Mama,' Lucy said. 'They wish to enquire how you are after playing.'

'Most obliging of them, but I would fare better were I not so hounded and allowed time to breakfast in private. It is most tiresome.'

By ten each morning I was in rehearsal, with two long plays to get through for me to play in that night. These lasted till three o'clock, after which I would rest a little, then dress at my lodgings before being taken to the house in a chair, Thomas running alongside. On the first occasion I settled myself inside and drew the curtains, as usual, but the wretches in the street told Thomas that if I closed myself in next time they would throw stones into the chair.

'I *will* not, *cannot* abide to have them gawping at me, or seeing what I am wearing for the performance and intruding upon my privacy in that manner,' I protested when he told me.

'Perhaps a veil, madam, and a cloak would serve instead?' Thomas suggested, ever considerate. 'We want no trouble.'

I was obliged to agree with him and the second morning settled for wearing a large loose gown over my dress, and a muslin veil over my face so that I could leave the curtains undrawn. This apparently satisfied the public curiosity, as they cheered and actually declared that they liked me.

'You're a good-natured lady, to be sure, and not proud like some we could mention,' they cried.

They meant Kemble, who had caused offence because some man had presented him with a bill he did not consider correct and he'd responded by calling him an Irish rogue. He'd suffered a poor benefit as a consequence.

The work was hard and the days long, and it would be past midnight before I was done and free to return to our lodgings for supper and bed. Sadly, however, the profits from this part of the tour were proving to be a disappointment, despite my sacrifice of privacy.

'We were too sanguine with regard to the profits of this engagement,' I wrote to the Duke. 'Apparently this is the wrong time of year, the weather insufferably hot for much of the time, which puts people off from attending. I do not think I shall make above £1,200.'

I promised, however, to send him some money in the next letter, as always.

As if all this were not bad enough, the constant commotion in the theatre was a severe drain upon my energy. 'But no matter how weak from exhaustion I am, I must go on or they will pull the house down.'

Lucy laughed, thinking I exaggerated. 'You have met with nothing but kindness and attention in private, and tumults of applause in public, Mama.'

'I will admit the houses, for Dublin, are good, and nothing could be more flattering than the reception I meet with every night. But there is a rather vulgar song very expressive of my feelings on those occasions: *without your cash your kissing won't do*. I shame to say that, Lucy, even to think it. And I fear at any moment they might change their view of me and throw bottles at my head!'

She gave her charming little smile, attempting to soothe me. 'I'm sure that would never happen. They adore you.'

'You may not have noticed, dear, but there is a continual warfare between the higher and lower ranks which they carry

even into the theatre. If the boxes attempt to applaud, it is a
signal for the galleries to hiss. It is quite shocking.'

'You are simply overtired, and must rest more.'

'I cannot sleep for thinking of home, of Bushy and the dear
children.' And my Billy, I thought, wondering where he was
and what he was about while I sweated here. 'I would not go
through this again if I were to reap thousands. I must therefore
in future cut my coat according to my cloth, and after this
remain with my family. I will not lose so much of them again.
What can pay one for such a sacrifice? Not anything in this
world.'

'I suspect your feelings against Ireland, Mama, were formed
long since, as a result of the bad experiences of your youth.
Let us relax and enjoy ourselves as best we can. Social invitations are pouring in and we can surely accept some. We are
to dine with Sir Jonah Barrington on Friday, which will surely
cheer you.'

Barrington claimed to have first seen me on the Irish stage
years ago in my youth, but I have no recollection of having
met him before this week. He was, however, kindness itself,
and most charming. He told me how he longed to send his
young son, Edward, to England to school, if only he knew of
a good one, and were fit enough to take him.

'I would be glad to help,' I offered, feeling the need to repay
the favour Sir Jonah had done me by loaning me the money
to pay my brothers' debts. 'The school my sons attended would,
I am sure, be glad to take him.'

'That would be most generous of you. The boy has hopes
for the navy.'

'Then the Duke could put in a word for him.'

From then on Sir Jonah Barrington became my champion,
for which I was most grateful. Later my gratitude paled slightly
when I found myself responsible for the boy's school fees. But
then how many times has my generosity been my undoing?

The manager came to me one day to say that Charles Lennox,
the Fourth Duke of Richmond, had requested a command
performance. 'His Grace makes this plea as he is so delighted with
your acting, Mrs Jordan, and may well ask for a second.'

I, of course, conceded to the summons, accustomed as I was to more royal commands.

The performance finished early for once, at about ten o'clock. Lucy was at the Barringtons', now being most friendly with Lady Barrington, and I sat waiting for Atkinson, as he usually came at that hour to settle the weekly account.

But instead of the manager, a Mr Parkhurst from Dublin Castle was announced, which at first surprised me, until I realized he might wish to discuss a possible reprise of the command. He at once embarked upon a praise of my performance that evening, and I quickly got to my feet to thank him. I let him chatter on for some minutes as he seemed a little nervous. Some people find addressing famous actresses somewhat overwhelming, which rather made me smile that, well past forty though I might be, I could still have this effect upon people.

After a little while I thought it best to interrupt politely as he was growing far too effusive. 'If this is to be a request for a second command, it should rightly be put to Mr Atkinson, the manager.'

He looked momentarily startled, but then flushed bright red, apologizing for not having come to the point. After another slight hesitation he at last proceeded to explain. 'I bring you the Duke's compliments, Mrs Jordan. He regrets that his situation prevents his doing himself the pleasure of calling upon you, but he should consider himself much flattered and extremely happy if you would allow him to call on you alone, at half past twelve this night.'

I stared at the young man for some moments in a complete state of shock. Could I have heard correctly? Was I actually being *propositioned* by the Duke of Richmond? Was this how I was perceived, as a piece of merchandise available to anyone who asked to partake of a taste? This was far worse than all the slings and arrows I had suffered at the hands of the press. I felt slightly giddy, as if my head were swimming, and an image of my dear children flashed before my eyes. I could not even find voice to speak. I put a hand to my head, certain I was about to faint, when the door opened and Atkinson burst in. He seemed to take in the situation at a glance and rushed to my side.

'Mrs Jordan, what is the matter? You look quite ill!' he said, turning to glare at Parkhurst, implying he was the cause.

I shook my head, too upset to speak, and sped from the room close to tears.

Atkinson came to my dressing room later, in a state of distress almost as great as my own. 'I bring a thousand apologies from Parkhurst. He is greatly shocked to have caused you such distress, and would not for the world have willingly upset you, but he could not refuse to bring the message.'

'I lay no blame upon Mr Parkhurst.'

'He will be relieved to hear that, Mrs Jordan. May I ask that this unfortunate matter be kept between ourselves? I would not wish His Grace the Duke of Clarence to think that you had been treated here with anything but the highest respect.'

I felt quite sorry for the poor man. Atkinson was clearly frightened out of his senses for fear the Duke should lay the blame upon him.

'Of course, I shall make no mention of it,' I agreed, wishing to appease him. 'These matters are far better not discussed, I always think, as they can grow into a veritable scandal in a breath.'

'I am most appreciative,' he murmured, most humbly. 'I wish only for your stay to be pleasant. I shall not have a moment's rest until I am certain of your safe arrival in Holyhead.'

Amen to that, I thought.

When he had gone, bowing as if I truly were a duchess as he backed out of the room, I turned to find Lucy's bright questioning eyes upon me and, once I had told her all, we both burst out laughing. If I had not laughed, I would have cried to think how badly my reputation was regarded, despite living a sober life with the one man I loved for what felt like a lifetime.

But I wasted no time, writing at once to the Duke to explain how deeply I had been offended even though I had learned to laugh about it since. Better *I* inform him than he hear of it from the scandalmongers.

Twenty-Six

'. . . that I am a better actress at this moment than I
ever was'

1810

Christmas that year was special as both my boys were home.
The house was alive with fun and laughter. George had suffered
from a wound and dysentery but was now recovering well,
and dear Henry returned to me as a seasoned seaman, no
longer the child I remembered. They went hunting and
shooting with their father, while the girls and I took carriage
rides in the park. There were games of charades and billiards,
reading ghostly tales to each other by a blazing log fire and
the traditional exchange of gifts. I played on my lute while
we all sang till we were hoarse, the girls showing off their
pretty new gowns as they danced. And we must have consumed
more than our fair share of plum pudding and mince pies,
port wine and sweetmeats, not to mention a haunch of venison,
goose and game. It was such a joy to have my family all around
me again.

But before the goose was picked clean, before even Twelfth
Night, I began to pack up ready for my next tour.

'You do not leave already?' the Duke asked, a scowl marring
his brow.

'I fear I must, dearest. The engagement paid too well to
refuse, and you know that I have tax to pay, and Lucy's dowry
still to find, not forgetting a pension for myself before I retire.
I fear I am too burdensome to you, but I assure you that I
want only to get out of debt then I shall indeed remain at
home with my family. One or two more good engagements
should set me quite free. I shall then convince you that neither
money nor pleasure shall take me from home.'

We kissed and said our farewells, and if his embrace lacked

some of the ardour I had once known I tried not to dwell upon it. I packed my bags and Lucy and I, ably supported by Thomas and Turner, set out into the cold once more.

January was spent in Manchester, where I performed in a most beautiful theatre almost as large as Drury Lane, which made me wonder if that national treasure would ever be rebuilt. Bannister and other friends were with me, and although I had much rather have spent New Year's Day with my family, I felt greatly appreciated. The applause was deafening.

A local Methodist minister may not have agreed with this generous acclaim as he sent me a letter solemnly accusing me of holding communication with the Wicked One, who had apparently bewitched me with charms, spells and magic.

I couldn't help but laugh about this to Lucy. 'They say the fault is entirely mine that they have been tempted against their will to come to the Devil's house six times, never having seen a play before, and hated all such abominations.'

'I did not realize you had such influence, Mama.'

'No more did I. But I apparently spirited the money out of their pockets and induced them to neglect their families and employments.' I handed her the letter, much amused.

Reading it, she smiled. 'It appears that you yet have a soul worth saving, if only you will give up your profession and intimacy with the Wicked One.'

'I shall certainly bear that in mind,' I said in mock seriousness.

As the month progressed we travelled from town to town: Rochdale, Blackburn, Chester and many more, huddled in shawls and warm coats, our frozen feet on a rapidly cooling hot brick. Fagging myself to death, as usual. My ankles were swollen and quite painful, so I took some time off at Kirkstall Abbey to refresh my spirits before going on to Halifax and Leeds.

There I played at the very theatre where first I had appeared in England after our long weary walk from Liverpool with Mama, only this time we stayed at the Grieves Hotel with a handsome bed and a good room for once. Then on to York where the theatre was as cold as ever and we all suffered from sore throats, but where on this occasion I was in favour with the ladies of that fine town.

Without doubt, what most fuelled my energy was a good audience. They seemed better than ever, every box taken. Dear old Wilkinson would have called it a 'thunderer', and I couldn't help a small satisfaction when I heard of Mrs Siddons playing to a house of but thirty-one. I might linger in the Green Room feeling exhausted, certain that I could not possibly go on. I would sometimes pace the stage a little before the curtain rose in an effort to prepare myself, but the moment the performance started it was as if a flame had been kindled inside me. I was afire with new energy, my step quick and light, all worries and family concerns gone from my mind, and I was reborn.

If I possessed any magic it came to the fore only on stage, not in the real world. Young actors and actresses would eagerly listen to every little instruction I gave them at rehearsals. They seemed to see me as a legend in my own lifetime, which was most flattering.

More offers came in, which I declined as civilly as I may, my thoughts of the Duke losing patience with my long absences constantly in my mind. I seemed to have no state of moderation. I was either deliriously happy or in the pit of despair.

And Lucy, I fear, found this a comfortless and weary life. She was quite right, for it is certainly that. We were glad to return to Bushy, where she soon informed me she had accepted the hand of Colonel Hawker. I was a little shocked, as he was in truth far too old for my darling girl, being a man approaching fifty.

'I hope you love him, dearest,' I anxiously asked. 'Do not accept him otherwise, and certainly not because you are father-less. I do so want you to be happy.'

'I shall be happy, Mama. The Colonel is kind and good.'

'But does he have passion?'

She gave me her patient little smile. 'I am not sure it is in my nature to seek passion, Mama, but he is certainly sensible and safe.'

'Is that important?' I was not entirely surprised by this prac-tical view she held of what was required in a husband, if a little disappointed by it.

'When I compare him with Fanny's choice of Alsop, yes, I dare say it is.'

A daughter's husband never does come up to snuff, I thought. But I made up my mind to be happy for her, and dear Lucy was married at Hampton Church in April, a quiet affair supported by myself, Henry and Sophy. There was further good news in May when Dodee gave birth to a delightful little girl.

By June I was again on tour, this time as far north as Edinburgh, travelling one hundred and thirty miles each day from five in the morning to ten at night. And as Lucy was with her new husband, Fanny accompanied me in her place. I received several requests for further engagements, including Glasgow and Bath, although I always checked with the Duke before accepting any of them.

'If it will answer my purpose better than Liverpool, I will do it, particularly as it will be the last time I shall leave you,' I wrote.

I knew in my heart that I could not test his patience for much longer.

I was playing Nell in *The Devil to Pay* in Glasgow at the end of June, when I received word that the Duke had been taken seriously ill with an attack of asthma. This was a regular occurrence, but far worse on this occasion. The managers kindly gave me leave, and although I would need to return to complete my contract with them I immediately set out for Bushy. We drove night and day, never leaving my carriage either to eat or sleep, and I was in the most dreadful state throughout the sixty-three hours of the journey. It was unbearable to think that something terrible might happen to my dear Billy while I was so far away.

But on my arrival at Bushy I found him already on the road to recovery, tended by Sophy, and by the royal doctors Dundas and Blane. Lucy had already left with the Colonel to join his regiment in Portugal, which almost broke my heart.

'Will she be safe?' I asked William, desperate for reassurance.

'Why would she not be, as she is with her husband?'

He sounded offhand, quite indifferent to my concern, perhaps because his spirits were low and he was not yet fully recovered. I changed the subject, thinking to cheer him. 'I have agreed to play one last time at Covent Garden for £100 per night. Great terms, I'm sure you'll agree. It will be my retirement performance there. After that I must pay the same compliment to other theatres, Bath, Margate, and so on. Then I shall most gladly retire.'

'If you feel the necessity. I thought you wished not to quit the stage?'

'I wish only to settle my debts first, then I will be more than satisfied to leave.' I had rather hoped this would please him, but as with his recent letters he was not showing the enthusiasm for my decision that I had hoped for. 'Were you not once of the opinion yourself that for the sake of propriety I *should* quit?' But seeing how he still breathed with difficulty, I put my arms about him to kiss his brow. 'I am tiring you, dearest. You must rest.'

'I shall go to Brighton,' William decided, of a sudden. 'The fresh air will do me good.'

'An excellent notion.' He did not offer to take me with him, or think that it might do me good to have a restful holiday by the sea. 'So long as the Prince does not lead you into more hard drinking,' I finished on a lighter note.

This brought forth the semblance of a smile and we parted on good terms, if somewhat more distant than usual.

'Please write to inform the boys that there will be no birthday celebration at Bushy this August,' the Duke casually announced one day, although he must have known I had been making preparations for the occasion myself for some time. 'The Queen has graciously decided to mark the day by giving me a fête.'

'Oh, how very kind of Her Majesty.'

William half turned away, avoiding my enquiring gaze. 'You know that you cannot be included in the invitation, Dora,' he added, and almost sighed with relief when I merely nodded, silently determined not to make the slightest fuss.

'What a very sensible woman you are,' he said, and I tried to remember the last time he had called me by my pet name of Little Pickle. 'Her Majesty has also granted permission for Sophy to go out into society, now that she is sixteen. Is that not most generous of her?'

I gasped, thrilled by this news, at least. 'It is indeed.'

'I shall naturally escort her myself.'

'Of course.'

I spent the Duke's forty-fifth birthday at Bushy. Quite alone. I sat in the garden in the sunshine and wrote to my son, explaining that the Duke had found it necessary to make some retrenchments and thought it prudent not to mark the day. I made no mention of the Queen's fête, although I did explain that the other boys were also away either at school or at sea, and the girls were out. I decided not to say they were at Windsor.

'If you see dear Lucy, I trust you will be able to prevail on her to remain at Lisbon. I am now quite alone, even Mely has taken her flight, and the house is so still that it does not appear like Bushy.'

I should have returned to Glasgow to finish my engagement but I was tired, and had lost heart somehow. I remained at Bushy for the rest of that summer.

I went on tour again in the autumn but Fanny was not the support my lovely Lucy was, constantly dissatisfied, as was her husband. I would frequently hear them quarrelling when they thought I wasn't listening, and generally about money. He was not my favourite son-in-law by any means. Alsop would do well, I thought, to learn from the prudence of March, dear Dodee's husband. The fellow was too full of himself and money slipped through his fingers like water. There were times that I feared for my daughter.

'I may become a concert singer,' she said one day as she brushed out my hair before I went on, as she had used to do as a small child so long ago.

'Your voice is pleasant enough, Fanny dear, but not in the top notch.'

'Then I shall act. I have before and could again. You aren't the only one with talent, Mama,' she grumbled, sounding so like Daly it brought a shiver to my spine.

'Of course you can act, darling, given the right part. But remember that as my daughter a great deal would be expected of you, and it would be humiliating were you not able to fulfil those expectations. Why not, for now, continue to help with the costumes and see how that serves?'

'Why are you never ready to see me progress?'

'This may be the wrong moment to discuss it, Fanny. I am rather tired after performing in the play, and must now go on in the farce. Nor have I been sleeping well lately, what with the boys away in the war and other worries I have on my mind.'

'You worry too much about them, and not enough about me,' she snapped.

'Oh, Fanny, that is not true. I would do anything to see you happy.'

'No one cares about me. I'm not even sure the Duke wants me at Bushy for Christmas this year. He is behaving most oddly towards me.'

Towards everyone, I thought, but said nothing more, and tossing her head she stormed off, leaving me to sigh and finish my hair myself.

The next day I woke very late and with a most dreadful headache. 'Goodness, I slept like a log, so why on earth do I feel so bad?'

'I put a few drops of laudanum into the warmed wine I gave you at bedtime. You said you needed a good night's sleep, Mama, so I made sure you would have one.'

'Fanny! You had no right to do such a thing, and certainly not without asking. A drop or two of laudanum leads to another, and another, and that way lies oblivion and madness. Don't ever do that again.'

'I can't see that it will do you any harm,' she huffed, but I watched her most carefully after that, and saw to my horror that she continued to take a drop or two in her own wine each evening. Again I warned her against it.

'My own Aunt Maria, who died before you were born, fell victim to laudanum and died early as a result. I pray you do not fall into the same trap.'

'It is but a drop, and only when I feel the need,' she coldly responded. 'I am not a child to be told what to do any more, Mother.'

And so I held my tongue, knowing anything I said would

only make her the more pig-headed. But it was another thing
to worry about. Sons may be a constant concern but daughters
are the very devil.

Princess Amelia died of tuberculosis on the second of November,
1810, and I know the Duke found the funeral a miserable
affair as the entire family grieved for the loss of this delightful
young woman. On hearing the news of his daughter's death
the King had collapsed, and fallen once more into madness.
Now over seventy and blind, few people expected him to
recover. Out of respect, Parliament had adjourned for two
weeks but running the country must go on, and so they
reconvened. William had felt it incumbent upon himself
not to miss a day in the Lords so that he could keep an eye
on events, knowing that his brother was already making
arrangements for the regency.

Sophy and Frederick accompanied him on this sad occasion
and, much to my relief, received a cautious welcome.

'Everyone was so kind to me,' Sophy told me. 'Especially
all the aunts. Why have I not met your family before, Papa?'

He half glanced across at me. 'They disapprove of your
Mama,' he said, somewhat bluntly.

I warmly clasped her hands in mine. 'I heartily wish things
could be different for you, my love, although I do appreciate
the efforts the princesses made in making you feel more
comfortable.'

Sophy was frowning, struggling to understand. 'Is that why
you were not invited, Mama? Because you and Papa are not
married and you refuse to give up the stage?'

'Something of the sort, but you are not to worry about me.'

'And they would not meet me because I am illegitimate?'

I winced. 'Do not even speak that word, Sophy,' I gently
scolded, shocked by the pain in my daughter's face.

'But if they disapproved of me before, why am I now invited
to so many functions? I have received two this week already,
both to balls.' There was excitement in her voice, which she
was striving to quell. 'Of course, these will not now take place,
with the King ill, but I don't understand. Why am I now being
so favoured?' She looked up trustingly to her father for an

explanation. He offered none, suddenly finding something of great importance he must do elsewhere that very minute.

Later I tried to offer him reassurance. 'Sophy is charming in mind and person and will make a clever and accomplished woman. Allow her to entertain for you, and to accompany you on social occasions as the Queen has suggested. She is now old enough to receive your friends – do, love, oblige me in this as it is what I have long wished. The company may amuse you too. I assure you it will give me the greatest pleasure to see her go out into the world.'

'There may be no royal blood in your veins, Dora, but there are buckets of warm generosity,' and for some reason his eyes filled with tears.

When I went back on tour I wrote to emphasize this point. 'But do give her a proper dress allowance. She must from circumstances cost you much more at present. Suppose you allow her the profits arising from the dairy and cheesing house towards the sum . . .'

I assumed that his current gloom must be connected with money, and I thought it my task to find a solution.

I returned in the late autumn to find the house empty of the Duke's presence. Not even darling Sophy was at home, or Mary. William came only on Sundays, but then he would be bound to be away more, now that he was escorting our daughters out and about. Even so, he seemed different, almost as if he were avoiding me, which made my heart pulsate with fear and pain. And if I made the slightest suggestion that he might stay home more, he would roar like a bull, or sulk for days.

I did once say to him: 'I believe when I am out of the gate at Bushy Park I am very soon forgot.' And where once he would have taken me in his arms and kissed me, calling me his Little Pickle, he merely smiled and said nothing.

I must retire soon, I thought, or I would lose him entirely. Although if I did lose him, I should need employment, as the allowance that had been part of our initial agreement would not be sufficient to cover all my responsibilities, even if his debts allowed him to pay it in full.

Christmas that year was the most melancholy I could ever

remember. Not a typically merry Bushy House Christmas at all. I was glad that Sophy was being taken out and about by her Papa, sometimes not getting home until five in the morning. But the thought of those who were absent spoiled it all. Where were my boys? Were they well? News of the King was no better and after a month at home spent largely with only Miss Sketchley and the little ones for company, I was glad for once to go back on tour, this time to Bath and Bristol, and the joys of a good house.

I missed my family, as always, but was happy to write to the Duke and inform him of my success.

'From the applause and admiration one would think that I had but started in the profession instead of being near the end of the race . . . I can for an hour or two forget you all and the various anxieties that in general depress my spirits. I really think, and it is the opinion of several critics here that have known me from my first appearance in London, that I am a better actress at this moment than I ever was.'

Twenty-Seven

'. . . a most injured woman'

I was seated in my dressing room at the Bath theatre when a note was brought to me. I stared at it, dumbfounded, hardly able to believe my eyes. I recognized George's handwriting instantly, and was so overcome I could not bring myself to open it. The thought which at once came into my head was that it had been sent to me as his last letter, and I should prepare myself for the worst.

And then the door burst open and there he was before me, tall and strong, healthy and very much *alive*! Oh, and so good looking that all the girls in the dressing room began to giggle and cluster around. But I did not let them near, not until I had gathered him in my arms first.

'Darling George, why did you not warn me you were coming? My heart is beating twenty to the dozen. I fear I may be about to have a heart attack from shock.'

He laughed. 'Then sit down, Mama, quickly, before you collapse,' and giving me a big bear hug in return he led me to a couch where we sat together grinning at each other like silly fools.

'You seem in high spirits, and good health.'

'I am indeed, and have been given leave although I must return to Portugal soon. General Stewart has told me he would rather have me than any other for his aide-de-camp.'

'Oh George, it is excellent to know you are so well regarded. I cannot tell you how pleased I am to see you. You have made a mother very happy.'

The young girls in the dressing room were also looking very happy to have this handsome young soldier in their midst, and while I went on stage I laughingly left my son in their tender care.

The next day we went shopping and he bought a whole

cargo of toys for his brothers and sisters. Then, while I sat and watched, he swam in the medicinal baths, a straw bonnet on his head, which made me laugh all the more. We had the most gloriously happy time together, and I tried not to lecture him too much about the dangers of smoking and drinking, gaming or falling into debt.

We discussed family matters, naturally, and he brought me news that Lucy was pregnant, but as she was still in Portugal, caught up the Peninsular war, she would have her baby before she could return to England. Henry, who had come so to detest the navy that his father had finally allowed him to leave, was now going to Marlow to prepare for the army instead.

'Will he be any happier?' I wondered aloud, to which George had no ready answer.

'We must hope so.'

He naturally asked after Papa and I urged him to pay a call. 'More than likely you will find him at St James's. Your father has been in town very nearly ever since you left us, with the exception of coming down on Sundays.' And sometimes not even then, I thought.

Oh, but what a joy it was to have my son to myself for two whole days. He quite restored my spirits. After he had gone on his way, promising to write more regularly, as boys always do their mothers, I set off on my travels once again, this time heading for Worcester and Coventry. I was greatly looking forward to meeting the Duke en route at Maidenhead, where I would tell him all about this wonderful surprise visit from our son.

But on arrival I received word that William would be unable to meet me due to a prior engagement. My disappointment was keen. Where is it that he goes, I wondered, that is so much more important than spending time with me? I was sensing a distance growing between us and my heart ached with loneliness, his letters no longer filled with love as they were in those early days.

I shook off my disappointment as best I could, and instead spent a most happy night with dear Freddles, who was granted time out of school to be with his mother. He wanted to stay in my room at the inn, and I did not feel inclined to refuse so gallant an offer.

In Worcester I wrote to tell William of the latest excellent offer I'd received, which would regretfully keep me a little longer from home. 'It would add £200 to my other profits. I know I am trespassing on your patience but trust you will forgive me.'

I did not, on this occasion, ask for his permission. I gave him a short account of my success, sent him money as always, and mentioned that as my lodgings were indifferent I was obliged to buy my meat and pastry from an inn.

I slept very ill in the weeks following, would rise early to take a long walk before I began rehearsals at ten. But as I did not have the company of either dear Lucy or the troublesome Fanny, I often felt out of spirits. 'The servants are very attentive and kind to me, but servants are not friends or children,' I wrote to the Duke.

There was a stubbornness settling around my heart as I felt an increasing need to protect myself, although I was not sure from what. My life seemed to be unravelling about me, spinning out of control. But my anxiety to enable myself to stay at home ultimately urged me to do as much as I could in the little time that was left to me before my retirement.

I seemed to be suffering from an ambiguity of emotions: I longed to be free of the travelling, the discomfort, the cold and the loneliness, and yet I relished every moment on stage. I was loved and applauded wherever I went, except by the one person whose opinion counted the most. Did he punish me with his neglect because of his disapproval of my touring, or was there some other factor at play, of which I was ignorant?

Sophy stood in the reception hall beside her father, together with his royal siblings, greeting guests as they arrived. It was the nineteenth of June, 1811, and the Prince of Wales was holding a great fête at Carlton House, ostensibly to welcome members of the French royal family to England, and to celebrate the King's birthday. But since His Majesty was in such a state of madness that he was unaware he even had a birthday, let alone fit enough to celebrate it, the true purpose of the event was to mark the start of the regency.

Two thousand had been invited, several lines stretching

through the hall and out into the gardens and Pall Mall beyond, where a stream of carriages blocked all other traffic. Matting had been spread upon the lawns to protect the ladies' shoes. There were covered walkways, lined with painted trellises and decorated with flowers and mirrors, along which the guests could promenade. The band of the Scots Guards played beneath the Corinthian portico, entertaining them with appropriate music while they chatted and waited.

The Queen had chosen not to attend, as she considered it inappropriate to celebrate anything while the King was so ill. The Regent's wife, Caroline of Brunswick, had not even been invited, nor was his fifteen-year-old daughter Charlotte present.

Sophy, to her great delight, had been fortunate enough to receive an invitation, the Prince of Wales even gifting her an elegant gown to wear upon this special occasion.

'I wish Mama were here to see this,' she whispered, as she watched the Princess Mary go by looking as beautiful as ever in an extravagant gown of radiant blue watered silk. 'At least the princesses have been let out of the "nunnery", as they call it, for the day,' she said with a giggle, referring to the name they used for their cloistered state. 'And there is Lady Hertford; is she not the Regent's latest mistress? Mrs Fitzherbert does not seem to be present.'

Her father ignored her comments, seeming distracted, but Sophy had heard from the gossip-mongers that the Regent's long-term mistress had refused her own invitation when she'd learned she was not to be permitted to sit at the top table with the Prince.

'Why wasn't Mama invited? She does not go on tour to Yorkshire until the end of July.' Sophy was having difficulty coming to terms not only with royal etiquette but the many puzzling rules of society. Not least the status of her own parent.

'Hush, child. You ask too many questions.'

She could see that he was longing to escape from this tiresome business of meeting and greeting, and that his eyes were searching the crowd, as if looking for someone.

The most honoured guests, numbering about two hundred, were seated at a long table which filled almost the entire length of the gothic conservatory. This room, designed by Thomas

Hopper, was lit by lanterns and an illuminated crown with the letters GR that hung above the Regent's mahogany chair. Sophy was deeply impressed by its regal splendour.

Behind the Prince's cushioned seat were numerous tables covered with crimson drapery, upon which was set a display of exquisitely wrought silver-gilt plate, tripods, epergnes, dishes and other ornaments, all filled with a wonderful array of food. Down the centre of the table a canal had been constructed on a raised plinth, its banks covered with green moss and aquatic flowers. Water flowed along it from a silver fountain, and gold and silver fish swam within. Never had she seen the like in her life before.

Her uncle, the forty-eight-year-old Prince Regent, well corseted and smartly attired in his new field marshal's uniform with the star of the Order of the Garter on his chest, an honour he had granted himself, sat at the head of the table above the fountain. The Duchesse d'Angoulême sat on the Regent's right, the Duchess of York on his left. She had prised all these details out of her father earlier, but he was again ignoring her, his attention elsewhere.

He settled himself on the seat allotted to him, and even as he began a conversation with the Comte d'Artois, his gaze was roaming the length of the two-hundred-foot table. Sophy wondered who he might be looking for, then saw his gaze fix upon a certain young lady.

A few delicate enquiries of her neighbour and Sophy discovered her identity. She was Catherine Tylney-Long, the daughter of Lady Catherine Sydney Windsor and Sir James Tylney-Long, Seventh Baronet of Draycot, who had recently come into possession of a large fortune. Seated beside her aunt and chaperon, Lady de Crespigny, she was attracting considerable attention, which Sophy didn't wonder at. Some claimed her annual income to be in the region of £40,000, others said it was but £25,000, but who would quibble over such a sum?

She was delicately formed, charmingly elegant, a veritable beauty indeed, but younger than her father by twenty years or more, so why would he be interested in her? Not that age appeared to be any bar to old men, who seemed rather to like young women. Colonel Hawker had not balked at carrying off

Lucy. It made Sophy shudder to suspect that her father might
be thinking along similar lines. Did not Papa love Mama? Sophy
frowned, thinking things through as she covertly watched him.

She had heard the Prince of Wales constantly advise her
father that the only way to settle his debts was through marriage.
Sophy disliked such conversations between them with a passion,
but always made a point of keeping quiet so that the royal
brothers would not realize she was listening. And she was
intelligent enough to understand the implications. Apparently
there was also increasing pressure from the Queen for her sons
to produce more legitimate heirs, of which the royal family
were in sore need.

'Men die in war, women in the lying-in chamber,' was Her
Majesty's caustic response whenever her father reminded her
that Charlotte was a healthy young woman.

And everything would change now with the regency.
Permission to override the Royal Marriages Act would easily
be obtained. Marriage to such a woman would resolve all her
father's financial difficulties. What then would happen to Mama?

It was the most sumptuous feast Sophy had ever seen. The
Regent's servants in their dark blue livery trimmed with gold
lace, patiently and graciously served hot and cold soups, roasts,
venison, game, cheese, jellies, custards and puddings to the
guests upon silver plate. There was iced champagne and fine
wines, and fruits including peaches, grapes and pineapples.

At last the meal was over and Sophy watched with a sinking
heart as her father hurried straight to the young woman's side,
then was actually dancing the quadrille with her. Sophy felt
she might vomit right there and then on the ballroom floor.
Steeling her nerves she edged closer, secreting herself behind
a pillar so that she could engage in her favourite pursuit of
watching and listening.

The dance ended and he escorted Miss Tylney-Long back
to her seat. 'Perhaps I may sign your card for another dance
later?' Papa was saying.

Catherine Tylney-Long flicked it open, giving it a brief
glance. 'I'm afraid there is not a space left upon it,' she told
him with an apologetic little smile, which Sophy thought
entirely false.

'Then perhaps we can at least talk a little, between dances.' He looked so disappointed that Sophy's heart plummeted with misery. Had he no pride?

'But of course, Your Grace.'

'Do call me William, no need to stand on formalities.'

Miss Tylney-Long merely inclined her head, but before he had the opportunity to say anything more, she was being led on to the floor by another gentleman.

'And who may he be?' the Duke demanded of his neighbour, a sour note in his voice.

'William Wellesley-Pole, the twenty-four-year-old nephew of the Duke of Wellington. They say she is quite smitten with him.'

The Duke scowled. 'Do they indeed?'

'He is not her only suitor by any means. There are any number, I believe.'

Sophy sighed with relief and slipped quietly away to seek a dance partner of her own. If the lady was being pursued by many gentlemen there was nothing to fear. Surely her foolish ancient father would have little chance of winning such a prize?

'Why did you make such an exhibition of yourself, Papa?' Sophy challenged her father as they drove home together in the early hours. 'I did not care to see you fawning over that woman. What of Mama?'

His answer was cautious. 'I'm sure your mother would understand. She is a most sensible woman.'

Sophy could hardly believe her own ears. 'But you love Mama.'

'Of course I do.'

'You have enjoyed almost twenty years of contentment together, as long as any marriage, brought up ten children, shared the joys and trials of parenthood. She has been your helpmeet, your wife in all but name. You surely would not betray her?'

'Yet she is not my wife, and never can be. You are too young to understand, dear child.'

'I understand well enough!' A bitter anger against her father, and strangely against her mother too, was beginning to fester and grow inside her. Why could they not have married like normal people? Why could they not at least be content together?

Why was her mother always taking herself off on tour instead of staying with her husband and children? Was it any wonder if people looked down their noses and refused to be friends with her? She was a nobody, a bastard!

'You can be sure, dearest, that were it not for other factors I must consider, I would not change her for the world.'

'Change her?' spluttered Sophy. 'You surely aren't thinking of offering for Miss Tylney-Long?' She was stunned, appalled by such a prospect.

William looked at his daughter, as if shocked by her presumption in asking such a question. 'I really do not think it is any of your business—'

'It is very *much* my business,' Sophy snapped. 'As your daughter, your *illegitimate* daughter.'

'Do not use that word.'

'Why not, when it is the true one? It wouldn't be right for you to involve yourself in a dalliance with a woman half your age, not when you are still living with *my* mother.'

The Duke flushed with annoyance and embarrassment at this apparent lecture on morality from his own daughter. 'Hold your tongue, girl.'

'I will not!' Sophy was her mother's daughter and knew how to stand up for what she perceived to be right. 'Think of Mama's sweetness, her generosity and liveliness which you have always loved. How often have you spoken of her practical good sense and excellent judgement, related to us the excitement of those early years together? I have heard the tale of how you pursued her, your love letters, the thrill of settling into Bushy House. How can you suddenly forget all that?'

'The King is seventy-three years old, suffering from terrifying hallucinations, considerable pain, sometimes talking non-stop for hours, entirely incoherent and often obscene, rarely aware of what is going on around him. Your Uncle George is carrying the heavy mantle of the regency upon his shoulders, and in twelve months the full power of that office will come into effect. But he has only one daughter to succeed him. Although he is fond of your mother, he too has urged me to consider marriage. It is my duty.'

Sophy considered this statement in furious silence for some

long minutes as the carriage drew up at St James's. 'So will you keep Mama as your mistress, even if you do take a wife?'

William cleared his throat, taking a moment before answering. 'I have considered that option, but feel it would be unfair after our long association. A clean break would be best, I think.'

She gave a little sob, unable to hold her emotions in check any longer. 'You will break her heart!' And without waiting to be handed down from the carriage, Sophy jumped out and ran to her room.

'I will break it to her gently,' he called after her, but Sophy was long gone.

A letter from the Duke was handed to me just before I went on stage. It was October, and I should have finished this engagement at Cheltenham by now but had agreed to play an extra night. I tore open the envelope, as I always did when I saw the Duke's handwriting, eager to read his news, to hear his voice in my head. But the words blurred before my eyes. He wished us to meet at Maidenhead – 'for one last time before we part'.

I couldn't take it in. What did he mean? There had been no word of our parting. Yet there it was in black and white: *for one last time before we part*. Was this then the moment I had so long dreaded?

'Starters please. Three minutes to curtain,' a voice called.

I pushed the letter into my box, out of sight, my heart pounding. I must have been in shock, for a kind of paralysis had come over me. I dabbed my nose with the powder puff, more by instinct than necessity. I was about to play Nell in *The Devil to Pay*, and the show, as they say, must go on.

Giving every appearance of calm I left the dressing room to go on stage, not feeling the least calm inside. There was a sick feeling deep in the pit of my stomach, a hollow sensation that seemed to be affecting my limbs; they felt weak and shivery, out of my control. Yet I did indeed go on and must have performed reasonably well at first. But in the scene where I was supposed to laugh out loud at some incident, and my fellow actor playing the role of Jobling would accuse me of being laughing drunk, I looked into his face and instead burst into tears.

He looked startled, as well he might, but then like the

trouper he was, said: 'Why, Nell, the conjuror has not only made thee drunk, he has made thee crying drunk.'

There were gasps from the audience, who seemed to sense that something was wrong, and how I finished the scene I have no recollection. It must have been entirely due to his skill.

I wasted no time in ordering my carriage and the moment the production was over, without even pausing to remove my costume or make-up, as these could easily be dealt with in the carriage during the journey, I stepped on board and set off for Maidenhead to hear my fate.

The Duke was pacing the chamber at the inn like a nervous schoolboy when I entered, and I instinctively knew, by the pallor of his face, what he was about to say. There were actual tears in his eyes, and he held out his hands to me in a helpless gesture. I did not take them.

'I am sorry, Dora, but the Queen has made it clear that she wishes me to do my duty and marry. The family has need of more legitimate heirs. There is only Charlotte, and you know that George has no intention of returning to Caroline. Frederick's wife is barren. I am next in line. I have no choice.'

My knees gave way and I half collapsed into a chair, fearful I might be about to faint. William made no move to help me, but rather kept his distance, perhaps knowing I was not the kind of woman to give in to hysterics. I clasped my hands tightly in my lap, and my voice, when finally I found it, was barely above a whisper.

'Then it is over between us?'

'Sadly, yes, it is over.'

'What of the Royal Marriages Act?'

'George will grant his permission, as Regent.'

'Of course.' A slight pause while I digested this. 'Do you have someone – a particular woman in mind?'

'No.'

I knew that he lied. I'd heard the rumours. 'I cannot believe you would put me through all this pain before you had even found my replacement.'

William too now found the need to sit, his fingers plucking at the buttons of his brocade coat in an agitated manner, tears rolling unchecked down his cheeks. 'Very well, I will confess that I have, although I was hoping to spare you more pain. There is a young lady, a Miss Tylney-Long.'

'Ah, the heiress. I have heard of her. Then this is all about money, is it, Billy?' I hadn't called him by this pet name for months; now I saw that it cut him to the quick. He was on his feet in an instant.

'It is about duty, Dora, as I have explained. Please do not make this any harder than it is already.'

I gave what might pass for a smile, a strange calmness coming over me that clearly unnerved him. 'But a rich young heiress will serve your needs better than an old actress, eh?'

'Don't even think such a thing. Money is a factor, I will admit. You know full well the state of my debts. But my duty must come above all else.'

'And what of the children? What is to happen to them?'

Perhaps he heard the fear in my voice, for he hastened to offer reassurance. 'Nothing will happen to them. They will need to be told, of course, but I would not deprive you of your children, Dora, I swear it.'

I closed my eyes for a second, breathing deeply, striving to maintain my dignity. 'Is there anything else you would like to say to me, William?'

'No, that is all.'

'Then would you please leave.'

He looked like a whipped dog, as if guilt were gnawing at his earlier confidence, reducing it to shreds of shame. He seemed quite unable to stem the emotion that was over-whelming him while I sat frozen with pain. Having informed me in his usual blunt, Jack-tar manner, was the reality of this callous announcement now slowly dawning on him?

A tear slid down my cheek which I was helpless to prevent, and he stepped quickly forward to take me by the shoulders. 'I cannot leave you like this,' he cried.

'Go,' I said, my throat choked with unshed tears. 'I beg you to go now!'

As he softly closed the door behind him, the sound of his boots echoing on the stairs as he walked away, that's when my sobs began.

Twenty-Eight

'. . . trifling most cruelly with my feelings and unfortunate situation . . .'

After a sleepless night, the worst I could ever remember, I wrote letters the following morning as if nothing at all had changed. There was still work to be done, after all, if not more so than ever. For I must protect the dear children, and my income for their sake. I wrote to Covent Garden, who had offered me an engagement for the winter season, and there were other offers requiring my attention. When that was done, and leaving my breakfast untouched since I had no appetite, I climbed back into my carriage and set out for Bushy.

What a joy when I saw the children come running the moment my carriage turned into the drive, and the instant I climbed out they flung themselves into my arms. 'Mama, Mama, you're home,' cried six-year-old Tus. His darling sisters too gathered round, eager for their own share of hugs. Eliza, at ten, was quite the young woman, but responded with warmth to my embrace. Augusta, or Ta as she liked to be called, was jumping up and down with the excitement of a two-year-old despite her eight years. Mely at four was looking slightly bewildered with her thumb in her mouth. Had she forgotten who I was during the long weeks of my absence? Tears filled my eyes at the thought. How much I had sacrificed for this man, and all out of love.

'Oh, it is so lovely to be home,' I cried, showering kisses upon them all, loving the feel of their small bodies against my aching heart. 'You must tell me all your news, what you have been up to since last I saw you.' When I thought of my own news I felt like crying, but was determined to put on a brave face in front of the children.

'We've been planting trees around the dairy. Come and look,

Mama, come and see,' shouted Tus, quite beside himself with happiness.

'Most of the soil seems to be in your hair,' I said, laughing as I rumpled his fair curls. My children all looked slightly grubby from their play, but rosy-cheeked and thankfully in robust health and high spirits. 'And how is dear Miss Sketchley?'

'All the better for seeing you, Mistress,' said that good lady, coming forward to offer her own welcome.

I clasped her hands in silent gratitude, but my eyes must have told her something of my inner turmoil, for she frowned, and putting an arm about my shoulders led me gently indoors.

'Come, you must be tired after your journey. Food and rest first, I think.' She was like a mother to me, and I was in dire need of one of those right now.

Fanny too had been helping to look after the dear children, and welcomed me in her typical off-hand manner. It felt so good to be back in the fold of my family. Did they not mean the world to me, and hadn't the Duke promised that no one would take them away from me?

That night, after I had tucked them all into their beds, I did the rounds as I so liked to do, telling them stories and listening to their prayers.

'God bless Mama, God bless Papa . . .' they chimed, reciting all the family members one by one, not even leaving out their favourite pet dog.

Tears came readily to my eyes as I listened, deeply moved by their innocence, for how could I tell them that our lovely family was no more?

The scandalmongers joined in the frolics, and were in full flow, discussing every personal detail of our lives. All my friends seemed to be bursting to disclose the latest tales they had heard, hoping I might enlighten them as to their veracity. How the Duke had pursued Miss Tylney-Long throughout that autumn while she was in Ramsgate taking the sea air; how he would call upon her every day, or 'accidentally' discover her walking with her mother and sister along the promenades and crescents, and eagerly join the ladies. Wellesley-Pole might be hovering nearby but the Duke would deliberately block him out, regaling his heart's desire with his lively sea yarns, as he once had regaled me. He apparently even offered to have the fellow drummed out of town.

'He is shameless, Mama,' Sophy told me. 'At a naval fête where all the ladies were dressed in red and white to honour his flag, Papa took advantage of his position to claim more than the two dances considered quite proper. However, Wellesley-Pole chose not to honour his precedence and laid claim to the dance himself. You should have seen Papa's temper flare. "I will not give her up to any man," he snapped, and danced on.'

'I'm not sure you should be telling me all this,' I protested, eagerly drinking in every detail, despite the pain it was causing me.

'Why should you not know?' And here Sophy adopted a pose. 'Seconds later Catherine fell to limping. "Oh my, I fear I have hurt my foot with hopping and skipping," she said. All a tale as she really does not care to dance with him, I can see it in her face. Papa is almost *fifty*, for goodness sake, and she in her early twenties! She begged to sit out the rest of the dance, but he refused to leave her side for the rest of the evening.'

I was on my feet in a second. 'I have heard enough. No more, please.'

'But there is a great deal more, Mama. People are sniggering and mocking him. It is so embarrassing! If you but knew the whole of it then you could do something to stop him making such a fool of himself, to save our family from destruction.'

'What could I do?' I felt helpless in the face of her optimism.

'I don't know. Tell him that you love him.'

'He knows that already.'

'Then perhaps you could stay home more.'

'Dearest, life is not always quite so simple.' How could I explain to this innocent child the complexities of a relationship, and the harsh realities of debt?

She grasped my hands and made me sit again. 'Later that evening, when he escorted her to her carriage, I followed and heard him say that he intended to write to her guardian, Lady de Crespigny, to inform her of the strength of his feelings.

"Would you like me to deliver any message?" he asked. And after the slightest hesitation, she said, "Give my aunt my best compliments." Papa asked if he might say that she had enjoyed a pleasant evening, by which he meant by spending it almost entirely with him. "You may add to my aunt I have had an *agreeable* evening," she said. It was not an answer that pleased him,' Sophy said with some satisfaction. 'I think she means to refuse him.'

And so it proved, after which followed much speculation on who the Duke might offer for next.

Ever tender to his needs, even to my own detriment, I had already warned him to proceed with caution for fear of disappointment. 'All women are not to be taken by an open attack, and a premeditated one stands a worse chance than any other.' Clearly he had not taken my advice, no doubt charging in with his usual boundless enthusiasm, like the royal Jack tar he is. Unfortunately, not every woman would find that aspect of the Duke's character as endearing as do I.

More of the story came my way via Miss Sketchley: how he claimed to be 'the first unmarried man in the land', assuring the aunt that he had broken off all connection with me. He even enclosed a copy of the 'generous' settlement we were in the process of agreeing. 'Which will I trust prove to your Ladyship I can justly value the conduct of a lady for twenty years . . .'

It did not seem to occur to him that his own conduct might be that in question.

As if all this were not bad enough, Cruikshank published several cartoons in the press which showed the Duke proposing to a pretty young lady, and myself standing by with the children clustered about me saying: 'What, leave your faithful Peggy?' At least Peter Pindar produced a poem in my support:

> What! Leave a woman to her tears?
> Your faithful friend for twenty years,
> One who gave up her youthful charms,
> The fond companion of your arms!

Brought you ten smiling girls and boys,
Sweet pledges of connubial joys;
As much your wife in honor's eye,
As if fast bound in wedlock's tie.

Return to Mistress J—'s arms,
Soothe her, and quiet her alarms;
Your present difference o'er,
Be wise, and play the fool no more.

I found all this hugely embarrassing. Worse, this kind of exposure meant that the other children had to be told: those old enough to understand, that is. The Duke left that task to me, playing the coward, avoiding telling the truth to George and Henry by saying only that he had a thousand places to go to and might not be home for Christmas. William did so hate anything difficult or unpleasant, as do all men. George was the first to comprehend what was happening, and I asked if he would break it gently to dear Henry, but it seemed his brother had already written to George in something of a state, asking if the rumours were true.

As for Sophy, since I declared myself unable to prevent this disaster falling about our ears, my darling daughter went back to St James's in a huff and stopped answering my letters.

Fanny, of course, claimed she had never liked him, and when soft-hearted Dodee met the Duke in town one day, she burst into tears. What misery had been brought upon us all!

So distressed was I by all this, that I wrote to my old friend and confidant Boaden. 'Money, money, my good friend, or the want of it, has, I am convinced, made him, at this moment, the most wretched of men. But having done wrong, he does not like to retract . . .' But I refused to blame him, and said as much to Boaden. 'Had he left me to starve, I never would have uttered a word to his disadvantage . . .'

While society whispered about me behind their hands I was in the midst of negotiating my settlement, a most unseemly business. Beset by lawyers on all sides I needed to protect myself, even though I had no one to advise me, save for Dalrymple, a loyal friend and neighbour.

In the end it was decided that I was to be granted £1,500 a year for the maintenance of my younger daughters and Tus, although he would soon turn seven and would then legally be in the care of his father, who would no doubt take full control of my little boy. For myself there was to be the same sum, and £600 for a horse and carriage. There were provisions too for my older girls, but there was also a proviso.

It was stipulated that in the event of my resuming my profession, the care of my younger children would revert to the Duke, together with the sum for their maintenance.

'Why is this an issue?' I asked Barton, the Duke's man of business. 'I thought he had agreed that I could continue with my profession so that I can settle my debts, and provide for my own pension.'

'Your continuing to work would reflect badly upon His Highness. It would look as if he had not properly provided for you.'

I thought of how my debts had mounted largely because of the Duke and his inability to economize, of the interest he still owed me in addition to the large sums I had lent him out of love and a tender heart. But my career, it seemed, was over, whether I liked it or not, so I said nothing further. I still loved him, and if there was nothing I could do to become respectable in the eyes of society, then I could at least ensure that I did not lose my children. In the aftermath of this melancholy business they would have need of a mother around.

So it was that on the twenty-second of November, 1811, my fiftieth birthday, I wrote to the Duke, carefully addressing him as 'my dear friend', for surely he would ever be that, and accepted the terms of the settlement.

Soon after that I decided to move out of Bushy House, as the memories were far too painful, and asked March to find us a house in town. It was time, I thought, for a fresh start.

But then, quite out of the blue, William Adam, the Duke's lawyer, called at Bushy and claimed not to be aware of any arrangement whereby my daughters could live with me. 'I regret you have been misinformed. I saw the Duke only last Thursday and no mention was made of this.'

I was devastated, and, suspecting some royal plot to oust me completely from the Duke's life and that of my children, I wrote at once to John McMahon, the Regent's private secretary. 'This is trifling most cruelly with my feelings and unfortunate situation . . .'

Oh, but I was angry. I had long ago learned to stand up for myself and resolved not to leave Bushy until the matter was settled to my satisfaction. All I wanted was to protect my family. I wrote also to the Duke, expressing my feelings on the arrangement *upon which we had agreed*. I addressed him as 'Sir', and signed it 'Your Royal Highness's dutiful servant'. All affection between us seemed to be dead.

Miss Sketchley informed me that my letter had greatly upset the Duke. 'He sensed your anger in every word. In fact,' she blithely continued, 'he has let it be known that he wishes you to be left in peace, and the children too. He apparently said: "She has ever been the best of mothers and I see no reason why our younger daughters should not stay with her until they reach sixteen." I am reliably informed, however, by McMahon, that the Prince Regent considers thirteen a more appropriate age.'

'It is the royal advisers who have conspired to deny me my children and career, not the Duke?'

'I fear His Grace has other matters on his mind now, madam. He is looking elsewhere for a bride, with no better luck. Most recently he offered for Mercer Elphinstone, daughter of Viscount Keith, not quite as rich as Miss Tylney-Long but young and good looking. To his chagrin she too refused him.'

'Poor William, he must be feeling quite humiliated, perhaps wishing he'd never started on this quest.' Not for a moment had he expected to experience any difficulty in securing himself a wife. He was a royal prince, third in line to the throne after the death of the King. Yet if he could find no rich heiress to marry, he would be obliged to consider foreign princesses, which wouldn't please him.

I wondered if he ever thought longingly of me, of the joy and comfort we had found in each other's arms, of how he had loved to see me in the cross-dressing roles, enjoyed my wit and mimicry, the warm, affectionate teasing between us. Did he, I wonder, ever regret having left me?

As if to confirm this might be so, Miss Sketchley went on to explain how he had instructed Barton to seek out any portraits of me which may be around. 'He wishes to see them hung on the walls of Bushy. For the children, or so he claims. No doubt he is reluctant to admit his own need to see your lovely smiling face again.'

I turned away, for there was only pain in that face today.

'He has now left the matter of the settlement in the hands of his men of business. But your allowance, they assure me, will be paid in full and on time.'

In view of the extent of the Duke's debts, that would be asking a great deal. I could but hope for the best.

Twenty-Nine

'. . . his liberality towards me has been noble and
generous in the highest degree'

I spent weeks preparing Cadogan Place for the dear children,
and almost began to despair that the Duke would ever allow
them to come to me, my spirits quite agitated by the delay.

'If it were not for the bustle of endeavouring to get the home
ready for the dear little ones, I should be found hanging some
morning in my garters,' I wrote to George, my only confidant.

But at length William brought them in early February,
delivering them to the back door of the house to carefully avoid
meeting me. I did appreciate it would be hard for him to part
with the children, but felt sad that our lives had sunk to this
level. Miss Sketchley came too, for we had become close
companions. I certainly needed her, as it was not easy coping
with the children in a small town house when they were used
to a place the size of Bushy.

Months had passed since the settlement had been agreed
and money continued to be tight, as I still hadn't received my
allowance from the Duke. Neither was I permitted to work.
Since I failed to get any response from Barton on the matter,
in desperation I wrote to the Regent for help, and to the other
royal brothers. The lawyers were not pleased, but later that
month the first payment was at last made.

'Now see what the rumour mill is accusing me of,' I said
to Miss Sketchley one day, shocked by what I had just read in
the latest scandalous news sheet. 'The Princess Charlotte is
saying that I intend to publish the Duke's letters. As if I would
choose to offend him in such a way!'

'They cannot understand how it is you continue to bear the
Duke such fond regard, after the way he has treated you.'

'To abuse his good name would be more than I am
capable of.'

But the incident so distressed me that I instantly packed up all the letters from him, save for the last four, and dispatched them to McMahon with a brief note expressing my dismay at such a charge, concluding with, 'Excuse this – for I am so ill I write from my pillow.'

What would those advisers do to me next?

I still had not heard from dear Sophy, but she was ever obstinate and I could only hope she would come around, given time. There was some good news at the end of the month when Dodee gave birth to a fine boy. But then one morning when Miss Sketchley brought breakfast to me in my room, she expressed concern over Fanny.

'She is waiting in the drawing room, come again to beg for financial assistance, claiming she and Alsop are in a most shocking state.'

I sighed. 'What is it this time? Does this young man imagine he married a bottomless pit of wealth with royal connections?'

'I fear that may well be the case, madam. The couple are ill-matched and constantly at odds. But there is something even more troubling about your daughter, I'm afraid.'

I looked sharply at her, my morning chocolate quite forgotten. 'In what respect?'

'You must judge for yourself.'

One glance told me everything. Fanny was hollow-eyed, as if she hadn't slept in weeks, and yet there was a lack of focus in her gaze, a slurring of her words as she put her plea to me, and I knew at once that she was again using laudanum. But what she had to tell me was even more terrifying. 'Alsop has admitted to debts amounting to two thousand pounds, which must be paid if he is not to escape debtor's prison. You must help us, Mama.'

My heart plummeted with fear, even as I put my arms about her. 'Fanny, my dear, there is nothing I can do. I do not have such a sum. How could I find two thousand pounds?'

She jerked away from me, her face crimson with fury. 'Were it your precious children by the Duke you would find it well enough.'

'I would not, my love, I *could* not. My savings are all gone in trust funds, insurance, dowries, tax and debt.'

'Don't you understand, we are to lose the house and have nowhere to live.'

'That at least is easily remedied. You can move in here, with me,' I said, even though the prospect of having Alsop live under my roof filled me with trepidation. I couldn't help but remember an elderly actress I met on tour, who had invited me to tea to reminisce about old times. She was very comfortably retired, living in perfect tranquillity on the Yorkshire coast. Would I ever find such peace? I wondered, as I smiled at Fanny. 'I'm sure we will all rub along perfectly well.'

Perhaps she caught the doubt in my voice for she began to rail at me using the most foul language, which could only have come as a result of the laudanum. Then she stormed from the room and the house. It was not the first time she had taken herself off in this way, but that did not spare me a great deal of anxiety until she returned a week later. By then her husband was well settled in, seeming not in the least concerned by his wife's erratic behaviour. Thereafter, Fanny lost no opportunity to remind me constantly that he would soon be incarcerated for debt if I refused to help.

'It is no good,' I said, pouring out my heart to Miss Sketchley. 'There is but one way I can help them and that is to go back on the stage and start earning again.'

She looked at me, appalled. 'But if you do that, you will lose the children.'

'I know, but Fanny has always suffered from being the odd one out. And she is right in a way, the younger children would be well taken care of by their father, and no doubt their royal aunts and uncles, even if they did not have me around every day.'

'Oh, madam, think what you are suggesting.'

I looked her squarely in the eye. 'I cannot refuse to help Fanny. She is my daughter. She envies me, her own mother. The theatre may be in her blood but sadly she has little talent, and will be the harsher judged for being who she is, so how can she earn the money needed to save her husband from prison?'

'She is taking laudanum, madam, her temper growing more and more unpredictable.'

I felt bone weary, as if a lifetime of striving had come to nought. 'I can see no other solution. Perhaps, if I am out of their lives, my children can be brought up without the slur of scandal attached. Will you stay with me, Miss Sketchley? They will have Mrs Cockles, but I should hate to lose your companionship.'

'You will never lose that,' she assured me. 'No matter what.'

And so my darling children were to return home to Bushy House. My heart was broken, but they went happily enough, not fully understanding what was going on. They were so well attuned to my peripatetic lifestyle that they simply assumed I was off on another tour.

'I can ride my pony again,' Tus yelled, jumping up and down with excitement.

'You can, dearest. Now see that you are good children for Mrs Cockles, and for Papa.'

'We will, Mama,' said Eliza, kissing me. 'And we'll see you soon.'

Nor could they know how difficult it might be in future for me to see them as much I would like, although the Duke had promised me ready access, when he was not at home. His advisers, however, would do all in their power to prevent me. Mely might have forgotten me altogether by then.

The day they left I fell into bed and wept. Never had I known such despair.

I returned to Drury Lane to great applause. I was even paid £600 owed to me from before the fire, but otherwise the offer was much less than I normally received, and at the end of that short engagement I chose instead to go back on tour. I went with heavy heart, filled with nostalgia for what I had lost. I missed the letters I used to receive from the Duke each day, which I would read so avidly, his thoughtful little gifts and the newspapers he would send to keep me abreast of London news and gossip. I was left with only my children for news, those who were old enough to correspond, that is, and they had busy lives of their own. In Sophy's case there was a profound silence, as she remained in a sulk, for some reason blaming me for her father's decision.

To his credit the Duke did what he could to help Alsop by securing him a post in India with Lord Moira, who had been appointed Governor-General of Bengal. Alsop was delighted. Fanny said she might follow him in due course, but I did not encourage her in this plan, for who would fund her journey? I tried yet again to persuade her to abandon the laudanum and pitch in her lot with me, perhaps a pleasant retirement together in the fullness of time. But she took to wandering the streets more and more, seeking her drug where she could, occasionally procuring theatre work, but not enough to sustain her.

Both George and Henry were happily pursuing their military careers in Europe, and Lolly started as a midshipman in March of the following year when he turned eleven. Lucy was content with her Colonel. Dodee and March also moved into Cadogan Place after their second child, so I was unable to let out the property to ease my load, and was also still paying them the promised dowry by instalments.

In February 1813, weary of touring and having an excellent offer from Covent Garden, I agreed to appear in Centlivre's play, *The Wonder: A Woman Keeps a Secret.*

I should have realized that returning to London was a mistake. After only the first night, *The Times* at once went on the attack. The paper implied that I was fat and old, no longer the talented actress I'd once been. It said that the audience had only come to watch me for the wrong reasons.

They likened me to a character in the play, saying I had been 'admitted to the secrets of harems and palaces, seen their full exhibition of nude beauty, and costly dissoluteness, the whole interior pomp of Royal pleasure, the tribes of mutes and idiots, sultans and eunuchs, and lavish passion and lordly debility'.

'Can you believe such language?' I asked of Miss Sketchley, who listened in mute horror as I read the piece to her. 'In effect, they are accusing me of living a promiscuous life, and also of vile avarice. They call me vulgar and degraded. They insult the Duke, and even criticize the fact that my children are now "strangely allowed to move among the honourable people of England, received by the Sovereign, and starting in full appetite for Royal patronage . . ." The paper's final claim is that I have brought "shame on those who must have it in their power to send me back to penitence and obscurity".'

'Oh, madam, that is quite outrageous!'

I was utterly mortified by the brutality of the attack. I had been pilloried many times in the past for the choice I had made in allying myself to a prince, but none quite so vicious as this.

I wrote a response, of course. I'd never been one to suffer in silence if I thought myself unjustly criticized. I sent my reply to a more supportive journal, hoping they would print it. It was long and impassioned, but this was the nub of it.

> In the love of truth, and in justice to His Royal Highness, I think it my duty, publicly and unequivocally, to declare that his liberality towards me has been noble and generous in the highest degree . . . He has with his accustomed goodness and consideration, allowed me to endeavour to make that provision for myself . . . This then, sir, is my motive for returning to my profession . . . having every reason to hope and believe that, under these circumstances I shall not offend the public at large by seeking their support and protection.

That, of course, was the question. Had I offended my public? Did they see me as 'vulgar and degraded'? Did they believe I would abandon my children for no other reason than avarice, that I lied when I stated that I thought their best chance in life was with a father who could provide and care for them better than I?

'How can I face the audience after such an attack?' I mourned to Miss Sketchley. 'I shall be booed out of town.'

'I will be in the wings with you,' she promised, quite unable to spare me such a humiliation but standing by me in my darkest hour. I hugged her close, grateful for her support.

That night as I waited to go on stage I was in a state of pure terror, suffering from the kind of stage fright I hadn't endured in years. Yet I refused to run away as I had done on that first occasion when I was but sixteen. I had lived a lifetime since then, faced the slings and arrows of fortune, and I would face whatever they threw at me now with fortitude and courage. I lifted my chin, hardened my resolve and walked out on stage. The audience were eerily silent, which, if anything, increased my sense of disquiet still further.

But when one of the characters spoke the lines, 'You have an honest face and need not be ashamed of showing it anywhere', the audience erupted. They leapt to their feet to cheer and applaud. The sound of their love and support filled the entire theatre while I stood bemused, tears rolling down my cheeks in disbelief. It was several minutes before I could even speak. My public had welcomed me back with open arms and loving hearts. I was home.

Author's Note

Very little is known about Dora's early life and no two sources agree on the date when she first appeared on stage. There is even dispute over the exact date of her birth, but I have opted for what seems the most logical. She became, against all odds, one of the greatest comedic actresses of her day, a noted celebrity earning the equivalent of thousands of pounds a week. She was an independent woman of great courage, if too generous-hearted for her own good.

Her letter in response to these last scandalous remarks, did indeed appear in every paper in the land, and *The Times* was obliged to do likewise and retract its earlier piece. There were no further attacks and her return to the stage was a success, although some of her sparkle had gone. Yet she retained a strong following, continued to work hard and be as generous as ever with her family. In 1814 she enjoyed a holiday in Brussels, where she was lauded as *la belle actrice*. The Duke kept his word and she did get to see her children occasionally during holiday periods, although at Lloyd's house, never at Bushy, and she was finally reconciled with her daughter Sophy. The Duke himself continued to sink into debt which soon reached over £50,000, kept solvent only with the help of the loyal Barton.

George and Henry suffered from a military disgrace and were sent to India. Fanny might have gone with them to rejoin her husband, but George refused to take her. She had been creating yet more trouble by writing threatening letters to the Duke. Dora banished her to Trelethyn, and while on tour left Dodee's husband, Frederick March, in charge of her affairs, particularly with regard to supplying Fanny with funds. Dora naïvely gave him blank cheques to perform this task, but on her return was shocked to discover that this second, most trusted son-in-law had cheated her out of several thousand pounds. With no direct access to the Duke she turned to Barton for support, begging him for help. Seeing his opportunity to be rid of what he perceived to be an embarrassment to the royal family, he urged her to leave for France to avoid being incarcerated in debtor's prison for the debts run up in her name. He promised to speak to the Duke and deal with them, at which point she could then return.

Dora believed him, took his advice and fled to France to avoid incarceration as she had once fled to Yorkshire. Miss Sketchley went with her. Barton also promised to forward her all letters from her children, but there is no evidence that he kept these promises. He never did tell the Duke the extent of her financial difficulties, and even though Dora wrote bright and cheerful letters every day to her children there is little evidence that she received many in return during the last months of her life, although until then they'd been regular correspondents.

Dora died in France on 13 July 1816, possibly of liver disease, with only the loyal Miss Sketchley at her side. The Duke was said to be so devastated by her death that he would not allow her name to be spoken in his presence for two years. He had proposed to the widowed sister of Tsar Alexander, who also refused him, and ultimately married Adelaide of Saxe-Meiningen. He succeeded to the throne as William IV in 1830, and it proved to be a happy marriage although she was not able to provide him with the legitimate heirs he needed. Queen Adelaide was, however, a fond mother to Dora's children, and insisted that the portraits the Duke had collected remain on the walls of Bushy House.

Furious over her mother's untimely death, Fanny attempted to publish a memoir about her, which was probably suppressed by royal advisers. The Duke paid for her to go to America and by then she had an illegitimate child, although it is not known what happened to him or her. Fanny died in June 1821 of an overdose of laudanum, officially classed as suicide.

Dora's other children were welcomed into society and all married into the English aristocracy. They did not have a smooth ride, because of their scandalous origins, and always carried a resentment in their hearts over the way their mother was treated. But their success would surely have delighted Dora, and perhaps made all her hard work and sacrifice worth while.